The Illustrated

Still Glides the Stream

Flora Thompson

In this her last book, published posthumously in 1948, Flora Thompson returns again to her childhood in the old countryside, and paints an unforgettable portrait of the people she knew and the lives they led. Unlike her bestselling trilogy *Lark Rise to Candleford,* however, *Still Glides the Stream* is entirely fictional, and in it Flora Thompson lets loose her imagination and artistic skills to wholly new effect. The book is like a magic carpet, carrying the reader back to the village of Restharrow where life was hard but values were solid and enduring.

THE ILLUSTRATED
STILL GLIDES THE STREAM

FLORA THOMPSON

CROWN PUBLISHERS, INC., NEW YORK

First published in this edition in 1984 by
Century Publishing Co. Ltd
Portland House, 12-13 Greek Street, London W1V 5LE

Still Glides the Stream was first published by
Oxford University Press in 1948

Published in the United States of America
in 1985 by Crown Publishers, Inc.,
One Park Avenue, New York, New York 10016

Designed by David Fordham based upon Nicholas Thirkell's
original designs for *The Illustrated Lark Rise to Candleford*
Picture research by Jenny de Gex

Typeset in 11½ point Ehrhardt

Printed and bound in Italy

ISBN 0-517-55841-6

10 9 8 7 6 5 4 3 2 1

First American edition

Thompson, Flora.
 The illustrated Still glides the stream.

 Originally published in 1948 under title:
Still glides the stream.
 I. Title.
PR6039.H653S7 1985   823'.8   85-3832
ISBN 0-517-55841-6

CONTENTS

I

THE FOOTPATH

THE Oxfordshire village of Restharrow has changed little in outward appearance during the last fifty years. Three of the old cottages have disappeared and to replace these, about half a dozen new pink-roofed bungalows have been built. The village inn has been brought up to date and its former frontage of oak beams and cream plaster has given place to one decorated with green glazed tiles and red paint; but it is still known as the *Magpie* and the old sign-board depicting that knowing bird with a gold ring in its beak still swings in its old position on the grass margin before the inn door. The old lollipop shop with bull's-eyes and barley sugar behind its dim green bottle-glass window has become the General Stores. On one of its walls a scarlet Post Office letterbox has appeared, with a notice above it stating that stamps may be obtained and parcels posted within.

One of the bungalows is occupied by a retired Metropolitan Police constable, another by the district nurse, and a lady who breeds alsatian dogs has had three of the old cottages thrown into one and installed a bathroom. The new schoolmaster is not expected to occupy the little two-roomed lean-to beside the school building which served a succession of schoolmistresses, but has his own house, remarkable for its well-kept lawn and flower-beds. The sound of his lawn-mower strikes a new note in the village symphony, but one which blends well with cock-crowing, birdsong, the clinking of buckets, and the shouts and laughter of children at play.

During the two world wars, at Restharrow as elsewhere, hearts must have been torn with anxiety for the absent, and, at the close of both wars, there must have been those those who mourned amidst the general rejoicings. But such scars as were left were personal and invisible; no bomb fell anywhere near Restharrow; no airfield or factory was established in the immediate neighbourhood; on account of the limited accommodation, evacuees were few, and the village retained and has since kept the air of peaceful seclusion now only possible in such places, far from towns, in the heart of the country.

It is a long, straggling place, consisting of what has always been known as 'The Street', though street it is not in the ordinary sense of the term, the cottages standing singly and in groups on both sides of a country byway with fields and hedgerows between. Some of the cottages stand on high banks with flights of stone steps leading up to the doors; others have been built so flush with the road that a passing wagoner, from the top of his load, might if he chose look into the bedroom windows. One here and there of the houses has a honeysuckle-covered porch, a pink or yellow washed front, or a gable end turned to the road, but the greater number are plain, square dwellings of grey limestone, only redeemed from ugliness by the mellowing effect of time and by the profusion of old-fashioned garden flowers which is a feature of the district.

There are many trees. Apple and plum and damson trees in the cottage gardens, laburnums and lilacs at cottage gates, and everywhere in the hedgerows wide-spreading oaks and elms. Around a roadside pond halfway up the village street stand old pollarded willows, the trunks hollowed by time to mere shells in which the village children hide, but every tree with its living topknot of silvery green leaves. A few white Aylesbury ducks still frequent this pond, though not so many as in former years, when, towards nightfall, little girls with light switches in their hands would go to the pond to call in those belonging to their families. *'Dilly, dilly, dilly, dilly!'* they would call, and the ducks would scramble up the bank and, with many a backward glance from their cunning little eyes, they would form two files and waddle off, one file up and the other down the street. It was as the children said, hard to tell which was whosen; but the ducks knew to whom they belonged. In twos and threes they would break from the rank

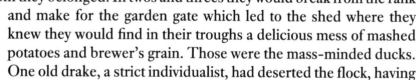

and make for the garden gate which led to the shed where they knew they would find in their troughs a delicious mess of mashed potatoes and brewer's grain. Those were the mass-minded ducks. One old drake, a strict individualist, had deserted the flock, having become so enamoured of his mistress that he followed her out of doors like a dog and, when she was at home, kept guard on the doorstep. His devotion had so endeared him to the woman that she could not bear to think of him in conjunction with sage and onions, and Mrs. Rouse, going to the well with her buckets suspended by a yoke from her shoulders, closely followed by her adoring Benny, as she had named him, was for years one of the sights of the village.

Now, as always, the majority of the Restharrow men are farm-workers. During the last half century the proportion of these has increased, for village tradesmen are fewer. The shoemaker who made, as well as mended, footgear and employed a journeyman helper and an apprentice is now represented by an ordinary cobbler; the blacksmith, the carpenter and the stonemason, who was also the sweep, have long ago shut up shop, and the notice board of 'Adam Strong, Tailor' was, years ago, chopped up for firewood. Adam Strong – 'Mus' Strong' to most of his customers, 'Adam' to a few, and plain 'Strong' to those of the gentry who employed him to do their repairs – had the reputation of being the best tailor for miles around. 'There's only one fault in your suits, Mus' Strong,' his customers would tell him; and, after a weighty pause, they would add: 'The stuff's so strong and the work so good that you can't wear 'em out nohow.' And Adam's invariable retort was, 'Try taking yours out of the box and going to church in it Sundays.' But only a small minority of the men were regular churchgoers; they left that to the women and children; and, after its first appearance as wedding attire, the best suit was folded away with lavender sprigs in its owner's clothes' chest and only taken out on high days and holidays, including the christenings, and, later, the weddings, of his children. Adam's suits cost three pounds, an enormous sum to men who, in those days, earned ten or twelve shillings a week, but the general opinion was that it paid to save up for one before marriage, for then, they said, a man had a decent coat to his back for the rest of his days, whatever betided.

Beyond the last group of cottages and the Manor House and the Vicarage, both set well back among trees, stands the church, a small grey building with a shingled belfry and a churchyard where the unmarked graves are as waves in a sea of long grass. The sound most frequently heard there is the moaning of wood pigeons in the surrounding elm trees, for that is the end of the village and few pass beyond the church in that direction.

The long flagged path bordered on both sides by tall, pointed clipped yews, leads from the church gate to the porch, and exactly opposite to the gate on the other side of the road is a stile. One August afternoon an elderly woman stood by this stile and saw that the footpath which crossed the meadow within had become faint from disuse. It was not entirely obliterated, but could still be discerned, winding up and over the gentle rise and dipping to the moist places. A disused footpath, especially one in a district far from towns and not on the itinerary of walking clubs, is to-day no uncommon sight, nor did this particular footpath appear to have any special feature to cause her to gaze upon it so long and intently. Neither was the meadow over which it wound in any way remarkable, being but a few undulating acres of turf, brightened just then by the golds and yellows of the common later summer flowers and closed in by dark hedgerows studded with elms.

Beyond the meadow lay a prospect of other fields, some dark golden with still uncut corn, others with corn in shocks, bluish green with root crops, or grassland; broken here and there by the dark bushiness of a copse, or by the line of tall herbage which marked a hidden watercourse. Overhead, the high, pale sky was flecked with moon-coloured clouds. Swallows darted and skimmed, white butterflies drifted with thistle-down on air currents. Except for the distant dot-like figures of men working in a harvest field, these were the only living things she beheld. Such a landscape may be seen from the window of a railway carriage in almost any part of the country at that season. Yet, though homely, such scenes never tire English eyes, for there is about them a quiet charm which can heal sore hearts and tranquillize tired minds. Demanding nothing from the onlooker, they bless alike the aware and the unaware. The woman at the stile had a special awareness. Her features relaxed and her expression was that of the deep satisfaction of one who in a changed world finds one beloved thing unchanged.

Though getting on in years, she was still pleasant to look upon; of good medium height; plump, but by no means unpleasing of figure, with wavy grey hair, fresh complexion, and clear, penetrating grey eyes. Women of her type are not uncommon in that part of the country; they serve you in shops, nurse you in hospitals, and welcome and make you comfortable at inns. Often, as cleaners or caretakers, they show you round churches or other old buildings. They have good memories and can tell those interested where in the neighbourhood the rarer birds or less common wildflowers are to be found. They can relate, and relate very well, the history of an old mansion or family, or describe, and sometimes interpret, a local custom. In cases of illness or accident, they are the first to be called upon for help by their neighbours. Chance-met strangers have been known to unfold for them the stories of their lives.

But the woman by the stile had not the appearance of an ordinary countrywoman; her neat grey suit, smart hat and good shoes were not in the country mode; neither had she the brisk, purposeful look of one going about some homely errand in a place where she knew everybody and was herself well known. That afternoon in the church and churchyard she had gazed long and intently upon objects which an inhabitant of the place might have been expected to pass unseeing, or with but a casual glance. And the graves beside which she had stood longest had not been the more recent ones, kept neatly clipped or planted with flowers, but those in the older part of the churchyard where long grasses billowed and even Clerk Tom himself had forgotten who was lying below. But she remembered; for she was a native of the village, a now-retired schoolmistress who, after an absence of many years, was revisiting the scene of her childhood. Her name was Charity Finch.

As she had passed through the village she had noted the few outward changes with a tolerant smile. The wonder, she had thought, was that they were so few when in the outer world all seemed to have changed utterly. What had touched her more nearly was that every face she had seen had been, to her, the face of a stranger. She had known where to look for those she had loved most dearly, or rather the low mounds

which covered their mortal remains; but other old friends and neighbours must still be living. Where were they? When she had set out that morning from the farmhouse in the next parish where she had found rooms, she had imagined men and women of her own age and older ones coming forward to grasp her hand and exclaim: 'Why, bless my soul! if it ain't Charity – Charity Finch? How be 'ee, me dear, how be 'ee?' but no one she had seen had recognized her and she had recognized no one.

Young women, many of whom might well have been born since her last visit to the place, stood in the doorways of cottages once occupied by well-remembered old neighbours. They hung their own artificial silk sets and the many-coloured garments of their children on clothes-lines in gardens where once rows of unbleached sheets and plain calico underwear had billowed, and called to their children from the old gateways. Some of them looked at her curiously, as if thinking, 'Who is this stranger and what is she doing in our street?' but though they were evidently now in possession they struck her as interlopers. That young person with a baby under her arm and a cigarette hanging from her lips at the door of what had been old Mrs. Burdett's cottage, a door always kept shut in those days, for Mrs. Burdett had been one of those who, as they said, kept themselves to themselves. And the girl in the skin-tight jumper bashing down apples with a clothes prop from the tree Jake Harding had planted. The apples would not be fit to eat, for the tree was an annual souring. Jake had favoured that apple because it was a good keeper, and had had several trees of that kind in his garden. Every year about Candlemas time he had gone round the village with a basketful of the fruit and handed out one apple for each member of the family at the doors of those who had shown him small kindnesses. 'Mind you bakes 'em well, missis, and you'll find they'll come up as white and as light as snow, and when 'em be done, you mash up the inners wi' a knob o' fresh butter and all the brown sugar you've got in the pantry, then you'll know why Eve stole the apple,' he would say. It was the nearest approach to a joke he had ever been known to make, for Jake was himself a bit of an annual souring. Well, Jake had gone, and all his apple trees save one had disappeared. But the girl seemed rather a nice girl really; she had smiled as she caught her eye and wished her good morning.

The children were coming home from school and their mothers were calling to them and they were calling back to their mothers, exactly as other mothers and children had called to each other long ago. But the sound of their speech had not the homely old Oxfordshire tang it was such as might be heard in any part of the country. The children looked better fed and were better shod and clad, and the women appeared more leisured than those she had known there, and she was glad to see that, though she sadly missed the old familiar faces. She had a feeling of unreality, of herself walking like a ghost on a scene where she had once been one of the living company which then held the stage.

But here, at the church stile, she felt at home once more. The little grey church was unaltered, every stone, tile, and weather-worn carving, were exactly as she remembered. The flagstones of the pathway had become mossed at the edges as if fewer feet trod them than formerly, but the yews looked not a day older, and the chestnut by the stile beneath which she was standing was no more widely spreading. The wood pigeons, descendants many times removed from those she had mocked in her childhood, 'Take two cows, Taffy! Take two cows, Taffy!' kept up the same perpetual moaning. Even the stile upon which she was leaning had not altered. It was still the same substantial structure, with high mounting-stools and a rounded beam for a top rail. "T'ould take a charge of dynamite

to shift this', her father had once said as he crossed it, and he had spoken authoritatively as a craftsman. The rounded top rail had been polished to glassiness by the Sunday trouser-seats of generations of village youths whose favourite perch it had been while waiting for the chimes to stop and the little *ting-tang* bell to tell them that the parson was getting into his surplice, when they would shuffle in a body up the flagstone path and tip-toe into the seat nearest the door, determined not to spend indoors a moment more than was necessary.

She saw again in memory those of her own day, heavy-footed, rosy-cheeked lads with honest eyes, wearing Sunday-best suits of pale plaids, and bright blue or pink neckties, their hair well plastered down and darkened with hair-oil, and in their buttonholes the largest and brightest flowers their parents' gardens could furnish. Some of them would wear a second flower in their hatbands. She had seen some of their names on the 1914-18 war memorial as she had passed through the village. Those of them still living must be grandfathers.

In the days of her childhood the footpath over the meadow had been a hard, well-defined track, much used by men going to their fieldwork, by children going blackberrying, nutting, or in search of violets or mushrooms, and, on Sunday evenings, by pairs of sweethearts who preferred the seclusion of the fields and copses beyond to the more public pathways. The footpath had led to a farmhouse and a couple of cottages, and, to the dwellers in these, it had been not only the way to church and school and market, but also the first stage in every journey. It had led to London, to Queensland and Canada, to the Army depot and the troopship. Wedding and christening parties had footed it merrily, and at least one walking funeral had passed that way. She herself when a child had trodden it daily, often with her skipping-rope, her white pinafore billowing, her long hair streaming, her feet scarcely touching the ground, or so it seemed to her now. At other times she had carried a basket, on an errand for her mother, to fetch a shillingsworth of eggs, perhaps; eggs twenty a shilling. Not very large eggs, to be sure – they were common barndoor fowls' eggs – but warm from the nest and so full of a delicious milky fluid that it gushed from the shell when the egg was tapped for breakfast next morning. Most often of all she had gone that way on her own errands, for a family of her cousins had lived in the farmhouse, which, to her, had been a second home.

She knew every foot of that meadow by heart. Beneath that further hedgerow violets had grown – white violets and grey blue-veined ones, as well as the more ordinary purple. In spring that dry slope had been yellow with cowslips, short-stemmed cowslips, but honey-sweet of scent. She had once helped to pick a peck of cowslips' pips there to make wine, and the flowers and their green rosettes of leaves had felt warm to her hand in the sunshine. The call of the cuckoo had floated over from Beacon Copse, and her mother had told her to wish, because, she had said, if you wish when you hear the first cuckoo of the year your wish will be granted – if reasonable. The little girl she had then been had wished for a kitten. She would have liked a white kitten, to be called Snow, but she thought it might not be reasonable to specify colour. The kitten given to her by a neighbour a few weeks later was a tabby with a white breast. She had to wait for the first of her long succession of Snows until she was grown up and could choose it from a cage in a pet shop.

She smiled at her own wandering fancy. More than half a century lay between to-day and that day's cowslipping. Long years which had turned the little Charity, or Cherry, as she had then more often been called, into the elderly Miss Finch. Years of hard work and many disappointments, a typical school-marm's life. But there had been compensations. One here and there of her pupils had shown the sudden gleam of comprehension, the mental and spiritual response to her teaching which sometimes in her lighter moments she had referred to when talking to her colleagues as 'plugging in', or 'taking the bait', but which in her secret thoughts she had treasured as her most precious experience. That, and the privilege of fostering such promise, had been the chief joy of her life; but there had also been material advantages, personal independence, a home of her own, books, friends and holiday travel. She had planned for herself a trip round the world the year she retired, but by that time the world was at war, and travelling impossible. Instead of voyaging round the world, she had gone back to her work and was only now free. A few weeks back she had been spending a weekend with a friend in her Essex cottage and, while there, she had smelled a bean field in bloom. The scent had so vividly

brought back to her the bean rows by the beehives in her father's garden that she had felt an irresistible longing to see her old home. She had no longer anyone belonging to her living at Restharrow and had not herself been there for twenty-four years, but the impulse was so strong it had to be obeyed.

She had that morning found unoccupied the thatched cottage where she had lived with her parents, and had gazed through broken and cobwebbed windowpanes at the old familiar rooms. Cold ashes filled the grate where cheerful fires had once burned; torn wallpaper hung in tatters on the walls; and the red-tiled floor which her mother had made cosy with rugs was mudstained and littered with straw. At the side of the house an outhouse door, hinges broken, stood wide open, exposing the seat of the earth closet within. Thistles and weeds choked the flower borders, the sprawling limbs of neglected shrubs blocked the pathway, and, although the day was warm and sunny, the air had the chill, moist smell of decay.

The desolation was no more than she might have expected. Men, she had been aware, were everywhere leaving the land and taking their families to live in towns, and those remaining would naturally prefer to live in one of the more convenient cottages. Still, dilapidated as it had become, the cottage had character and it was roomy; she herself could live happily there, and she had spent some time thinking out what improvements could be made and what furniture would look best in the different rooms. She still had several of the old family pieces which had helped to furnish the house in her childhood, and she felt she would like to see them back in the old positions. It was a daydream, of course, a daydream! She could not put back the clock. Cliffbourne was now her home; there she had her nice little flat and her friends and her committee work and her evening classes. She was too old to be retransplanted. And yet —

Her dreams were dispersed by a polite cough behind her; she turned and saw standing in the road a countryman with a scythe upon his shoulder. She scanned his face hopefully, for he was a man of about her own age, but again the face was that of a stranger. 'Good arternoon to you, ma'am,' he was saying, then, perhaps thinking to save her a fruitless walk, he added: 'That path over the stile there don't lead nowhere.'

'But it was used a good deal at one time,' she said, and he, perhaps taking the statement for a question, replied, 'Yes, I dare say. There used to be a farmhouse over there, but they had a bit of a fire and what wasn't destroyed outright went to rack and ruin afterwards. Nobody's lived there since.'

Charity remembered the fire. Would she ever forget it! But all she said now, and why she said it she did not know, was, 'What kind of people lived there?'

The man smiled good-naturedly. 'Ah! now you're axin' me summat,' he said. 'It all happened years before I come here – I'm a Launton man myself. "Launton, God help us," they call it, though God knows why!' Charity knew, but she did not enlighten him, and, after a few moments' consideration, he went on: 'I've bin told that the farmer hisself didn't live at the farm. He'd got a better and bigger place at t'other end o' th' village and had put some of his workfolks into th' old un. So they wer' just folks, I s'pose, what wer' livin' there. Just folks, same as anybody else might be, just folks!' and, scythe on shoulder, he plodded on.

Just folks! How well that described those she had known there. Just folks like anybody else might be who for the short term of a lifetime had held a lease of their world with all the pride of permanent possession; then, when their time had expired, they had disappeared and others had taken their places. The green fields, the footpath, the village street, had known them no more, a new generation had taken possession and even their names were forgotten. Forgotten by all but her, the one living survivor of the family. In her memory they still lived, moved, and had their being. In imagination she still heard their voices and saw them in their accustomed haunts, and to her, at that moment, they appeared more vividly alive than many of the still living.

Before her inward eye the footpath became once more a well-beaten track, the meadow yellowed over with buttercups, the hedgerows frothed with may. And who were these coming towards her? Two tall girls in their teens, her cousins, Bess and Mercy, and the small, fat child who swung on their hands between them, her feet now off the ground, now on it, was little Polly. Pollywaddles, they used to call her because she was such a soft, dimpled, roly-poly little thing and late in learning to walk. To encourage her now and to help her along, Bess was singing an old country rhyme:

> *All in a row, a bendy bow,*
> *Shot at a pigeon and killed a crow,*
> *Shot at another and killed his brother,*
> *And then went home and told his mother,*

and Charity, as in fancy she rushed to meet and fall down with them among the buttercups, took up the strain, *All a row, a bendy bow*!

A bended bow! The only bow known to those children was of the homemade kind, used with a pointed stick for arrow by boys for shooting at sparrows, and the story behind the lines they sang conveyed to them nothing of the tragedy they apparently commemorated. Echoed for centuries by children at play the rhyme had become meaningless, mere words, a jingle to hop, skip, and jump to. Theirs had been the day of the bayonet and the Gatling gun, of horse-drawn gun-carriages and balloon observation, of soldiers fighting in tight-necked scarlet tunics. The most gallant among them knelt before a gentle, white-handed woman to be decorated. Some had spoken of her as Victoria the Good; others, more flippantly, as the Widow of Windsor; but all spoke of her with affection, for had she not said that she loved every soldier in her forces as her own child? Their world had seemed to them to be a modern, progressive world; but now, looking back upon it over the vortex of war upon war, the simple life of that time was seen to be in all but actual time nearer to the bow-and-arrow age than to that of the bombing aeroplane.

The fighting man she now envisaged was a tall, leggy youth in a scarlet tunic who crossed the meadow at a run, leapt the stile, and, finding on the farther side a small girl in a blue Mother Hubbard bonnet, snatched her up in his arms to lift her over, then paused with her in the air above his head to exclaim: 'Why, Cherry, how light you are! You don't weigh no more than a feather. I believe your bones are hollow, like a bird's. I could put you on my shoulder and run with you all the way to Banbury. You'd like me to take you to Banbury Fair, wouldn't you, Cherry? You wait till I come home from India, you'll be a big girl by then, and I'll squire you to Banbury and buy you a silk handkerchief with the Queen's picture on it and as much toffee and brandysnap as you can eat, you see if I don't!' And he passed from her vision, as he had passed from her sight on that long-ago misty morning when he had swung off down the village street to meet the carrier's cart at the crossroads.

Then Bess, the grown-up Bess, in her fresh pink gingham and shady hat, came, swinging her blackberrying basket, her round, freckled face as innocent-looking as if, as they said, butter wouldn't melt in her mouth. Who, seeing her cross the meadow so leisurely, could have guessed she was off to the pond to meet the young squire and by so doing to start a train of events which would set every tongue in the village wagging?

And Charity's uncle, Reuben Truman. He had used that footpath all his life, for he had been born in the parish. When a child he must often have played in the meadow; as a youth and young man he had crossed it to his work in the fields, and, later, for thirty years, the footpath had led to his home. She saw him now as she remembered him best, a shortish but solidly built and erect man, somewhat past the prime of life, his dark hair and beard sprinkled with grey, and the eyes in his honest countryman's face clear and steadfast. He was wearing his decent churchgoing suit of an old-fashioned pepper-and-salt mixture, and under his arm he carried his old family Prayer Book with its gilt-edged leaves shut tightly in with brass clasps. In his hand or his buttonhole there would be a stalk or two of lavender, or a sprig of southernwood, thyme, or some other sweet-smelling herb. In his childhood it had been a general custom to carry such sprigs of sweet herbs to church, and he loved to keep up the old country ways, including regular churchgoing.

And others, old neighbours and friends and relations, came thronging into her memory, and countryside figures all dead and forgotten, even by her, until to-day. As she walked back through the fields to the farmhouse where she was staying, their faces, their actions, words and expressions, long forgotten or not consciously remembered, were recalled; and seen in the perspective of time and in the light of mature experience they took on a new significance. The dead lived again, the missing peopled their former haunts, and for her, for one sunset hour, the past and the present merged in one pattern of living.

On her first arrival the farm people had welcomed her effusively; they were young people, interested in education, and far in advance of herself in many of their ideas. They declared themselves intolerant of social snobbery, yet, after learning from herself something of her local antecedents, they had cooled visibly towards her, and for

the next few days after her first visit to Restharrow she seldom saw for more than a few moments any other than the maid who brought in her meals. In her present thoughtful reminiscent mood this suited her well. During

her long solitary walks, in bed at night, or with an unread book propped up before her at table, her mind continued to explore the past. She went again to Restharrow and, after making inquiries, found still living there a few survivors of her own and her parents' generations. When talking over old times with these, they supplied her with details she had forgotten, or had not known, and from their varying viewpoints threw crosslights on happenings already in her mind, though none of them appeared to have retained more than a few isolated impressions

She found herself being addressed by these old neighbours as 'Miss Finch', or 'Ma'am', and although she repeatedly asked them to call her 'Charity', as in the old days, the usual response was, 'Oh, no! I couldn't; not now! You says you be and I knows you be, or was, that little gal of George Finch's, but it don't seem as if you can be, somehow.'

'I assure you I am that same person,' Charity would say with a smile; but, although she so frequently stated the fact, she herself found it increasingly difficult to identify that same child with the woman she had become. She attributed the feeling of detachment which grew upon her to her long absence and to the world-shaking events of the later years; but she discovered afterwards that her experience is one not uncommon to age, looking backwards in time.

Then, one afternoon, while sipping tea in a hop-covered arbour in the farmhouse orchard, her only company web-spinning spiders and a robin pecking up the crumbs of her biscuit, herself thinking of quite irrelevant matters, such as the proper airing of her bed at home in her flat at Cliffbourne, it suddenly occurred to her that the part of the child Charity had been that of a learner, an onlooker, rather than that of an actor on that bygone scene. Her then companions had been living their lives fully; hers had not properly begun. They were eventually to close their eyes for ever on an order of living they had at birth found firmly established and which they had accepted as inevitable, never suspecting that already its foundations were crumbling and that in a very few years it would have become but a fading memory. Long after they had passed from this earthly scene, her own life had gone on, through the disruptions of war and change, into a new world of marvellous discoveries, overturned idols, changed values, and a new conception of human relationships. Though she was by no means aged as age is considered to-day, her own life had bridged the old and the new worlds, and now, while appreciating the new resources and rejoicing in the new opportunities and new freedoms, she could still look back on the past with loyal affection.

The world of her childhood had been a narrow world, inhabited by simple people whose lives had been restricted by poverty and other hardships and deprivations; yet it had held something of beauty, of unselfconscious simplicity and downright integrity that seemed to her worthy of remembrance.

II

MISS FINCH REMEMBERS

THE cottage where she had been born and had lived as a child with her parents was the first on the right hand side when coming into the village, and stood at the point where the narrow, tree-shaded lane which led to the crossroads widened into the village street. Between the house and the road a brown path zigzagged over a stretch of rough turf and, to reach the gate, the brook which ran below the garden hedge had to be crossed by way of a plank bridge with a handrail. In summer this small stream was so choked with willow-herb and water-mint that its gentle murmur could barely be heard above the humming of the hive-bees. After the autumn rains, on quiet winter days, pauses in the conversation within-doors were filled by the sound of running water. Even in the hottest summer the stream never dried up, and this, she was told, was because it was fed by well-springs. Charity's father called the house their castle and the brook their moat and laughed when a neighbour asked him how he could a-bear to live in such a lonesome old place, adding that to live there would have made him feel unked.

At that time village houses had no numbers or names, the names of the occupants being sufficient distinction, and Charity's home was usually spoken of as 'Finch's', though some of the older inhabitants persisted in calling it 'Gaspar's'. Tradition said that a white wizard of that name had once lived there and that he had made a fortune by charming away illnesses, finding lost things, and telling people their lucky days. He had either died suddenly or disappeared, and was supposed to have left his hoard hidden beneath the thatch or under the floor-boards. But although Charity searched hopefully, she never found anything of more value than a coil of wire, a pewter spoon, and a King George III penny. When she found the penny her father laughed and told her to take care of it, for it was the first coin that had ever come into their family without hard labour.

He must have intended that as a joke, for he was the last man in the world to make

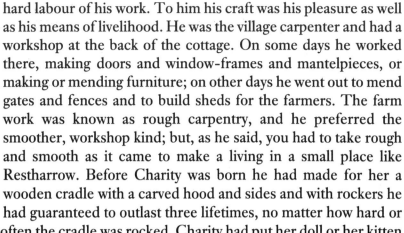

hard labour of his work. To him his craft was his pleasure as well as his means of livelihood. He was the village carpenter and had a workshop at the back of the cottage. On some days he worked there, making doors and window-frames and mantelpieces, or making or mending furniture; on other days he went out to mend gates and fences and to build sheds for the farmers. The farm work was known as rough carpentry, and he preferred the smoother, workshop kind; but, as he said, you had to take rough and smooth as it came to make a living in a small place like Restharrow. Before Charity was born he had made for her a wooden cradle with a carved hood and sides and with rockers he had guaranteed to outlast three lifetimes, no matter how hard or how often the cradle was rocked. Charity had put her doll or her kitten to bed in it until her mother had given it to a very poor family, who, after their last baby had outgrown it, had used it as a washtub and left it out in the rain. Her mother would have preferred one of the more fashionable wickerwork cradles, lined with pink glazed calico covered with spotted muslin.

The cottage was an old-fashioned, countrified place standing in a garden crammed with fruit trees, vegetables, flowers, and lavender bushes. Inside, it had none of the conveniences now considered essential to comfort. Water had to be drawn up with a long hooked pole from a well in the garden; paraffin lamps and candles lighted the hours of darkness, and the sanitation was primitive. There were red-tiled floors in the downstair rooms, and the only fireplace besides the small oven grate in the kitchen was the parlour grate, of the high, bow-barred, basket-shaped kind under a high mantelpiece now seen only in old prints. But the unenlightened Finches found their house comfortable enough; indeed, they rather prided themselves upon living in one of the most commodious cottages in the village, with a parlour and three bedrooms, whereas most of their neighbours had but one room downstairs and two, at most, upstairs. The tiled floors were made warm and comfortable with home-made rugs and long strips of red and brown matting, and the low price of coals made it possible to keep up roaring great fires in cold weather. 'I'm going to make this house as warm and snug as a chaffinch's nest,' her mother had said one day, while spreading out on the floor a handsome new black-and-scarlet rug she had been making, and that idea had pleased her small daughter, for weren't they themselves Finches, and was not the cottage their nest? She liked the idea of a nest better than that of a castle, for a castle she had never seen, and there were nests in every hedgerow.

People in the neighbouring villages, speaking from the superior standpoint of those living one, two, or three miles nearer a town, used to say that the Restharrow folks were

a rum lot, and it may be that, secluded as they were from outside influence, they had lagged behind in the march of progress. Many of the old country customs, dead or dying out elsewhere, were still honoured at Restharrow. There were the Christmas mummers, the May Day garland; broad beans were planted in gardens on Candlemas Day. *Candlemas Day, stick beans in the clay. Throw candle and candlestick right away*, they would quote. But they no longer heeded the second admonition; they lighted their paraffin lamps and stayed up until nine or ten. If a lamp burned low or smoked, the older ones would say, ''Pon my soul, this lamp's no better than a farthing rushlight!' and describe to their grandchildren how their own mothers had dipped and dipped and dipped a rush from the brook in melted fat to form the tiny, twinkling candles of their childhood. 'You young uns be a lucky little lot,' they would say. 'You'll never know life in the rough with all these wonderful inventions.'

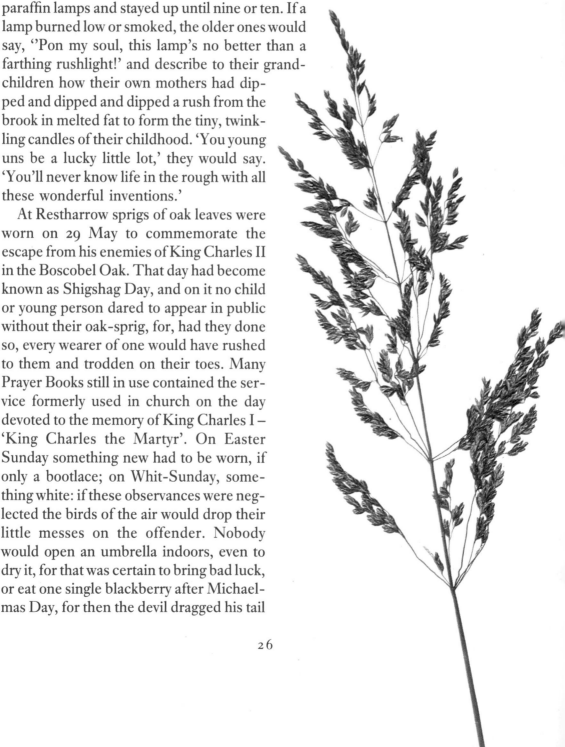

At Restharrow sprigs of oak leaves were worn on 29 May to commemorate the escape from his enemies of King Charles II in the Boscobel Oak. That day had become known as Shigshag Day, and on it no child or young person dared to appear in public without their oak-sprig, for, had they done so, every wearer of one would have rushed to them and trodden on their toes. Many Prayer Books still in use contained the service formerly used in church on the day devoted to the memory of King Charles I – 'King Charles the Martyr'. On Easter Sunday something new had to be worn, if only a bootlace; on Whit-Sunday, something white: if these observances were neglected the birds of the air would drop their little messes on the offender. Nobody would open an umbrella indoors, even to dry it, for that was certain to bring bad luck, or eat one single blackberry after Michaelmas Day, for then the devil dragged his tail

26

over those left on the bushes. But the observance of such customs and superstitions was not as yet so singular as to mark the participants as rum. That reputation was probably founded on a certain untamedness, a closer-to-earth earthiness, a hanging together in clans and regarding outsiders as potential enemies, shown by the older inhabitants.

As was then usual in small country places where little happened to crowd out of village memory the events of former years, old traditions were cherished and old stories re-told. Village memory was long, very long. In the eighteen-eighties an aged man told Charity that his great-great-grandfather, when what he described as 'a girt, lolloping lad', sat on a field gate on a Sunday morning and looked on at the Battle of Edgehill – a family tradition which may or may not have been founded on fact. Charity, after working it out on paper, decided that there should have been at least one more 'great' in it; on the other hand, the correct day of the week gave a circumstantial touch to the story. Another aged man remembered the arrival in this country of the news of Napoleon's defeat at Waterloo and the bonfires lighted to celebrate our victory. Everybody over sixty remembered Queen Victoria's Coronation, and the Crimean War and the Indian Mutiny were spoken of by many as if they had happened but yesterday.

The village families had intermarried for generations and three surnames served for quite half the population. Relationships were involved; there were first, second and third cousins and, after that, those who were known as 'a sort o' cousin'. A gossiping woman could spend a diverting if not very profitable morning determining the exact degree of affinity of some about-to-be-married couple. 'His aunt what brought him up,' she would say, ticking her off on her finger, 'she's his aunt on his mother's side, but on his dad's she's his step-grandmother. And, to her', meaning the bride, 'he's a full cousin on his mother's side and a sort o' cousin on his dad's. But it's all right', she would conclude authoritatively, 'there's no blood relation, for I've puzzled it out in the Prayer Book.'

In past times these mixed marriages had produced a wild, lawless race of sheep-stealers, poachers, and fighting and drinking men. Stories were still told of pitched battles with gamekeepers, or the men of neighbouring villages, in which knives and bludgeons had figured. There were stories of murder, almost openly committed, for which no one had been brought to trial, for none would give information lest by doing so they brought down upon themselves and their families the vengeance of the murderer's relatives. The most horrifying of these was that of a man who was said to have murdered his stepson, a boy of five. The charred remains of the poor child had been found in the big bread-baking oven in the wash-house wall of his mother's cottage. It had never been actually proved how he had got there, but his stepfather had been known to dislike the child and to have treated him badly and all in the village were convinced that he was responsible for the crime. At the inquest the man, when asked how he supposed the boy had got into the oven, had said he supposed he must have climbed into it to hide and have accidentally banged to the door, which could only be opened from the outside, and when it was pointed out to him that even a child of five should have known better than climb into a hot oven, he had said that anybody might have thought so, but young Amos was a stubborn sort of child and if he once made up his mind to do a thing he'd do it, if only to aggravate. Though the Coroner and his jury must have had their suspicions, there was no evidence upon which the man could be sent for trial, and a verdict of accidental death was returned. But the villagers were convinced of his guilt and, from that time on, he was an outcast among them. After a time he left the village – some said that he had taken to the road as a tramp – and nothing was ever heard about him afterwards. But for forty years the story survived, and a piece of broken wall, half buried in nettles, where his cottage had stood was avoided by most people after nightfall. Strange noises were said to have been heard there for years; then, about the time when the stepfather might have been expected to die of old age, they had ceased. 'For why? The wretch had gone to his account,' they told their children.

The more certain perpetrators of lesser crimes had usually escaped punishment. One old woman told Charity that when she had been left a young widow, forty years previously, a neighbour who had so far appeared well disposed towards her had taken her late husband's tools from a shed at the side of the house and pushed them off on a wheelbarrow in broad daylight. She had watched his proceedings from an upstairs window and, although indignant, she had not gone out to re-monstrate, because, she said, he might have blackened her character by telling folks lies about her. That was the woman who once described the Restharrow of her youth as a regular little rogues' harbour.

That was long before Charity's time. In her childhood there was an occasional bout of fisticuffs outside the inn after closing time on a Saturday night; one man was known to do a little mild poaching, and fruit sometimes vanished from trees and vegetables from gardens after dark, but nothing worse happened, and, on the whole, Restharrow was as peaceable and law-abiding a place as any in the country. Peaceful and law-abiding; though, as they said of themselves, its inhabitants were not all cut to the same pattern. The State had taken in hand and was educating and smoothing out oddities in the younger generation, but many of the older people had been born too soon to have come under its equalizing influence, and among these there were individuals of the kind then described as 'cards', or 'characters'.

About half a dozen old men who, having become too infirm for fieldwork, had yet managed to keep out of the workhouse, made their headquarters on the bench provided by the landlord for more paying customers beneath the swinging signboard of the *Magpie*. When one of them happened to be in funds, a pot of beer would be called for and passed from hand to hand; when, as more frequently happened, not one of the company had (as they said) a couple of coppers to rub together, they cut chunks

off their rolls of twist tobacco and chewed. When there was a horse to be held or a message to carry, the more active among them would spring up spryly, for on such casual earnings they depended for their pocket money. Twopence was the usual reward for such small services; if there was a garden hedge to be trimmed or a path to be weeded the pay might be sixpence. Between whiles they discussed life in general.

The spirits of the little assembly depended mainly upon funds. Over a pint of beer the conversation grew lively. On beerless days rheumatism, lumbago, bad weather, and the deterioration of the world since their own young days were the staple topics. The married old men, told to be home at certain time, would frequently drag their old-fashioned turnip watches from their trouser pockets; the lone widowers had only to consult their own inclinations. When the talk became lively one old man of a timid nature would glance over his shoulder and the others would rally him, 'No, she beant a comin' and she can't hear us neither,' they would say. Poor old Ben had a regular tartar

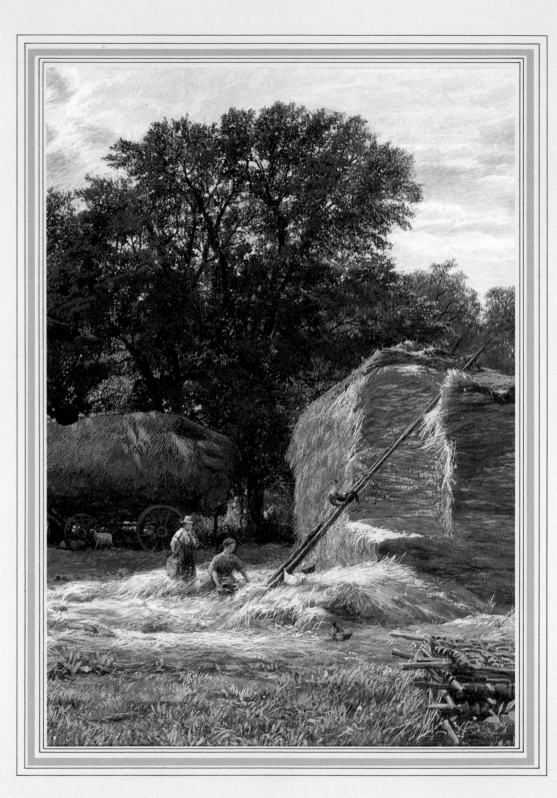

of a wife. Once Charity, passing by on the roadway, saw her, a big, sour-looking old woman in an enormous pink print apron, steal silently up to the back of the bench and seize old Ben by the shoulder. 'Off you go and clean them winders,' she shouted. 'I'll larn 'ee to set her gossiping while I work me fingers to the bone!' and Ben followed her meekly.

But that pair was an exception; most of the poor old men and their poor old wives lived together in quiet decency. A few in affectionate intimacy. Old Ambrose Moss paid but a short morning visit to the benchers, and when he thought his wife had had time to make all snug at home he returned to his own fireside, only crossing the road once more towards nightfall with a jug for their supper porter. Mrs. Moss was a tall, thin old woman with a dark upper lip who strode in her walk like a man. Both of the couple were slightly deaf and at seasons when doors and windows stood open their conversation could be heard by any passer-by on the road. Charity, standing on a neighbouring doorstep waiting for her basket to be filled with damsons for jam-making, once heard Ambrose exclaim: 'You doant remember Aaron? Him what married the pub at Asbury with th' landlady thrown in as a makeweight – 'ooman wi' a face like a pickling cabbage, weighted sixteen stun if her did an ounce. You surely can't've forgot the two of 'um!' and Judy roared back that, though she could not call the couple to mind, she was glad that the young feller got a good makeweight, and they sat by their fire guffawing over their stout like two jolly old men.

These had all been landworkers. They had known all their lives that in their old age parish relief and any help that their children could give them were all that would stand between themselves and the workhouse. There was another old man in the parish, not one of the benchers, who had earned good wages as a craftsman and had in his time saved money and yet in old age was incomparably worse off than the poorest of them. Thomas Hearne was a native of Restharrow, a stonemason, who, after spending his active years working for a firm of builders in a distant part of the county, had in his old age drifted back to the home of his childhood. Hearne had in his day been a first-class workman with experience, skill, and that something beyond skill which is a compound of taste and imagination. His firm had valued his services. When there had been a difficult or a delicate job to be done, it had been given to Hearne as a matter of course. Specimens of his workmanship stood, and some must still be standing, all over that countryside, in the renovated stonework of restored churches, the arches of bridges, stone piers at entrance gates, and on the façades of mansions. He had in his day instructed two generations of apprentices.

But by the eighteen-eighties Hearne's day was over. Physically he was past his prime, though still hale and hearty and capable of a full day's work at his bench in the shop, or of walking, toolbag on shoulder, three or four miles or more to an outside job. But times and ideas had changed and his fastidious, painstaking methods were out of date. Speed had become more important than craftsmanship and the artistry which aimed at nothing less than perfection was little esteemed. The more important jobs were being given to younger men, smart fellows who knew all the latest dodges for saving time and materials. Young workmen, apprentices but yesterday, would take upon themselves to instruct him in his craft. It had been all very well in his day, they told him, to go in for all this undercutting and finishing, but who was going to wait or to pay for it now? and the kindly disposed would bring their mallets and chisels over to Hearne's bench and show him what they called the tricks of the trade.

But Hearne had no use for tricks. He preferred to work as he had been taught to work, leisurely and lovingly, striving always to approach as nearly as possible his own version of perfection. For a few more years he continued to use the bench which for more than a quarter of a century had been known as 'Hearne's', working steadily at such jobs as were given him, consulted by others less often than formerly and respected less, but never abating his own self-respect. In his home village he was liked and respected as a man with a good trade in his hands, who had a good wife and a pleasant, cheerful cottage, and there were some there who envied him those blessings, for it was a poor agricultural neighbourhood.

This state of things might have lasted until his working life had ended in the natural way had not his old employer, the head of the firm, died and his son, a young man with modern ideas and a determination to increase his business, come into possession. The firm was reorganized, the latest and cheapest methods were instituted, and in the new scheme there was no place for Hearne as leading mason. He was called into the office and told that a younger and smarter man was to have his bench in the shop. The young builder was about to add that he had no idea of cutting adrift an old servant like Hearne, that as long as he was able to work there would still be a job in the yard for him, an old man's job with an old man's wages, but, before he could speak further, Hearne took him up sharply. 'Is anything wrong with my work?' he demanded. His young employer hummed and hawed, for he had no wish to hurt Hearne's feelings. 'Well, since you ask me,' he said, 'I'll say that you're a bit too finicking. You put in too much time on a job to justify your wage in these competitive times.'

'But look at my work!' cried Hearne. 'Look at that east window tracery in Tisley

Church, and the new keystone I let into the Norman arch at Bradbury, and that bridge over the Ouse at Biddingfold; masterpieces all of 'em, though I says it as shouldn't. Other jobs, too. You've only got to take a walk in the cool of the evening and use your eyes and wherever you go in any direction you'll find summat worth seein' with my mark 'pon it,' and this he said, not pleadingly, but rather by way of a challenge, and as he spoke he stretched out his arms as though to call the whole neighbourhood as witness.

The young builder was in a difficult position. 'I know all that,' he said. 'I'm not denying you've been a good mason, a first-rate man in your day. But those were the days of my father and grandfather and those times have gone, the world's on the move, and the truth of the matter, though I'm sorry to say it, is that you do your work too well. You take too much time over it, and that doesn't pay in these days. We've been out of pocket by you for years.'

Hearne's fine dark eyes flamed and his long, thin old figure shook with rage. 'Too much time over it!' he shouted. 'Too much time! And how d'ee think good work's allus been done? By hurrying? By scamping? By begrudging a stroke here or a moment there? Look at the churches round here. Bloxham for length, Adderbury for strength, and Kings Sutton for beauty! Think they grew out o' th' ground like mushrooms? Or were flung together by slick youngsters such as yourn? Let me tell yer, young feller-me-lad, I learnt my craft from them as made a craft o't, not a come day go day means o' puttin a bit o' bread in their mouths, and I ain't goin' to alter my ways and disgrace my upbringin' for nobody. I'll make up my timesheet and you can put one o' your slick youngsters at my bench, for I've done with th' firm. And this I'll say before I've done with you for ever: th' work of my hands'll be standin' to bear witness for me when you and your like be frizzlin' in the spot old Nick keeps specially hotted for bad workmen!'

Old Hearne neither starved nor entered the work-house. For some years longer he made a poor livelihood by replacing roof tiles, building pigsties, setting grates, repairing walls, sweeping chimneys, or any other odd job which could be regarded, however remotely, as included in his own trade. When his wife died he left the village near the town where he had

worked and returned to his native Restharrow, where he still owned the cottage in which he had been born, and there carried on his humble occupation of jobbing mason. On chimney-sweeping days he was grimy, but, at other times, he went about his work in the immemorial garb of his craft, corduroy trousers scrubbed white, or whitish, white apron girded up round the waist for walking, billycock hat and nondescript coat powdered with stone and mortar dust. He had become, as they said, as thin as a rake, and his fine dark eyes, into which the fire of fanaticism was creeping, had become so sunken that his forehead looked like that of a skull. By the time Charity first remembered him, he had become queer in his ways. Harvesters going to the fields at daybreak would meet him far from his home, wild-eyed and wild-haired and dew-soaked. When asked where he had been he would whisper confidently that he had been out all night, guarding some church or other building, but who had set him to guard them or what they were to be guarded against he would not say. Otherwise he talked more freely than he had been used to do and with many a 'he sez' and 'sez I' he would relate the story of his last interview with his former employer to anyone he could buttonhole. Everybody in the parish had heard the story, though few with sympathy, for it seemed to most of his listeners but an instance of a man throwing away a good job in a fit of temper, and, to save themselves from a third or fourth recital, when they saw Hearne in the distance they would turn aside to avoid a meeting. The more kindly spoke of him as 'poor old Tom Hearne', the less kindly as 'that tiresome old fool', and the children would tease him by calling after him, 'Tom! you're slow! You're too slow for a funeral! Old Slowcoach! Old Slowcoach!'

But there were still a few who respected him, craftsmen who, though compelled by changed conditions to modify their own methods, had not entirely lost the ideals of former days. Charity's father was one of these. He would listen patiently to Hearne's rambling talk, fill his tobacco pouch or ask him in for a drink, and once when his wife remarked that a fat lot of good the old man's fine workmanship seemed to have done him, he said quite angrily that money was not everything, there was the satisfaction of knowing you'd turned out a good job. Charity, upon whom Hearne's story had made a deep impression, concluded that his best friend in that house was her father, and that her mother disliked him and only did him the few little kindnesses she could because, to her, kindness came naturally.

Then, one Sunday morning when her father was hearing her repeat her Catechism in readiness for Sunday School and her mother was stuffing a fowl at the table, Hearne passed their house with a mob of teasing boys at his heels. People used to take the law into their own hands in those days, and George Finch ran out and dispersed the

ringleaders with a cuff or two. 'That'll larn 'em!' he said when he returned. 'Now Charity, get on, "My duty towards my neighbour"?' 'My duty towards my neighbour is to love him as myself and to do unto all men as I would they should do unto me —' Charity was fairly launched when her mother heaved a prodigious sigh. 'Aye, there's my bosom snake!' she exclaimed. 'To do unto all men.' 'Just hark at the woman!' said her husband. 'You'd think she was the chief of sinners! Your bosom snake, my girl, if you've got one, must be about the size of a cheese mite!'

'It's that poor old Hearne,' said his wife. 'I think and I think about him, living all alone with nobody to do as much as a hand's turn for him, and us with that good attic and a crust we should never miss.'

'Well,' said her husband decisively, 'if that's your bosom snake you can scotch it, once and for all. Your duty to your neighbours begins with them nearest to you, and that's me and Charity. We should neither of us be any the better for havin' a poor old death's head like Hearne sittin' with us at table and talkin' us upstairs and downstairs and out into the garden. Ask him to dinner on Christmas Day, send him a plateful of anything tasty you've cooked any time, knit him a pair or two of socks for the winter, or anything of that sort, but don't bring him into the house for good for I couldn't stand it!' Again Mrs. Finch sighed, but this time it was a sigh of relief rather than one of regret. ''Twasn't that I wanted him here myself,' she said. 'I only thought perhaps 't would be Christian.'

'Christian or heathen,' said her husband, ''t'ldn't be natural. Now Charity, get on with that "Duty towards my neighbour", and you, Mother, see that you put a sprig of marjoram in that stuffin', and if you've a mind to send Charity up street with a bit of dinner for Hearne when 'tis done, I've got nothin' to say against it, 'cept that she'd better have her own before she goes or she won't get any.'

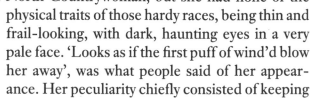

Living as they did a little removed from the rest of the village, the Finches had no very near neighbours. In the house nearest to them, one of a row facing the road, lived an elderly widow who was often spoken of as peculiar; by some as 'eggcentric'. She was Mrs. Burdett, the widow of a ganger who, a few years before, had come to work on a section of a new railway which passed through the district and had met with his death in circumstances which had obliged the Company to give his widow a small life-pension. Mrs. Burdett was by birth a North Countrywoman, but she had none of the physical traits of those hardy races, being thin and frail-looking, with dark, haunting eyes in a very pale face. 'Looks as if the first puff of wind'd blow her away', was what people said of her appearance. Her peculiarity chiefly consisted of keeping herself aloof from her neighbours, of taking long, solitary walks in the fields and lanes, and of what the neighbours considered excessive letter-writing.

Her aloofness might have passed with little comment, for there were other women in the village who kept themselves to themselves, as the saying went; and the walks, though singular in a place where walking for walking's sake was unheard of, might have been excused on the ground of the want of other employment; but why she should be seen sitting in front of her window, bending over a paper, pen in hand, every time a body chanced to pass by her house, was, as the bodies said, a puzzler, 'and her without a chick or child of her own to write to, and herself not gettin' a letter once in a month o' Sundays. Besides, whoever saw her post one o' them she'd written?' The only person who could have explained that matter was Mrs. Burdett herself, and nobody cared to ask her to do so; for one thing a direct question was not 'manners', and, for another,

she might have told her interrogator to mind her own business, as she had once told somebody who had asked her another question about her affairs. 'Pardon me, but that is my business,' she had said, as grand in her manner as any duchess, the neighbour had reported. With her neighbours generally, Mrs. Burdett had little to do. If she met one of them face to face in the street she would pass the time of day with them and pass on, never stopping to talk. If anyone made occasion to knock at her door, she would reply civilly to what they had to say, but never herself started a topic or asked them inside. Naturally, she was not a popular person. People said she was proud and stand-offish, though what she had to be proud of God only knew, and her with but a paltry pension of seven and sixpence a week and lookin' as if a good meal'd do her no harm, and as to her craze of strolling the fields, and at her age too, it looked to them as if her wits were going.

Charity's parents liked Mrs. Burdett. They said she was the kind of neighbour they

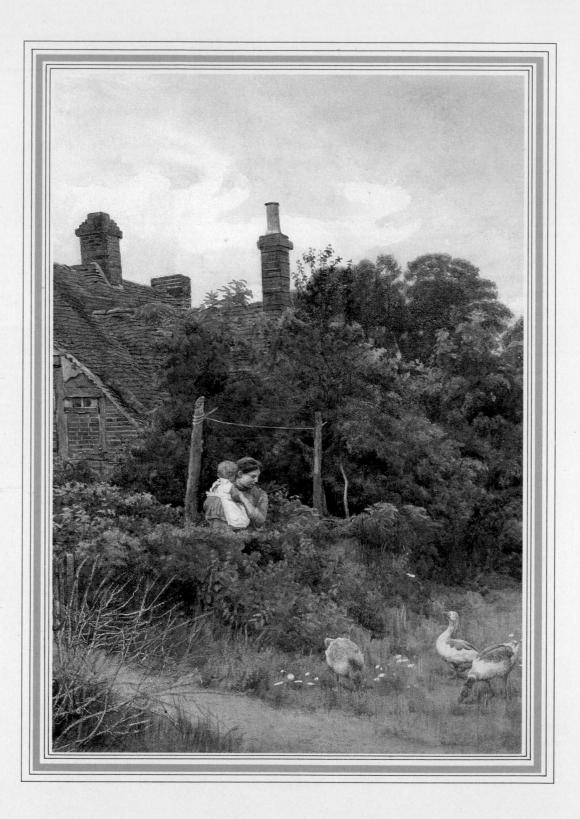

preferred, civil but never intrusive. When Charity's father sent her a few green peas or a vegetable marrow from his garden, she accepted them courteously and even seemed pleased, and when her mother said to her one day that if ever she fell ill, or needed any other kind of help, she knew where to send for it, she thanked her with some show of feeling. But those were their nearest approach to intimacy. With Charity she was a little more communicative. Once she had met her when the child was searching for violets in a deserted green lane out in the fields and had shown her a blackbird's and a thrush's nest back to back in the same stump, and, afterwards, had lent her a book with coloured pictures of birds which, she had told her, had been written by a country clergyman named Gilbert White. But, on the whole, Mrs. Burdett appeared to be one of those reserved, self-contained natures whose only wish as far as their neighbours are concerned is to be on polite but by no means familiar terms.

Close by Mrs. Burdett lived another old widow, but a widow of a very different quality. Mrs. Sykes had lived at Restharrow all her life and knew everyone who lived and everything which happened there, including some things which happened only in her own imagination. She dressed in the old 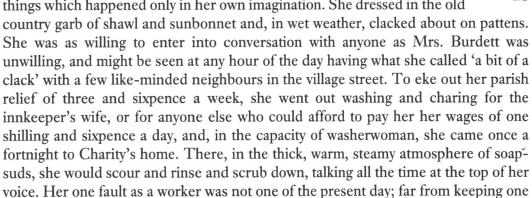 country garb of shawl and sunbonnet and, in wet weather, clacked about on pattens. She was as willing to enter into conversation with anyone as Mrs. Burdett was unwilling, and might be seen at any hour of the day having what she called 'a bit of a clack' with a few like-minded neighbours in the village street. To eke out her parish relief of three and sixpence a week, she went out washing and charing for the innkeeper's wife, or for anyone else who could afford to pay her her wages of one shilling and sixpence a day, and, in the capacity of washerwoman, she came once a fortnight to Charity's home. There, in the thick, warm, steamy atmosphere of soap-suds, she would scour and rinse and scrub down, talking all the time at the top of her voice. Her one fault as a worker was not one of the present day; far from keeping one eye on the clock towards finishing time, there was no getting rid of her without telling her directly to go. If she had been permitted to do so she would have stayed on till midnight. When, at last, she had unwillingly edged out of the door, still talking, her employer would feel almost as exhausted as if she had herself done the day's washing.

If it could have been taken in moderation, much of her con-versation would have been entertaining, for she knew everyone in the village and all that had happened there for the previous fifty years, and had the history of each family and all the ramifications of the involved relationships by heart. When, after Mrs. Sykes had gone, Mrs. Finch com-plained to her husband of having been talked to death, he would laugh and say that, exhausted or not exhausted, she seemed to have picked up a lot of information. Which she had; she could not help doing so when all that had happened or was thought to have happened in the village since the last wash-day had been related, with copious illustrations drawn from the happenings of other days, and with nothing lost in the telling.

Mrs. Sykes was superstitious and believed not only in charms and omens, the meaning of dreams and the telling of fortunes from tea-leaves, but even more firmly in witchcraft and ghosts. And she was not at all choice in her language. Mrs. Finch had often to *S-s-s-sh!* her when Charity was by, and afterwards to excuse her by saying that in Mrs. Sykes's young days country-folks were an ignorant, broad-spoken lot; and, taking her all in all, she would add, she was a cheery, good-natured old soul and an excellent washerwoman.

She might not have thought so well of her had she heard some of the stories Mrs. Sykes told her small daughter when she happened to be alone with her for a few minutes. After hearing some of these tales, Charity could not sleep at night for thinking of the sheep-stealer on the gibbet, calling aloud all night to his mother to save him, *Mother! Oh, Mother!* or of the woman, laid out for dead, who came downstairs in her grave-clothes. Mrs. Sykes had a ghoulish mind. Once, after a child had died in the village, herself sitting, fat and rosy, at the kitchen table having what she called her 'bavour' of bread and cheese and beer while Mrs. Finch hung out the clothes to dry in the garden, she said meditatively: 'Six weeks to-day since little Anna Parminter died. Poor little lamb! six weeks in the pitty-hole! By this time th' worms've gnawed at her; you'd never know little Anna if you seed her now. When I wer' a little gal, like you, I once seed a bone ole Clerk Moss'd turned up, diggin' a new grave —' Fortunately, at that moment Mrs. Finch came in, but Charity had already heard enough to give her some nightmarish evenings in bed that winter.

The then Vicar of the parish, Mr. Penpethy, was said to be, and no doubt was, a very learned man, and he had all the queer, absent-minded ways popularly associated with learning. Often, in cold or wet weather, he would be seen walking in the fields and lanes in his old library cassock and slippers, having forgotten to put on his coat and boots before leaving home. On such walks he would talk aloud to himself, checking off what may have been the feet of verse on his fingers; or he would stand silent, gazing at the earth at his feet, apparently lost in meditation. At such times he would fail to respond to the greetings of his parishioners, not from ill-will or disdain, but because he did not observe the bobbed curtsy or the pulled forelock. He would forget that he had to conduct any but the regular Sunday services, and wedding and funeral parties

40

would have to wait in the church porch until he had been found and reminded of his appointment. He once christened a child by an entirely different name than that given by the godparents. At that time the upper servants in big houses were called, not by their Christian, but by their surnames, and the mother of the child had had a favourite fellow servant named Veness, after whom she wished to name her new baby, but this was pronounced at the font Venus, and the clergyman, after shaking his head and whispering, No! No!, declared loudly, 'Mary, I baptize thee —' He told the mother afterwards that the name she had chosen was unsuitable for a Christian child. 'Perhaps you do not know that Venus was a heathen goddess!' he suggested. 'Oh, no, sir, she wasn't,' the mother said tartly. 'She was the cook at Finchingfield House, for I knowed her!'

Mr. Penpethy was said to be poor – 'as poor as a crow' was the village expression – and he lived alone in his big, silent Vicarage without any other attendance than that of the parish clerk, who, officially his gardener, was actually his man-of-all-work. Except for one small plot in what had once been the kitchen garden, kept cleared by Clerk Savings for the growing of vegetables, the Vicarage garden was a jungle of weeds and thistles and untended shrubs and fruit trees. Grass grew on the carriage drive which led to the locked and barred front door. The villagers when they wished to put up their banns of marriage or had to arrange for a funeral went to the back door, and Mr. Penpethy's only other known visitor was one of the neighbouring clergy who was said to have been with him at college. The Vicar, indeed, was as near being a recluse as is possible for a parish priest. He was a small, nervous man, prematurely grey, and with a habit of pausing in mid-speech and gazing into the distance, as though he had lost the thread of his discourse and was seeking it there. But, when once his attention was attracted, he was not unkindly and the villagers rather took a pride in his oddities than resented them, feeling that to have a parson so very unlike other parsons, one who never interfered or bothered people about going to church, and could speak Greek and Latin (as they said) like a native and read old books written, very likely, before Noah's flood, conferred distinction on the whole community.

Of course, no coal or blankets or soup in winter, or little delicacies for invalids, could be expected from that quarter. For these the Restharrow poor had to look to the lady of the Manor House, and even from thence such bounties came in a trickle, rather than in the steady, generous stream known in more fortunate villages. 'Poor and proud' was the local description of the Manor House family, which family at that date consisted of Mrs. Maitland herself and one son, away at school, and afterwards at Oxford. Her daughters had married and gone to live in other counties.

At one time the Maitlands had owned the greater part of the parish; but, farm by farm, then field by field, they had had to sell their property, until only the house and grounds, some of the village cottages, and a few acres of what had been the home farm remained. It was said that by that time all would have gone had not the late squire, Mrs. Maitland's husband, met with a comparatively early death in the hunting field, leaving their baby son and the shrunken remains of the family estate to the able, determined management of his widow. Now, it was thought, she had so far retrieved the situation that her son, when he came of age, would be able in a modest way to maintain the establishment. Charity had sometimes seen the young squire when home for his school holidays and, later, from Oxford, riding his pony, or carrying his gun or fishing tackle, a tall, slender youth with smooth dark hair and friendly brown eyes. He had always a smile for the children playing in the road and a cheerful greeting for the old men and women, and he had once given a huge pike he had caught to Mrs. Taverner, who had a family of twelve, including herself and her husband. It was Master Roger, too, who had got old Bowden's thatched roof repaired. At first Mrs. Maitland had said that as the Bowdens paid but a shilling a week rent and were six months behind with that, she could do nothing, even if they did have to fix up an umbrella over their bed. Then, according to the parlourmaid at the Manor House, Master Roger had offered to pay for the work with his pocket-money, and his mother had said of course he must not; that she herself was sorry about the rain coming through on their bed, but an active old fellow like Bowden could, if he liked, borrow a ladder and repair the thatch; he was a lazy old scamp, old Bowden. However, she would give orders that the work should be done at her own expense.

When Charity first remembered her, Mrs. Maitland was a tall, tight-lipped, aristo-cratic-looking middle-aged woman. Her son, Mr. Roger, was the youngest of her family, a late-comer after a long interval. Although she was what the village called

'near' in money matters, her own dress was of the richest descrip-tion, of dark-coloured silks and velvets with real lace at the neck and wrists and with skirts of a length to trail slightly. In summer weather she carried a parasol with a long carved ivory handle which she held between her thumb and first finger with the air of a queen holding her sceptre. Her carriage was majestic, her ideas were feudal, and her heart, if she had one, was deeply hidden. No one in the village had ever seen her moved or excited. She lived in her grand house, removed, as it seemed, from the trials and vexations of lesser humanity. Although she had entertained little during her stewardship, she had kept up her county connexions, and any fine afternoon might be seen driving out in her old-fashioned carriage to pay calls. Twice a week she went to the

village school to examine the girls' needlework and to hear the younger children repeat the catechism. She visited regularly the poorer cottagers and was said to be very good to the sick and aged.

She had never been to Charity's home, for the Finches belonged to the class then known as the comfortable poor, and, as such, were supposed to have no need of her ministrations. Perhaps, too, she felt some degree of personal distaste for that particular family. George Finch, called in to repair some floorboards in the Manor House drawing-room, had told her frankly that patching would be of no use, for dry rot had set in and a new floor and wainscoting were necessary. 'I'll patch up the planks if you wish, Ma'am,' he had said, 'but if you take my advice you'll make a complete clearance.'

At that the lady had, as he had expressed it, reared up: 'You will please do the work I have ordered,' she commanded. 'But when once this here dry rot sets in —' he had begun, his craftsman's soul troubled by the ruin he envisaged, but he was talking to an empty room; the lady had gone and he heard the silken rustle of her skirts on the stairs.

He had felt his experience slighted and had taken offence. It did not occur to him that the lady, quite probably, had gone to her bedroom to face in privacy what may have been to her an appalling expense. Or that her pride and hauteur might have been a shield and the woman behind it as vulnerable as anything human. It must have been gall and wormwood to her pride to feel herself hated by her maids for her frugal housekeeping and to imagine the comments of the villagers when her bounty did not come up to their Big House standard. Like many elderly ladies of her day, she no longer attempted to keep up with the changing fashions, and her rich clothes may have seen long service, for such materials as she favoured would with care last a lifetime, and her furs and real lace were probably family possessions. But her gallant stand to save her son's inheritance was outside the range of village sympathy. The real poor cannot be expected to sympathize with the difficulties of the poor-rich, and the general view of her economies was expressed when they said she was one of them who'd skin a flint for a farthing, if she spoilt a good knife over the job.

Pride and poverty had soured Mrs. Maitland. The more typical country lady of her age and social position was, if somewhat masterful, kindly, and often showed genuine affection for her poorer neighbours. Once in her childhood Charity had an opportunity of studying one of these ladies closely. Restharrow stood in the midst of good hunting country; hounds often met near the village and the hunt in full cry over fields and hedges was a familiar sight to its inhabitants. One mild, misty December morning a middle-aged lady had taken a toss in a field near the Finch's cottage and had been brought there to rest while her carriage was fetched to take her to her own home in a distant village. She had escaped injury, but felt, as she said, a little shaken. 'Not as young as I once was,' she told Mrs. Finch. 'Ten years ago I should have taken that fence like a bird. But I mustn't grumble, I've had forty-five years with the best pack in the county and enjoyed every run. I'm now sixty-two and it's time I gave up the huntin' and stayed by the fireside makin' flannel petticoats for my old women.'

'Excuse me, my lady, but I can't see you sitting indoors sewing on a hunting morning. It doesn't seem natural, somehow,' said Mrs. Finch, who, down on her knees on the hearth-rug, had been pulling off the lady's hunting boots and now slipped on her feet a brand new pair of carpet slippers she had in readiness for her husband's birthday. As she rose, the lady looked her full in the face. 'By all that's holy, it's Alice!' she exclaimed, seizing her hand, and from the conversation which followed Charity soon gathered that the lady sitting in her father's armchair with the skirt of her habit turned up over her knees and her feet on the fender was no lesser person than the great Lady Travers who reigned over the distant village which had been her own mother's birthplace.

Mrs. Finch's offer of refreshment was welcomed. 'That fool of a groom' who had taken the two mounts and gone for the carriage had carried off with him his mistress's sandwich case. So a pot of tea was quickly made and the table was spread with a modest repast to which Lady Travers did full justice. Over the meal old times and old friends were discussed. So-and-So was married and the father or mother of so many children, or had emigrated to Australia and was doing well there, or had not been heard of for years. Poor old Mark Allen had died at last, this very winter, ninety-eight. Pity he couldn't have stayed the course and made his century! Sir Thomas had intended to celebrate his hundredth birthday, with a tea-fight for the whole village, with Mark as the guest of honour and a birthday cake and whatnot, but it was not to be. 'Yes, I will have another cup, please. I know it's my third, but never take more than one cup before starting to a meet. It doesn't do with a long day on horseback before one. And I'll have another of your excellent sandwiches, if you don't mind, and you need not bother to

cut the bread or the bacon too thin, I'm sharp set, as you see, sharp set! There!' as she wiped her lips with her pocket handkerchief, 'I haven't enjoyed a meal so much for an age. I must say you know how to cure a side of bacon. Ours has never been quite so good since Saunders left. Oh, yes, she's gone, pensioned off two years ago and living in that little cottage in the park where poor old Trent spent his last days. You remember Trent? He died two years last Christmas. Eighty-seven. We still miss the old fellow. Ah, Alice, we have had many changes of late. You heard about our own poor boy?'

Alice said she had read in the newspaper at the time that the Captain had been killed in the Sudan and had been sorry. 'Yes,' said the lady. 'It is always saddening to see a young life cut short. And this was one that could ill be spared – heir to an estate like ours and full of ideas for improving the property – intended to sell out and leave the Army when things quieted down again; but we must not murmur, God knows what is best for us.'

Charity, making herself scarce on the window-seat, herself unnoticed, but with the handsome, hooked-nosed profile of their guest in view, was amazed to see one big tear course silently down the weather-beaten cheek. Then the lady blew her nose loudly and said in her ordinary, cheerful tone, 'Thank God he died for his Queen and country!' Then, with barely a pause, 'You've got a nice little place here. Just the kind of little place I should like myself if the time should come for me to retire. Our Dower House, as no doubt you remember, is bleak and bare and far too large for one old woman. And your girl does you credit, but why only one? Ah, yes, of course, I understand, and a nasty time you must have had, I'm sure. And you've got a good husband, I hope?' Alice said that she had the best husband in the world and was rather surprisingly told that she was lucky, for good husbands were few and far between; certainly there were not enough of them to go round.

'She's a fine-spirited one is Lady Travers,' said Charity's mother after she had gone. 'I remember once when I was a child she was out with the guns and stepped in a hole and broke her ankle. They said Sir Thomas was all of a dither and white as a sheet, but though the pain must have been awful she laughed and told him there was no need to make a fuss; she wasn't killed, only wounded. "Get me home and send for the doctor," she said. "It's certainly a bit painful, but if I can't bear a bit of pain at my time of life I'm no sportswoman." And the gentlemen carried her home, bandy, two at a time, in turns. Of course they ought to

have got a hurdle or something to carry her on and have kept her foot up, but the keeper didn't like to tell 'em so, and off they went over the rough ground with her foot going dangle, dangle, and swelled to the size of vegetable marrow by the time they got her home, and not so much as a groan.'

That hunting morning, before she left the Finch's cottage, Lady Travers said lightly, 'Where's the child's money-box?' and Charity, not understanding her mother's forbidding headshake, fetched it, as she thought, merely to be inspected. Her ladyship turned up the skirt of her habit and, from some interior pocket, produced a bright half-sovereign and slipped it into the box. She knew that to have offered payment to her hostess for her hospitality would have given offence; yet she could not have brought herself to have consumed so much of Alice's excellent bacon and make no recompense, so she did what she would have called 'the right thing', gracefully and unostentatiously, talking all the time of other matters.

There were several other such gallant old ladies at that time still living about the countryside. One Lady Louisa was still riding to hounds at the age of near eighty. Keen sportswomen, good neighbours, kind though exacting employers, bounteous to the poor in their own villages, they ruled over their own small worlds as by sovereign right and, when they died, they were mourned by whole neighbourhoods. And they had their counterparts among their poorer neighbours. Women who also knew how to do the right thing in their lesser degree. Learned only in country lore and the Holy Scriptures, but keenly intelligent, they ruled over their own families, fulfilled their personal obligations, and used their spare energy in helping their neighbours. Racy of tongue, forthright in manner, firm believers in the cakes-and-ale side of life, with big, comfortable bosoms and fat sides, often shaken with laughter, they slapped life into the newly born and sped the dying with words of homely comfort. Their day has passed and they have passed with their day; there is no place for Lady Bountiful or Dame Smith in this modern world. But in their own day they served their world well. In the family vault and the unmarked grave, peace be to their ashes!

III

WATERSIDE FARM

IN a small village like Restharrow, everyone knew everyone and all were counted as neighbours; but there was one family which concerned Charity and her parents more than the rest. It was that of her uncle, Reuben Truman. Reuben was a farm bailiff who occupied part of a farmhouse at the farther end of the village. His wife had been Mrs. Finch's dearly loved elder sister. While Charity had been quite a small child, she had died, leaving her husband with three daughters, the eldest at that time fifteen, the youngest but two years old. As Waterside stood out in the fields beyond the farther end of the one long, straggling village street, a distance of nearly a mile separated the two dwellings. But this distance had never been allowed to restrict communication; when Charity's aunt was alive, she and her mother had met almost daily, for, besides being sisters, they were the closest of friends and did nothing without consulting each other. On Sundays it was the custom for the two families to take tea at each other's houses alternately, and on weekdays there were garments to be cut out, jam or pickles or home-made wine to be made, or some important family letter to be written in collaboration. And, almost every day, between school hours, one or other or both of Charity's elder cousins would come running over the grass plot in front of her home with a book, or the newspaper, or the paper pattern of some garment, or to borrow or bring back something, or with what they called a 'taster' of something their mother had cooked. If they happened to come at a mealtime, they would draw up a chair to the table as a matter of course, and Charity was just as much at home at their house, for, as the neighbours sometimes said, the two families were like one family.

One of Charity's earliest recollections was of her eldest cousin, Bess, racing across the grass patch with hair and pinafore flying and, in her hand, a covered basin, calling, 'Cherry curds! Cherry curds, ho! Old Daisy has calved and I've brought some cherry curds for our Cherry,' and Cherry sat down on a little, low stool and was given a spoon and ate her curds, just like little Miss Muffet. Only there was no nasty great spider to

bother her; it would have been difficult to find a spider or a spider's web in Mrs. Finch's clean, tidy house. The spiders lived in the workshop, up in the rafters, where no one disturbed them unless someone got a bad cut, when a handful of their dark, thick webs would be reached down and clapped on the wound to stop the bleeding.

After the girls' mother had died and Bess had had to turn house-keeper, Cousin Mercy was the usual messenger. She would come in, puffing and panting with hurrying, for she was a sturdy, thickset girl and fattish, and say, 'Please, Aunt Alice, how long ought our Bess to boil that breast and hand of pork?' or 'What groceries ought she to get

when the wagon goes to Banbury?' or, unrolling a bundle, 'Please, Aunt, our Bess says would you mind ironing our Polly's Sunday frock. She's washed and starched and rough-dried it, but she can never get the frills to set nohow,' and the advice or the help was most willingly given, for Mrs. Finch felt she could never do enough for those she spoke of as 'those poor motherless girls'.

When Charity was old enough to be trusted out alone, she was often sent to the farm. 'Now, be sure not to get run over,' her mother would say, snapping the elastic of her hat under her chin, and she would promise to be careful, though it would have been difficult for a much more venturesome child than her to have got itself run over on a road where the most dashing equipage was the Manor House wagonette with, between its shafts, the old grey mare, which at other times pulled the lawn-mower. The doctor's gig, an occasional farm wagon, the baker's van, or the coalman's cart were the only other wheeled vehicles she was likely to meet. She might see a horseman or a horsewoman, a tinker with his barrow, or a herd of cows ambling peacefully homeward towards milking time, but seldom anything more dangerous. Once, indeed, on a grey, misty, September morning, she had suddenly been confronted by a large flock of geese being driven by road to market. She had not stopped to say 'Bo!' to them, but had crept between the lower rails of a field gate, for she knew that geese had a nasty way of stretching out their necks and hissing at small girls. When they had passed and she had ventured out of the field, she found the wet road patterned all over with webbed footprints, and that pleased her. She was one of those children who notice such things.

Usually she saw but a neighbour coming from the well with her water-buckets, or a youth riding sideways on a farm horse, *clop, clopping* along with jingling harness from field to field, or, out of school hours, children playing marbles or hopscotch in the road. They usually played together near their homes, but, once, on a cold windy day, she had met a big fair boy of seven, in petticoats made from an old plaid shawl of his mother's, his knees blue-mottled with cold, marching alone in the middle of the road, drumming on an empty treacle tin and shouting:

Wake up the dead! What ho! What ho!
How sound they sleep who lie below,
Never heeding poor mortals who walk aboe,
Wake up the dead! Wake up the dead!

and, really, she thought, Johnny Tuffrey was making enough noise to awaken them. Charity knew the lines; she had read them, written in pale brown ink, on the fly-leaf of an old Prayer Book at home; but to hear them shouted aloud close by the churchyard wall seemed to her shocking. Suppose the sleepers within should hear him: what then?

Poor Johnny himself with his bold blue eyes and massive knees was soon to join the sleepers. A few years later, a month after he had started work, the horses had moved on prematurely and he had been flung, face foremost, from a loaded wagon in the harvest field. One moment he had been brimming with life and high spirits; the next, not all the noise in the world could have awakened him. Poor Johnny!

After the footpath had crossed the meadow it merged in a little green lane which led to the open fields and a farmyard where elaborately thatched and pointed stacks stood on stone straddles. From this, past a long apple orchard, a rutted track led by a less direct route than the footpath to the road which passed the church. The farmhouse was built of grey limestone and half covered with creepers, including a monthly rose trained round the parlour window, which, except in frosty spells, could show a few pale pink blooms nine months out of the twelve. In June it was covered with blossoms; the girls used to pick great bunches out of the bedroom windows to give to their friends.

Waterside Farm had been so named because of the stream which flowed, with the road between, in front of the house and the farm-buildings. It was the stream which as a brooklet ran before Charity's home, but in the course of its windings and turnings back upon itself through the fields it had grown deeper and wider. In front of the stable yard at Waterside a dam had been made, with, beneath it, a round pool that had been scooped out for the horses to drink from, and the water falling over this ledge into the pool kept up continually a splashing, gurgling, waterfallish sound which Charity afterwards remembered as one of the distinctive voices of Waterside. When after more meanderings the stream reached the next village, it had increased sufficiently in depth and width to be known as 'the

51

river'. And as the river it continued, threading the rich, flat, corn-growing country, with water-lilies on its breast and bulrushes by its margins, past quiet villages and peaceful, prosperous little towns, until at last it came to and was merged in the North Sea, known at that time as the German Ocean.

The farmhouse was a roomy, rambling old place. In the older, back portion, stone steps led up into some of the rooms and down into others. A long, stone-floored passage ran through the house from the front door to the back door, and opening off this, near the back door, was the big living kitchen, also stone-floored, though cheerful and cosy-looking, with its two windows, brightly coloured rag rugs, good fires and well-filled dresser. Next to the kitchen door was a glass-panelled one which opened out into a small walled garden. Tradition said that in the palmy days of the house, before it had become a farmhouse, this garden had been the ladies' herb garden. But that was probably a guess, for no one living remembered that time or who had lived there. When Charity grew older, as a girl in her teens, she often marvelled that of all the people who had been born, lived and died in that house, nothing whatever was known, not even their names, though to have occupied a house such as that they must have been people of some importance. It may be that the big altar tomb surrounded by iron railings in the churchyard belonged to them, or the other graves with sculls and cross-bones, or cherub's heads, carved in high relief on the headstones. Rain and frost had obliterated the incised inscriptions.

Surrounding the back courtyard were many out-buildings – wash-house, brew-house, dairy, and cheese-room – reminders of a time when the farmhouse had been the headquarters of the farmer himself. Now that the herd of cows had been moved to grazing grounds nearer their owner's present abode, dairy and cheese-room stood empty and were kept locked to save cleaning. Through the dim, cobwebbed panes glimpses might be caught of old, forgotten utensils once in use there, stone slabs, rusty dippers, and wooden milking-pails, falling to pieces. The brewhouse had been abandoned long before the dairy, and the only out-building still in use was the one known as the pump-house, where water was obtained for domestic purposes. The front part of the house had at some time been rebuilt and the rooms there were large and well-proportioned, with long sash windows with window-seats and white panelled inside shutters, high ceilings, and handsome mantelpieces. In one of these rooms stood an immense oak settle which had been found too large and heavy to be removed

with the other goods belonging to the farmer, and that was the only furniture in either of the two front parlours, for neither of the present tenants had sufficient to half fill one of them, and they had chosen smaller and, to them, more homely apartments.

Although Charity's uncle lived in what seemed to her a very fine house, it must not be supposed that he was a rich or in any way an important person. He was but a working bailiff, or foreman, who, when the farmer had moved with his family into a newer and more convenient farmhouse, had been given part of the old one instead of a cottage. His duty it was to set the men employed on that part of the farm to work on the tasks decreed by the farmer and to visit them from time to time in the fields to see that they did their work properly. Between-whiles, he kept all in order about the farmstead and, when called for, he would often appear, wearing the old smock frock he called his yard smock, with a shovel, or a broom, or a polishing-rag in his hand. When he rode out to inspect the work of the men on the grey, long-tailed pony the farmer had provided for his use, he discarded his smock and appeared in the usual bailiff's garb of rough tweed coat and cord breeches and gaiters. Reuben Truman was a countryman through and through, a sturdily built man with greying hair and beard and the healthy complexion of one who had never had a day's illness in his life. His expression was serious; some might have thought it severe, save when something was said or done which brought the twinkle to his eyes and the countryman's slow, cautious smile to his lips. He had a passion for horses and liked to see the teams turned out in the morning well-groomed and with plaited manes and tails and shining brasses, as if, the men said, they were going to a fair, instead of to a hard day's ploughing. As only a young carter was kept, any extra work involved fell upon Reuben himself. He would cut big squares of hay from the hayrick with a great flashing knife to fill the racks above the mangers, give the stable floors an extra cleaning and bed them down with clean straw. If a horse was unwell, he would doctor it himself, only calling in the vet for serious cases, when he would play the part of nurse to the other one's doctor. When old Captain, the big grey carthorse with feathered fetlocks, had pneumonia, Reuben sat up all night poulticing its chest. He had the management of the mares when foaling and of the breaking in of young colts, and for these duties he received a money bonus. His standing wage was thirty shillings a week. His hobby was that of acquiring and keeping well-polished the brass horse-ornaments which decorated the foreheads and reins of his favourites.

There were those in the village who did not like Reuben. They said he was too solemn and strait-laced and 'a durned sight too particular' as to how the work was done, 'Jest for all th' world as if the land was his'n and all the profits went into his pocket. Give me a bayley like Muster Radley o' Shaplands,' they'd say. 'Wi' him, if things look all right they be all right, an' none o' y'r pokin' an' peerin' an' as like as not findin' fault, an' ready to crack a joke or to drain a pint pot wi' th' next man,' and when Mr. Radley disappeared suddenly from the neighbourhood on account of some shady dealings with a corn-merchant, they continued to speak of him as the poor man's friend. Those who had nothing to fear from inspection of their work liked and respected Reuben for his readiness to give credit where credit was due, and for his thoroughness and downright sincerity. Those who had found him a friend in trouble loved the man.

From the time she had been a small child, Charity had loved her Uncle Reuben. No matter how busy he might be about the farmyard, he would always find time to show her the new foal nozzling in the straw beside its mother; or the fat old sow with her family of little pink piglets. Or he would reach her down a ripe pear from the tree, or find her a freshly laid egg, warm from the nest, to take home for her breakfast next morning. Such small kindnesses please children, and she loved him for them; but she loved him more deeply for what he was in himself, though at that time she could not have defined what appealed to her in his character.

Her parents spoke of him as 'Reuben', or, to her, as 'your Uncle Reuben', as of one so firmly established as he was then in their lives and thoughts that a Reuben at any other age or in any other relationship was unthinkable. Charity, looking back in later years, thought how little they had really known about him. He had married Mrs. Finch's sister comparatively late in life, his age at that time being forty and his bride's twenty. She had been a newcomer to the village, as had the rest of her family. Even living in a remote village and working on the land, no man can reach the age of forty without going through many experiences. By the time he has reached that age, what most people would regard as the best years of his life have passed, and in most lives those are the most eventful years. Reuben had been a boy, a young man, and a man in his prime before they had known him; he had not always been just 'Uncle Reuben'.

Reuben Truman had been twice married. Charity had learned this one autumn afternoon when she had gone to the churchyard with her mother to plant bulbs on the grave of his second wife, her own Aunt Marianna. The graves of his two wives were far apart, for the poor of that parish had no choice of a burial plot; their dead were buried in long rows and the latest comer was given the next vacant plot after the last burial. 'A nice tidy arrangement, but a bit of a mix up,' Mrs. Finch had remarked, energetically digging and prodding with the little fork she had brought with her to plant her snowdrop bulbs. 'Old enemies lying side by side quite as often as good neighbours. Those two at the end of that row there were always at it, hammer and tongs, in their lifetimes – but of course you remember Mrs. Pulbrook and Caroline?'

Charity remembered them well and saw them again in imagination: Mrs. Pulbrook, large, pink-cheeked and placid-looking, when untroubled by her foe, and Caroline, about five feet high and dark as a gipsy, with snaky curls and spit-fire eyes and a voice which, as the neighbours said, went through your head like a knife. The two had lived side by side in a pair of semi-detached cottages, like two matchboxes set end to end under one covering of thatch. The two front doors were but a foot or two apart and the

best of good neighbours might have found such propinquity a strain on their neighbourly feelings. To Mrs. Pulbrook and Caroline it was fatal. Between their contests they were not on speaking terms and, after Mrs. Pulbrook had whitened her doorstep in the morning, her door was kept closed for the rest of the day, so that she might not see Caroline lounging on her own untidy doorstep and, as she said, be tempted to set the mark of her ten finger-nails on her impudent face. But the two back gardens had no dividing fence and, with wood to be chopped, pigs to be fed, and washing to be hung on the line, they were bound to come face to face almost daily. And when they did, as the neighbours said, the feathers began to fly. 'As good as a poppy show, any day,' was the comment of a man who had chanced to witness one of their encounters. 'Poor old Ma Pulbrook, as red as a turkey cock and tremblin' like a leaf, and Caroline – you ought to've seen Caroline, the little devil! dancin' round and round an' shakin' her fist at the poor old soul; baitin' her, reg'larly baitin' her!'

When and how the feud had begun nobody knew; but whatever the cause of their original difference, at the mere sight of each other it revived. Charity had been told never to go near when she heard their voices raised, for their language, especially that of Caroline, was what her mother called 'not pretty for a child to hear'; but as she had to pass their gate four times a day on her way to and from school, she could not always avoid hearing. As it happened, she heard what must have been one of their last contests.

Mrs. Pulbrook had been to fetch water from the well, and the two heavy buckets, suspended by a yoke from her shoulders, had no doubt tired her, for she had set them down on the path inside their gate and was standing with her hands on her hips, panting, when Caroline came out and accused her of blocking the pathway. Caroline had had her say – there was no stopping her once she had started – then, without permitting Mrs. Pulbrook to get in a word edgeways, she screamed what she intended as a parting shot: 'And now you get along indoors, you old so-and-so, and cry y'r so-and-so eyes out, same as you did the last time I told yer a bit o' God's truth,' and Mrs. Pulbrook, who had not caught what she had said and perhaps had lost some of her old spirit, for soon afterwards she fell ill of the complaint which carried her to the churchyard, turned weakly and said, 'Eh?'

'Ay – Ay – Ay!' jeered Caroline. Then chanted: *'Ay for 'osses, straw for cows, milk f'r little pigs, and wash for gert ole sows* – like you!' And, stung by the insult, Mrs. Pulbrook rallied and retorted, *'You mind your own business and I'll mind mine. You drink the pigs' wash and I'll drink wine!'* Whether or not this rhyming back-chat was extemporized is hard to say. Probably not, though Charity had never heard it before and never heard it again. In either case it made a neat ending to their long contention.

A few days later Mrs. Pulbrook was taken ill and the next time Charity saw Caroline she had a clean face and was wearing a nearly clean apron, and was stepping from her own doorstep to that of Mrs. Pulbrook with a covered basin in her hand. 'Tendin' her night and day, same as she might her own mother,' people said of Caroline. 'Shows she can't be a bad gal at bottom, f'r all her tantrumy ways.' When Mrs. Finch repeated this to her husband, he remarked rather dryly that he had no doubt there was some good in everybody, but you often had to be dying before you got down to it. Mrs. Pulbrook died, and a few months later Caroline was knocked down by a cart and fatally injured coming back late on a Saturday night from Mixlow, and, as hers was the next death in the village, she was laid by the side of her old enemy. 'But what's the odds?' said Mrs. Finch cheerfully while planting the snowdrops. 'They're quiet and peaceful enough now! And, mind, not a word to the girls about me planting these snowdrops. I want it to be a surprise to them when they come out next February.'

It was like Charity's mother to think less of the dead than the living. She had dearly loved her elder sister and had shed many bitter tears when she died. But that was five years before the day when she planted the snowdrops, and she had long ceased grieving and had even ceased saying, 'All the grieving in the world won't bring the dead back to life again,' though her care had never slackened for those her sister's death had left motherless.

The graves of Mrs. Pulbrook and Caroline could easily be distinguished, for the grass had not had time to engulf them; but, beyond them, the low, unmarked mounds were swallowed up in a green tide and Charity was afraid she would step upon one as she tiptoed behind her mother between the long lines to the older part of the churchyard.

'Here we are,' said her mother at last. 'It's easy to find because of the headstone,' and Charity read aloud, stumbling a little over the Christian name, which was new to her:

Lavinia.
The Beloved Wife of Reuben Truman.
Who departed this Life
November 23rd, 1856.
Aged 19 years.

and her mother told her that Lavinia had been buried with a little day-old baby on her arm which could not be mentioned on the headstone because it had not been baptized. 'But,' she continued, 'that's only what I've been told. It all happened long before any of us came to live here, and your uncle's never mentioned her to me, nor I to him. I expect he felt losing her at the time, but a lot has happened since then and very likely he's forgotten all about her. Men are like that.'

After that, Charity would sometimes wade through the churchyard grass to Lavinia's grave, and she several times noticed a trail other than her own from the path to the grave. In spring the grave was covered with forget-me-nots, like a lovely blue counterpane over a bed. At the time she thought that the flowers had been planted long before and seeded and renewed themselves year after year; but in later life she concluded that, though she had been dead thirty years, and he had married again and had children and again been widowed, Reuben had not forgotten Lavinia.

The grave of Charity's own Aunt Marianna was as homely a sight to her as their own front garden bed at home. She often went with her cousins to place flowers upon it, and when on one of these occasions little Polly said, 'I wonder what Mother was like,' she was able to tell her. She remembered her Aunt Marianna best as she had been on the day of Polly's christening, a small, plump woman with a kind smile, and dark hair which, for all her smoothing, would escape at her temples and the nape of her neck in tiny, round curls. That Sunday she had been wearing a dress of her favourite plum colour, with lots of little frills, and before she had taken the baby up from the cradle, she had turned back her skirt and made a lap on her white embroidered petticoat, 'For fear of accidents,' she had said.

Charity remembered all this because Polly's christening party stood out as one of the first landmarks in her childhood. She and her parents had, of course, been invited, but all the morning the sky had been dark and lowering and she had feared that it would rain and her mother would say they must stay at home. 'There's snow about. I can smell and taste it, and by the look of that feather-bed sky we're going to have a lot of it before we're very much older,' her father had said as he held open the garden gate for her mother and her to pass through.

'Oh, dear!' her mother had exclaimed. 'I wonder what we'd better do. I don't like taking Charity out if it's likely to snow, and her bronchitis so bad last winter, and yet I don't see how we can stop at home, me being one of the godmothers, and having promised to meet them in the church porch.' And she stood stock-still on the plank bridge, looking upward, as though for guidance.

'Oh, come along, do!' urged her husband impatiently. 'We can't stand here all day sky-gazing like a lot of ducks in a thunderstorm. It's not often I go to church, and now I have got into my best suit I'm not going to turn back for a few snowflakes,' for, even as he was speaking, the first fine flakes had come powdering down and Charity's mother had opened her best umbrella.

'We shan't have much yet awhiles,' spoke the voice of authority; 'and if we do we're not made of sugar; we shan't melt. Here, take my arm, and Charity, you take hold of my other hand.' And thus linked together, with snowflakes floating around them, they had trudged churchward.

The village street was deserted of all but themselves. Firelight flickered on the cottage window-panes, every door and window was shut fast; evidently it was the 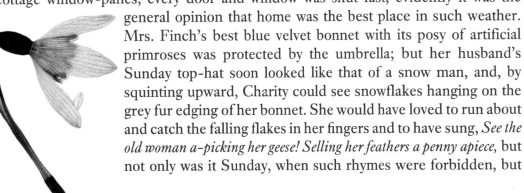 general opinion that home was the best place in such weather. Mrs. Finch's best blue velvet bonnet with its posy of artificial primroses was protected by the umbrella; but her husband's Sunday top-hat soon looked like that of a snow man, and, by squinting upward, Charity could see snowflakes hanging on the grey fur edging of her bonnet. She would have loved to run about and catch the falling flakes in her fingers and to have sung, *See the old woman a-picking her geese! Selling her feathers a penny apiece,* but not only was it Sunday, when such rhymes were forbidden, but she also feared to draw attention to herself before they were more than halfway up the street and nearer the church than home. If they take me back after starting, she thought, my heart will be broken. She had recently heard for the first time of a broken heart. So she made herself as small as possible and walked very quietly, consoling herself the while by licking the snowflakes off the fur edging of her tippet.

After they had passed the *Magpie* one other churchgoer appeared. It was Luke Atwell, a stocky, red-faced youth of eighteen, who had been asked to stand godfather to the baby. He was waiting for them at his mother's gate, dressed, most unsuitably for the weather, in his all-the-year-round reach-me-down suit of pale grey, with a brand new bright magenta necktie, bought specially for the occasion. His large red hands hung bare by his sides and his peaked cloth cap was but poor protection for his carefully oiled and parted crop of light flaxen hair; but he looked so well pleased with his appearance that it seemed almost cruel of Charity's father to say, 'Surely you're not going out in this weather in that rig-out? Where's your top coat, man? You'll need it before you get back.' Luke, ever obedient to the voice of authority, even when, as now, the authority was that of age alone, went back indoors and reappeared wearing the old black waterproof he wore at his work. It was the only overcoat he possessed, and that, like his suit, had become too small for him. 'Button up the collar, or you'll get a sore throat,' advised Mrs. Finch, and, obedient still, though reluctant, poor Luke extinguished the glory of his bright new tie. Why did not grown-up people understand a person's feelings better, thought Charity.

Luke had begun to work for his own and his widowed mother's living when he was ten years old, at first scaring rooks from the corn, then as a ploughboy, leading by the rein great carthorses which, as the ploughmen told him, could have eaten him up, bones and all, at one mouthful. In time he had become a ploughman himself, and now was working under Reuben as carter at Waterside, earning man's wages, as his mother told people proudly. But as those wages were only ten shillings a week – although Luke and his mother had become as well off as most other people in the village and better off than some, for they were but two in family – after they had paid their rent and for food and firing, they had little left over for clothes. Reuben had asked Luke to stand godfather to the baby because, he had said, 'Luke's a good, willing, hard-working chap and deserves encouragement,' and his wife, who was one of the sweetest-natured creatures on earth, had dismissed from her mind her own more ambitious plan of asking the farmer to honour them, and said, 'Yes, to be sure, and such a good boy to his mother.

spirits soon made him a general favourite, not only with his adopted family, but also with the neighbours. Reuben had hoped that he would stay at the farm and work under him on the land, but Oliver had an adventurous nature, and in those days and in that place the only way to gratify this was to enlist in the Army. Oliver had enlisted, and by the time of Polly's birth he had been a year on foreign service.

On that snowy christening Sunday, Charity, trudging along between her two cousins, had been thinking of her mother's promise that when the baby was undressed for bed that night she should hold it on her lap. Being an only child, she had never seen a small baby without its outer wrappings, and the prospect of holding and touching one was exciting. And how happy she felt that after her day-long fears and in spite of the snow they were actually on their way to Waterside. She was so much younger than her companions that a great deal of their talk went on over her head, but when Luke began telling the story of the ghost which had recently appeared in the churchyard at midnight, she listened. It was a negative kind of ghost, a floating figure in white, without shape or form,  name, story, or sex, that Bill Gaskin said he had seen hovering over the churchyard when he had returned at midnight from a visit to his sick sister. The more matter-of-fact were inclined to think that all Bill had seen had been mist, or a gleam of moonlight on a tombstone; but the superstitious majority were, or affected to be, terribly upset, and nobody was disposed to go near the churchyard after nightfall.

'I bet you'd be afraid to come this way after dark,' Bess was saying, and Luke, who was a truthful lad, admitted that he'd rather not. 'But,' he added, 'I'd come like a shot in the middle of the night if I'd summat to come for – if one of th' 'osses wer' took bad an' Muster Truman sent for me, or if one of th' 'ayricks got fired, or anything.' And Bess laughed and said he could well afford to make rash promises, because he knew very well that if every horse in the stable got colic at once, her father would not send for him, but for Mr. Virtue, the vet.; and as to the hayrick firing, that was not likely to happen; their hay was well dried before it was stacked. 'So, there, young Luke, that means you dursent go at all, not even with one of your grand turnip lanterns to light you! But what are they stopping for?'

The couple in front with the baby had stopped and Mrs. Truman was calling and beckoning. They could not hear what she was saying at that distance, but her husband's strong voice took up and repeated her call: 'Bess! Bess! Bes-sy!' and Bess hurried on to where her mother and aunt were waiting and apparently was given some instructions, for she ran on at top speed towards home, raising and letting fall her arms in the long cape sleeves in imitation of a bird flying.

Soon they were all in the big, warm living kitchen, their damp outer garments removed, and their faces, burnished by a rough towelling, reflecting the blaze of the fresh log Bess had thrown on the embers. The blaze shone on the brightly-coloured crockery on the dresser shelves and the brass candlesticks and red-and-white pottery dogs on the mantelpiece and lighted up the festive-looking tea-table, which had been left ready spread with the best china and with dishes of bread and butter and scones and jam, and, to crown all, in the middle, the christening cake which, the day before, Charity's mother had iced and inscribed in pink sugar piping: *Mary Alice.*

But there was a surprise to come. When, in the semi-privacy of the chimney-corner, Mrs. Truman had fed Mary Alice with food more suitable to her age than iced cake and laid her in her cradle, 'Now, Bess', she said. 'Look sharp with the forks and spoons.' Then, to the company at large, 'You'll never guess what I've got for your teas.'

Her sister, with her head on one side, studied the forks and spoons Bess was placing on the table, then said in the conventionally reproachful tone called for in such circumstances, 'You've never gone and cooked a ham?' 'No,' said her sister. 'It's not ham; nothing so common. It's something you've never heard of for tea before, christening or no christening. But you wait a minute and you'll see,' and, after girding herself with a white apron, she went out to the back kitchen and soon reappeared carrying a pudding of noble proportions. 'Now, pass your plates,' she said, seating herself at table. 'I'm not going to tell you what's in it; you must find out,' and she stuck her knife into the rich, flaky suet crust, releasing a stream of brown gravy, and began to spoon generous helpings on to the plates.

'You could make a good meal on the smell alone,' said Charity's father, sniffing the air appreciatively. But what was that within the pudding which smelt so delicious? It was not beef, for it was cut into joints, and the joints were not those of a rabbit. Charity's parents looked puzzled. Luke was licking his lips and staring round-eyed. Then, as Mrs. Finch began cutting up Charity's portion, she exclaimed, 'Upon my soul, our Marianna, I do believe it's a fowl! Who ever heard of such extravagance!' And Marianna said modestly, 'I thought you'd all be as hungry as hunters this cold day, so I got Reuben to kill a couple of those cockerels.' By the terms of their agreement with the farmer, who kept no poultry at Waterside, the Trumans were permitted to keep fifteen fowls, which, it was understood, would live chiefly, or more likely wholly, on

68

their own gleanings of corn from beneath the mangers and about the farmyard, and the cockerels then sacrificed, probably belonged to a late brood which had brought the number beyond the limit. Which may have accounted for the extravagance, though not for the brilliantly original idea of putting them into a pudding.

If her guests had not felt hungry before, the sight and smell of the cockerel pudding had given them good appetites. In a very short time the last remnant of suet crust, with the last scraping of gravy and oddments of pork, were being spooned on to Luke's plate to accompany the last pickings of his drumstick. Then every vestige of the meat course was cleared from the table by Bess. 'Take pepper and salt and everything,' her mother said. 'Then I'll cut the cake. We must have a genteel tea-table when Mrs. Pocock and Stella come in.'

Mrs. Pocock and Stella were the mother and daughter who occupied part of the farmhouse. Mr. Pocock had been a former bailiff who had died from injuries caused by being tossed by a bull, and the farmer, as compensation, allowed his widow a few shillings a week and rent-free quarters at Waterside. There was plenty of room for the two families, and, as they had separate kitchens, they were able to live together amicably, though without being particularly friendly. ''T'ld never do for us to be running in and out each other's rooms at all hours of the day and telling each other everything, living at such close quarters as we do,' Mrs. Truman had said when discussing the matter with her sister, and Mrs. Pocock appeared to be of the same opinion, for she seldom came into the Trumans' living kitchen unless invited, and still more seldom invited them into her own upstair sitting-room. Which was just as well, for Mrs. Pocock and Mrs. Truman, in nature and ideas and ways of life, were as dissimilar as the proverbial chalk and cheese.

That being a formal occasion, Mrs. Pocock and Stella had been asked to the christening tea; but as they were at present attending the services at a church in the next village, Mrs. Pocock having recently decided that those at the church in her own parish were too high, they were late in returning, and she had said that they were on no account to wait tea for her. Stella and she would look in for a cup later.

Presently there came a small little rat-tat at the kitchen door and Mrs. Pocock and Stella entered. Fresh tea was made, which Mrs. Pocock sipped genteelly, her bonnet strings thrown back over her shoulders and her white hand-kerchief spread on her lap to keep any chance crumb from her Sunday skirt. She was altogether a genteel little woman, being what was known there as a 'better-most person'. The bettermost person, who was always a woman, never a man, was not, as might be supposed, one belonging to the upper ranks of society. Those at the top of the social tree were always spoken of as 'gentry' and, after them, came several grades higher than the bettermost. That term, in that locality, was used to describe anyone in ever so slight a degree removed from the general level of poverty, provided that she herself showed by her manner of living that she was conscious of her own supposed superiority. The bettermost person did not stand upon her doorstep to gossip; she invited another of her own kind to tea behind starched white lace curtains. When she went shopping, she took as her right the front seat beside the driver in the carrier's cart and turned her back, if not always a deaf ear, on the gossiping crowd in the back seats. For church or market she always wore gloves, usually of black kid, and, wet or fine, carried a neatly rolled umbrella. Mrs. Pocock was such a bettermost person, and that afternoon, in her black silk blouse, with lace at the neck and a locket suspended on a thick gold chain at her breast, she had the true bettermost appearance. Her first act on coming in had been to blow into each separate finger of her black kid gloves and place them carefully near the fire to finish drying. She had a pale, worn face, smooth, greasy-looking black hair, and remarkably small grey eyes, set closely together. Hers would not to-day be considered an attractive face, nor was hers an attractive nature; there were many of the poorer neighbours who said they couldn't abide that Pocock 'ooman, although at the big houses where she went sewing she was, according to her own account, a great favourite.

Although she could keep silent – deep as a well some people called her – she talked a great deal about herself and her own affairs, and that day, as the guest of honour at a christening tea, she evidently felt it behoved her to make conversation. They had had a blessed time that afternoon, she said; Mr. Gosney had excelled himself in his sermon. Pure Gospel, none of your popery and monkey tricks, such as crossing and curtsying, and no drifting off into Latin or Greek, like some parsons nearer home she could mention. Meaning by that not like their own eccentric, absent-minded old vicar, who had a habit of introducing Latin quotations when preaching, though, to do him justice, it must be said that he usually followed these with a translation.

Lady Aline had not been in church herself – who could expect her to be here in such weather? – but she had sent by her own maid, Miss Perkins, who had been present, a message to her, Mrs. Pocock, asking if she would kindly oblige by undertaking the young ladies' mending while the schoolroom-maid was away nursing her mother. Miss Perkins thought she had cancer and, if so, the girl might be away weeks, months even,

and how tiresome that would have been for her ladyship if she had not known to whom to turn in such an emergency. Of course, with all her own engagements, it was difficult to arrange for three days a week at Norvale House, but she meant to fit it in somehow. She didn't see why she should put herself out for folks such as Mrs. Eaton, the doctor's wife at Radley, who expected her to make her boy a suit out of one of her own old skirts and actually found fault if it didn't fit to a T. Such as her would have to wait. But she must spare one day for Mrs. Mercer at the farm; they were killing a pig on Thursday and were inclined to forget the little bit of griskin they gave her if she was not on the spot. Mrs. Mercer had said some time ago that she wanted that sea-green alpaca of hers made over for Miss Emily, and now was the time to see about it.

Marianna and Alice listened to all this with patience, if not with much sympathy, putting in Ah's and Yesses and Noes at appropriate intervals. Reuben and Luke had gone to the stables to see to the horses, and Charity's father, after asking to be excused, had retired to the chimney corner with the newspaper and a candle. Mercy and Bess were washing up the tea-things in the back kitchen, and Charity, mindful of the maxim, 'Children should be seen but not heard', sat silent on a low chair beside her mother.

Boring as Mrs. Pocock's monologue might be supposed to be to a child, Charity had not found it boring, for it had gone in at one ear and out at the other. All her attention had been concentrated on Stella Pocock, sitting at the table beside her mother, saying nothing and doing nothing, but simply being herself. Eyes of speedwell, hair pale golden, a skin like alabaster, fairylike lightness and grace of form – all were Stella's. At nine years old she was already the one perfectly beautiful person Charity was ever to see in her life, and it was sufficient pleasure to her merely to gaze upon her. When she had come in that day, fresh from the cold outer air, the ordinary lily pallor of her cheeks had been tinged with pale pink, and her hair, carefully arranged in long, fat ringlets by combing round her mother's finger, had been scattered by the wind and clung in tiny gold tendrils to the rich, dark fur of the little sealskin cap she was wearing. Her mother had hurriedly removed the cap and smoothed down the hair, apologizing for what she called Stella's untidiness, but not before Charity had absorbed an impression never to be forgotten. Looking back in after life, she sometimes wondered that, even taking into account a certain coldness of perfection in Stella's looks, her beauty had not attracted more attention. The villagers were quite ready to admit that Stella Pocock was pretty, but they usually qualified the admission by saying that hers were not the sort of good looks they admired. Too set and stiff-starched, they said, too much like an angel on a gravestone; give them a gal with a good colour in her cheeks and a bit of life and fun in her. The ladies at the great houses where her mother went sewing and where she often took Stella must have

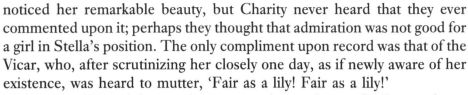

noticed her remarkable beauty, but Charity never heard that they ever commented upon it; perhaps they thought that admiration was not good for a girl in Stella's position. The only compliment upon record was that of the Vicar, who, after scrutinizing her closely one day, as if newly aware of her existence, was heard to mutter, 'Fair as a lily! Fair as a lily!'

Though her mother was a widow and poor, Stella was always prettily dressed. From the houses where she worked Mrs. Pocock returned laden. The lady of the house gave her left-off clothing for herself and for Stella; the cook filled her basket with left-over food, the gardener with fruit or choice vegetables, and even the gamekeeper made an occasional contribution of a brace of rabbits. The three upstair rooms they occupied were filled to overflowing with furniture others had discarded, and padded with carpets, cushions and curtains that had seen better days, but were still presentable. Even Stella's name had been given her by one of her mother's ladies, when graciously consenting to be her godmother. 'And may I have the honour of naming her after you, m'lady?' Mrs. Pocock had said; and the lady had replied, 'Certainly you may if you wish.'

The reason for Mrs. Pocock's popularity with such people no one knew, though there was plenty of speculation about it, some saying bluntly that she was 'a reg'lar old creeper', meaning by that she had a flattering tongue and was ready to make a doormat of herself when she saw it would be to her own advantage.

That Sunday evening Stella said little. She was at no time a talkative child and was always less communicative than usual when her mother was present. When Charity asked her if she had been permitted to hold the new baby, she said 'No', and added that she did not think she would like to as it might mess her frock. And when Charity, suddenly conscious of her own bad manners in staring so long and fixedly at Stella, suggested that they should go out to the other girls in the back kitchen, she again replied, 'No, I don't think I had better, not in my new frock.' That gave Charity the opportunity to say how pretty the frock was and how well it suited Stella. Which it did, being a perfectly plain, straight garment made of a deep sapphire velvet, which had been one of a pair of window-curtains given to Mrs. Pocock by one of her ladies, who had found that, when hung, the colour of the curtains did not harmonize with the rest of her room. Rich as the lady was, had she seen Stella in the frock she might have regretted that she had not thought of using the material to make a frock for her own daughter. But perhaps she had thought of it and decided that sapphire was not the colour to bring into close juxtaposition with the big dark eyes and sallow complexion of little Lady Anne, who at that time showed small sign of her future beauty.

After Mrs. Pocock and Stella had retired to their own part of the house, the christening party drew into a circle round the fire and the men drank beer, heated by thrusting down into the hot coals the point of the long, conical vessel there known as a hooter, while the women and girls sipped elderberry wine and ate hot roasted chestnuts. Luke held the shovel containing the chestnuts over the fire and when they were roasted handed them round in strict rotation, though the largest and best-cooked nuts seemed always to fall to Bess's share, and these, before passing them to her, he shelled. His face was almost as red as the live coals and sweat glistened upon his brow, but his broad smile betokened pure happiness.

The baby had been washed and dressed for the night and her mother and aunt took turns at holding her in their arms and rocking and singing to her. She ought, long before, to have been carried upstairs in her cradle, but, as her mother said, it was her day of her christening, and why should she be put to bed in the dark while the rest of the family was celebrating. Once or twice Luke put out his big hand and touched the tiny fingers of his godchild. Since the demand for roasted chestnuts had slacked he had become thoughtful. He opened his mouth as though about to speak, then closed it again and fidgeted with some coins in his pocket. His silence and unease became so marked that Charity's father exclaimed, 'Why, Luke, what ails you, man? You've been fidgeting this last ten minutes like a cat on hot bricks. If you've got anything to say, out with it!' and, thus brought to the point, Luke dipped into the pocket with which he had been concerned and brought out a sixpence which he  deposited upon the little round chimney-corner table beside Mrs. Truman.

'A sixpence! A bright and shining new sixpence!' she said, raising her eyebrows, 'But why? And what for?'

'For her,' stammered Luke nervously, indicating the baby. 'To – wet her hair and to bring her good luck.' His elders gazed at him in silence for a moment. They were in a delicate position. Luke's offering was a considerable amount out of his small spending-money and it could not be refused without hurting his feelings. Yet, on the other hand, they all, except Reuben, prided themselves upon belonging to a new and unsuperstitious generation which abominated such old heathenish practices as wetting the head of a newly-born child with spirits. Charity's mother especially objected to the custom still observed in the village of wetting a child's head with gin immediately after its christening; before, as she said, the blessed water was dry on its forehead.

They stared in silence at Luke, and he, never dreaming that any objection could exist to a custom observed by his parents and grandparents, and relieved that he had fulfilled his last duty as a godfather, without, as he had said, making a fool of himself, beamed back upon them. Then Mrs. Truman took up the sixpence – she said afterwards that it was nearly red hot from his constant handling – and said warmly: 'That's real good of you, Luke, and 'twill bring little Polly good luck, I feel certain. But, myself, I haven't much faith in the gin, and she does so badly need a pair of little woolly bootikins to keep her little tootsies warm, so, if you're sure you don't mind, I'll get her a pair with your sixpence next time I go shopping and you shall come in and put them on for her the first time of wearing. What colour would you like me to get, pink or pale blue?' Luke turned to Bess for advice as to colour and the episode ended happily.

Soon afterwards the christening party broke up, and Mr. and Mrs. Finch and Luke set out for their homes and bed, Mr. Finch teasingly telling Luke that he must take Mrs. Finch's hand when they came to the churchyard, or the ghost would get him.

Charity, tucked up in Bess's bed in the room overlooking the farmyard, said as Bess sprang up from saying her prayers, 'I think I can hear the brook.' Bess stood for a moment in her long white nightgown. 'Yes, that's the brook,' she said. 'You can hear it in this room at night when everything's quiet, but I'm so used to the sound I never notice.' And she jumped into bed and caught Charity in her arms and the two snuggled down in the deep feather bed.

Outside, far away in the snowy fields, a dog-fox barked sharply; an owl drifted across the window of their room, *Too-hoo-oo!*-ing; one of the horses in the stable shifted its hooves uneasily; then all was still but the stream, which stole, babbling and gurgling, all night past the silent house with its sleeping inmates.

IV

POMPADOUR APRONS

THEIR mother's death after only a few days' illness was a great blow to Bess and Mercy, and they thought and said that life could never be the same again. But they were young. Bess had her new responsibilities to cope with, Mercy her honest hard labour, while the care and management of their little sister occupied the time and thoughts of both; and, as time went on, their first painful grief became softened to a wistful regret, tempered by everyday cheerfulness.

Under her aunt's guidance, Bess became a fairly good housekeeper. She was inclined to do things by fits and starts, not keeping to a particular day for particular work. At times the whole place would be in such a ferment of activity that her father, standing in the living kitchen doorway, would call out, 'Haven't you got so much as a spot where a man can set down the sole of his foot when he comes in to dinner?' But he said it with an amused smile in his eyes, for he was mindful that Bess was still little more than a child. Although somewhat lax in the routine of housekeeping, there were other ways in which Bess excelled, especially in the eyes of the younger children. She became quite an expert at cake and pastry making, and sometimes, when in what the other girls called her good moods, she would make treacle toffee in the brass skillet over the open fire, the kind of toffee known as stick-jaw, which could be pulled out in long threads and ribbons; or she would give Charity papers of sugar and currants and rice to play shops with Polly, or make sweet, brightly-coloured drinks with fruit juice, which they all sipped out of what had been her mother's best wine glasses.

Her rule over her younger sisters was also spasmodic. At some times she treated Mercy as an equal partner and consulted her in difficulties; at others she ordered her around as though she had been a servant. People in the village began to say that Bess Truman put upon that sister of hers; but Mercy did not feel herself put upon. Beneath her somewhat stolid exterior she had an immense store of energy, and hard manual work was a pleasure to her. 'I know I'm not good-looking or clever, like our Bess,' she told her aunt, 'but there are some things I can do a lot better than she can, and I like to see a job that's got to be done well done; it gives me a sort of satisfaction,' and her satisfaction was shared by all who saw her cherry-red brick floors, her well-scoured deal tables and shining dish-covers. Mercy was one of those who love doing better than thinking or talking. She would listen to the conversation of others, seldom putting in a word herself, but nodding or smiling at appropriate intervals to show that she missed nothing. When her opinion or advice were directly asked for, it was found that neither good sense nor good judgement were lacking, and as to good nature, that was never in question, for all knew that she would, as the saying went, have given her own head away if she could have unscrewed it from her shoulders.

With Polly, Bess would one day be indulgent, letting her do as she liked and giving her whatever she asked for, allowing her to run upstairs with muddy shoes or to play with the parlour ornaments, and laughingly excusing her little misdeeds. The next day she would say that the child was getting unbearably spoilt and scold her severely for the very transgressions which, the day before, she had found amusing. Bess had always been inclined to spoil Polly. When, as a baby, she had not been allowed to have her own way and had fallen into one of her tantrums, in which she would stiffen her spine and

scream herself red in the face, and her mother had put her to bed in a darkened room as both cure and punishment, Bess would steal into the room and kiss and cuddle her. With less opposition, Polly had become better-tempered, but only on condition that she had her own way in everything, and, though she no longer kicked and screamed, she was still often tiresome. But Bess adored Polly, and it was her delight to see the child grow, to teach her her prayers and pretty manners, and, above all, to dress her prettily.

Bess was a good needlewoman and spent much of her time making or altering her own and Polly's clothes. The sewing machine stood almost permanently uncovered on the kitchen side-table, and partly made garments and scraps of material from cutting out often littered the sofa and chairs. 'You and your fal-lals!' her father would say, clearing a chair for himself before drawing it up to the table; but he never came nearer than that to reproaching her for what some fathers might have thought waste of time or extravagance. Indeed, he loved to see Bess wearing the pretty clothes she made for herself at surprisingly small cost. Although his whole being was rooted in the past, and though he practised all he thought good of the old customs, Reuben was in some other respects in advance of his age. 'Every tub must stand on its own bottom', was one of his homely ways of expressing the individual independence desirable in children.

He maintained that, no matter how loving and wise parents might be, they could only guide their children up to a certain point. After that point was reached, the child must be held responsible for its own opinions and welfare. He was a good friend to Charity when the time came for her to choose her own profession. 'You can't live her life for her. It's her life and she's got to live it; you can only help by giving her a start in the way she's inclined,' he told her parents.

Reuben was just in his money dealings with his daughters. A few weeks after he had lost his wife he began giving the two elder girls a small sum weekly, for which he refused to take credit, saying that it was well earned and only their right. These allowances were, of course, very small, but in those days of now almost unbelievably cheap dress materials – cotton prints for instance, at a few pence a yard – a clever home dressmaker, such as Bess, could dress nicely on very little. Her father's generosity did not end at the weekly allowance. It had been his custom throughout his married life to divide his bonuses, extra to his standing wages, between his wife and himself, and he now gave Bess and Mercy quarter shares. But though in such matters he took care to treat his elder daughters exactly alike, and tenderly as he loved his motherless babe and appreciated Mercy's good qualities, there was no concealing the fact that Bess was his favourite daughter. He had great faith in her judgement and soon fell into the habit of consulting her on his business affairs, as he had done her mother. Bess was the only person on earth who did not take Reuben too seriously. If she did not agree with something he said, she would say so and give her reason for disagreeing. She would laugh at and tease him about some of his old-fashioned country ideas. In their blooming season, he liked a few marigold heads in his mutton broth, and tansy flowers in his rice pudding, and he liked his cabbage or greens boiled with the bacon, not in a separate saucepan, and Bess, who was beginning to pride herself upon her up-to-date ideas in cookery, as in other things, would tell him that taste had changed and people no longer cared for such strongly flavoured dishes. But, for all that, she always took care that, when available, a few marigold heads should float on her father's basin of broth and that at least once in the season there should be a tansy pudding made from the old country recipe.

At that time Charity had affairs of her own to occupy her mind. She was learning to read and to write, and the names of dozens of the less common field and garden flowers, and to lay the table for meals and to wash and dry the tea-cups without breaking them, and to iron her doll's clothes with the small-sized iron her father had bought for her from the scrap-iron merchant, and to sweep the floor with her little broom, going carefully into the corners. She never quite grasped the reason why the corners were so much more important than the middle of the floor; surely, she thought, it should be swept well all over, but her mother seemed to think that the corners were most important. Bess said Aunt Alice was an old fidge.

Stella Pocock, as she grew older, spent most of her time out of school hours with the Truman girls; otherwise, with her mother so often from home, her life would have been a lonely one. Though she was approaching what was known as the awkward age, there was nothing awkward about Stella; perfect beauty, perfect grace, were still hers. She was not as silent as she had been, at times she would become quite animated, talking and laughing with the other girls about things which interested or amused them. Bess and she had always plenty to talk about, for both were interested in dress and the fashions, and of Polly she appeared to be really fond. When the talk turned to more serious subjects, Stella had less to say, unless it was something irrelevant, and Charity was beginning to wonder that one so lovely should have none but common-place ideas. Still, it gave her a shock when Miss Fowkes, their schoolmistress, said one day that Stella Pocock was a stupid girl, 'as these great beauties so often are,' she added, a remark which some hearers might have attributed to the inborn jealousy the plain woman is supposed to feel for the well-favoured. Poor Miss Fowkes herself certainly could boast no beauty of feature or colouring, though by that time her face had become so dear to Charity that, for her, it had its own peculiar beauty. Stella did not share Charity's feeling for their schoolmistress; she positively disliked her, and the rude remarks she made about her and the ugly names she called her behind her back made Charity feel that, for all her loveliness, she did not like Stella as much as she had once done. Other small, disquieting things, many of them mere trifles, occurred to widen the cleavage.

Occasionally Bess would join in Stella and Charity's games with Polly. Charity especially remembered one summer afternoon when they were playing in the orchard and Bess, who must have been in one of her best moods, brought out their tea and her own on a tray and sat down with them to partake of it in the shade of the apple tree. Stella was wearing a white embroidered dress which had once belonged to Lady Anne, and a cushion had to be fetched from the house for her to sit upon to guard the frock from grass-stains. The others sank down into the tall grass with the earth for a seat and ragged robin, sorrel, and moon daisies as a curtain. The day had been hot, the cool air beneath the apple boughs was refreshing, and the taste of food eaten out of doors was a delightful novelty in those days before picnics became popular.

After tea, they played hunt-the-thimble, the 'thimble' being on that occasion a battered old pewter pot from the harness-room window-sill. Bess entered into the game with zest. She was wearing a washed-out lilac print dress which hung limply upon her and was made so long that she had to hold up the front of the skirt when she ran. She was then eighteen and had reached her full height, though light and springy as ever of figure and gait. After she had given her father his tea, Mercy came out and joined in the game. In looks she had altered little, being still short and stocky, with apple-red cheeks. Over her dark afternoon dress she wore an oatmeal cloth apron, upon the bib and pockets of which Bess had embroidered poppies and wheat ears in the then fashionable crewel stitches.

From the beginning of the game Stella had distinguished herself, as she often did at hiding and finding games, by always being the first to spot the hidden article. Even when Bess stood the pot in the fork of an apple tree, unconcealed, but above the range of vision of the seekers, it was Stella who called out, 'I spy!' 'Oh, Stella, how lucky you are!' cried Charity, and Stella said modestly, 'It's only because I've got an eye for finding things.' It was then Charity's turn to hide the pot and she was thrusting it down into a thicket of raspberry canes when, for no particular reason, she glanced back over her shoulder. Bess had turned her face to a tree trunk and only the long sweep of her lilac dress and the back of her head with its bunch of escaping curls at the nape of her neck were visible. Mercy had both hands in front of her face, and Polly's eyes were screwed up as tightly as sleeping daisies. But it was not on account of any of these that the scene imprinted itself upon Charity's memory; that was due to her instantaneous impression of Stella hastily lifting her hands to cover her eyes. She had been looking.

Charity told no one of what she had seen, for, according to the country code, telling tales of each other was almost as bad as cheating at games, but the knowledge that Stella was not quite straight widened the breach between the two girls.

To a differently brought up child than Charity, Stella's defection might have seemed trifling, but to her her discovery came as a shock; the game in the orchard lost all charm and she felt quite relieved when, soon afterwards, someone whispered, 'Here comes Mr. Virtue.' At the mention of that name, Bess suddenly remembered that she had something to do in the house and departed. Mercy went with her and the younger girls followed, for although they as yet had heard nothing to prejudice them against Mr. Virtue, they were not very fond of him, and also had tired of their play.

No picture of Restharrow or of Waterside at that time would be complete without mention of Mr. Virtue. In those days of heavily stocked farms and when horses did the work now largely done by tractors, the veterinary surgeon was an important man in all country districts, and Mr. Virtue, the Mixlow vet., had other qualities besides his profession to make him conspicuous. Tall, lean and weatherbeaten, straddling in his walk, bold of feature and bolder of eye, wearing the distinctive garb of his calling – loud, check-patterned suits, well-polished leggings, a four-in-hand tie with a horse's head tiepin, and a cloth cap set at a rakish angle – for forty years he was a well-known figure about that countryside.

Mr. Virtue's Christian name was Emmanuel, a name which, when she first heard it applied to him, Charity thought blasphemous; but none of the villagers ever spoke of him by his Christian name; he was 'Mus' Virtue', or 'sir' when present; 'Dog Virtue' or 'Old Dog' only when they spoke of him among themselves. The men liked him well enough. Not so the women, for he had a way of looking at anything in petticoats in such a manner that some of the women and girls declared it made them blush to the backbone.

Though said to be hard as nails in his dealings with human beings, he was marvellously gentle with sick animals, and, although horses and cows were his speciality, he would just as readily examine and prescribe for the cottagers' pigs, cats, and dogs – for any animal, indeed, which was suffering. There was a tortoise at the Manor House, said to be over a hundred years old and nearly blind, and on this he worked a marvellous cure simply by washing its eyes with a lotion he had brought with him for the purpose. And the strange thing about this, as people thought, was that he would make no charge. He said that he would as soon have thought of taking a fee from Methuselah. He asked no fee of the cottagers for advice when their pigs or pets were

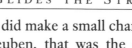

ailing; but he did make a small charge for medicine, because, he once told Reuben, that was the only way to insure that the creatures got their regular doses. Something for nothing, he said, was not valued.

As a man, Mr. Virtue was not so much esteemed as he was as a vet. He was reputed to be what was then known as 'a loose liver'. A girl living in the poorer quarter of Mixlow was said to have her rent paid by Mr. Virtue, who was also credited with being the father of her three children. There were other tales, too. People said they couldn't think how his poor wife stood his goings on; perhaps she had never heard of them; the person most concerned is usually the last to hear of such things, and many seemed anxious for her enlightenment.

It happened that about the time when Charity was old enough to hear of such things, a Restharrow girl was in service with the Virtues. A dangerous position, her mother's neighbour maintained, though Sally had never complained of her master's attentions. She had been with the Virtues some years and had become devoted to them when her mistress's illness began, and there was a note of triumph in her tone when she told of her master's patience and kindness. 'Night and day,' she said, 'night and day, anything he can do for her he will do. "How do you feel, darling? What sort of a day have you had? Let me put another cushion under your head," or "Do, just to please me, take a spoonful of this soup," or "a sip of this claret". And when she wanted him to go and sleep in the spare room, so as not to be disturbed by her groaning, he wouldn't. "No," he says. "You might want something in the night, and I know you wouldn't ring your bell. Besides, after twenty-five years together, I'm not going to leave you alone to suffer. I'll keep to my shakedown in the corner" – that's what he calls his camp-bed in her room – "and then, even if you don't want anything, you'll know I'm there and ready and waiting to get you anything"; and, if you ask me, I don't believe he's had his clothes off these five nights.' Such was Sally's testimony, and although it made little impression upon those who wished to believe Mr. Virtue the villain of the neighbourhood, it was probably truthful. There may have been some truth in the other stories, too; human nature is a strange mixture.

At thirteen and a half Charity was appointed monitress at school, with a salary of two pounds ten a year and, as her badge of office, a short, light cane, known as a pointer, officially intended for pointing out the letters of the alphabet on the big wall card to her class of infants, but equally useful for banging the desk to give emphasis to her instructions. To help her support the dignity of her new position, her hair, which had hitherto hung loose upon her shoulders, was plaited into a long, thick pigtail. Her skirts were brought down from her knees to her ankles and, over them, instead of a white pinafore, she wore a small black, or coloured, apron. Instead of as 'Charity' or 'Cherry', as formerly, the children of her class were told to address her as 'Teacher', and this trifling rise in status gave her great satisfaction, for she felt she had taken the first step towards realizing her long-cherished ambition of becoming the mistress of a village school, like her own Miss Fowkes, whom she greatly admired.

Her parents had had other plans for her than teaching; but when they found that her heart was set upon it, they consented to her plan, though not before Miss Fowkes had been to the house and employed her superior powers of persuasion. The shilling a week, her mother conceded, would certainly keep her in shoeleather, and the extra education she would obtain would do her no harm, but where the money was to come from to send her by-and-by to training college, she did not know; she could make no promises. It was not an encouraging consent, but it served to launch Charity on the career she had chosen.

During the midday break, after bolting her own dinner at home, she returned to the school playground for games with her infants, and after school in the evening she had her own lessons to prepare for Miss Fowkes, so her days were well filled. Not so full, however, that she saw less of her cousins. Saturday afternoons she always spent at Waterside, on Sundays there were the family tea-drinkings, and on light evenings and even on dark ones, the moment her lessons were done, she would dash off up the street and over the meadow to see Mercy and Bess. By that time they were both grown up. They wore their skirts down to the ground and their hair wound round and round in little plaits at the back of their heads, like a flat cap that had slipped back or an inverted saucer. But, though both had an abundance of hair and they wore it arranged in the same style, the effect was dissimilar, for Bess's goldy-brown locks still rebelled against close confinement and escaped in masses of soft, light curls at the nape of her neck and her temples; while Mercy's hair was tightly strained back and as smooth as wetting and brushing could make it. But, for all her strained-back hair, which left a good deal of her forehead exposed and gave her grey eyes a watchful look, Mercy at twenty was not uncomely. She had her admirers. One afternoon, when the two sisters had been shopping at Mixlow, and on their way home had passed the school gate as Charity came out of the door, Charity saw the old road-mender leaning on his scraping tool and gazing after the two girls. 'That second gal o' Reuben's is a-going to make a fine figure of an 'ooman,' he was saying to a passing neighbour. 'Fe-ace as red as any rose in th' garden, and look 'ee, now she's raisin' her skirts! There's a fine leg for 'ee! Makes the shanks of t'other gal look like a robin redbreast's against a gatepost! 'T other's a poor, puny scrag of a critter to my way o' thinkin'. Give me a gal as has got a bit o' colour in her cheeks and a leg she needn't be ashamed of anybody seein', an' she's the gal for my money!' And although the neighbour said somewhat sourly that he ought to be thinking of his own latter end and not of gal's legs at his age, and that they, for their part, mud or no mud, had no business to hold up their skirts to their knees, he only showed his toothless gums in a broad smile and continued to gaze after the two retreating figures – Bess, light and buoyant, picking her way daintily between the puddles, and Mercy, with the heavy marketing basket in one hand and a bulging umbrella in the other, trudging along stolidly.

Polly was no longer the fat, dimpled, roly-poly child she had been. She had grown into a tall, thin little girl with her hair in two plaits, who went to school and to choir practice and had her own ideas and interests. 'A reg'lar little madam,' some said, when speaking about her, meaning by that one who was over-fastidious about her clothes and her personal cleanliness and had, altogether, a too good opinion of herself. Polly was an intelligent child and did well at her lessons; but outside school, in the playground, she was not at all popular. She was too fond of telling the other children what they ought to do and exactly how it should be done. If the other children of her own age were making what they called a house by laying stones on the ground to represent rooms and Polly came up, she would at once take charge of the proceedings and decide which room was to be the kitchen, which the parlour, and where the fireplaces were to be put, and, after the house was completed, who was to be father, mother, and baby. Although her ideas were often an improvement on the original plan, she was not liked any the better for that, for young builders are no more willing than older ones to change their own plans for those of another, however superior. But Polly had her good points. She was practical and quick-witted. If a child fell down in the playground and barked its shin, it was Polly who produced a clean, or nearly clean, handkerchief and bound up the injured member. When Miss Fowkes was at her wits' end for a new flower to work on the samplers, it was Polly who remembered that her father had a pair of carpet slippers at home with a pattern of pansies, and Polly who copied the pansies on her own sampler first, then showed the rest of the class how it was done.

To save her the walk home in all weathers, Polly brought her dinner to school with her and ate it at Charity's home. Her readiness to join in the grown-up conversation and to give her opinion on all manner of subjects often irritated Mrs. Finch. But she was just a woman, and she often remarked that it was a marvel how much Polly knew, and how clever she was in thinking of things.

One day after he had submitted to what almost amounted to a lecture from Polly, Charity's father remarked, 'Our Lammas lamb seems to be turning out more of a sheep dog.' He smiled at Charity as he spoke and Charity smiled back at him. They often exchanged such private glances, for Mrs. Finch had a differently constituted mind to theirs. On that occasion she remarked, 'I do hope our Polly's not going to grow up one of these strong-minded women you hear so much about nowadays.'

'Her mind'll be a regular giant for strength if it goes on growing,' said her husband. 'But, as you're always telling us we are all as we were made, and it takes all sorts to make a world. To my way of thinking, a few strong minds among womankind are just what's needed to stiffen up the bulk a bit. Charity's mind's all right, and yours is all right in a different way, but the minds of most women I meet are like thin porridge, some sweetened and some unsweetened, but all weak and watery,' and, without waiting for further discussion, he went back to his work.

'Did you ever hear the like?' said her mother to Charity. 'But, there! men do say queer things.'

The one thing about Polly that no one ever criticized was her singing. Her voice was quite out of the ordinary. Even before she was able to speak plainly she had caught up and could repeat in her baby way any tune once sung in her hearing. It had never been any trouble to Bess to get Polly ready for church, for the church services were her treat of the week on account of the hymn-singing. At eight years old she led the church choir of schoolgirls and at ten she sang 'Caller Herrin' ' at one of the village concerts. The few strangers who came to the Restharrow Church services remarked on her voice, and one gentleman, said to understand music, actually saw her father about it and said that it ought to be properly trained. That, of course, was out of the question, but his interest pleased Reuben, and also, it must be said, increased Polly's already high opinion of her own powers. Kind Miss Fowkes, who, in addition to her duties as schoolmistress, played the harmonium in church and trained the choir, gave Polly what singing hints she could, and, for several years, on Easter Sunday and Christmas Day, Polly sang an anthem: a great event in the village life, especially as while one half of the congregation enjoyed it, the other half objected and said it was popish.

Those were the days of the pompadour style of dress, a style which no doubt had originally been inspired by pictures of the Marquise de Pompadour and other ladies of the Court of Louis XV, though probably not one in a thousand of the wearers and

admirers of the style had ever heard the name of the king or his Pompadour. To the feminine inhabitants of Restharrow, pompadour was the name of the fashionable flowered print which could be bought from any draper for sixpence or eightpence a yard. To begin with, in more fashionable circles the name had been associated with the polonaise of brocade or flowered silk, made with wide panniers and a bunched-up back and worn over a skirt of some harmonizing plain material. For those who followed fashion at a distance, cotton prints took the place of the richer materials, and soon everybody who was anybody, as they said, was sporting a pompadour polonaise. Eventually the name was transferred to all printed cotton goods with bright patterns, and there were pompadour bedspreads, pompadour chair covers, pompadour frocks, and even pompadour aprons.

At Restharrow the pompadour apron had a tremendous vogue, for there were few who cared for fashion who could not afford to spend a shilling or so to be in the swim. Another advantage was that anyone who could use a needle could run up their own pompadour apron in an evening; it being but a three-cornered piece of print with the upper corner made to pin at the breast as a bib, and the sides caught together by means of wide strings, tied in a bow at the back of the waist. Sometimes the strings were arranged to tie a few inches below the natural waist line, with the dress skirt bunched up a little above the bow, and this style was considered exceptionally smart and graceful.

Stella and Bess had made for themselves pompadour polonaises which they wore to church on Sundays, but neither they, nor the other girls, including Charity, had a pompadour apron, and it caused quite a flutter of excitement among them when Charity's mother came home from shopping in Banbury with the material to make them one each. The print was not in one piece or of one pattern. Mrs. Finch was too good a shopper for that. She had chosen short lengths of the patterns and colours she liked and she said that when she had made the aprons the girls were to choose, except Polly, whose apron had to be made smaller.

A few days later, when Charity came in from afternoon school, her mother had finished making the aprons and had laid them in a row on the parlour sofa for her to choose her own and for her elder cousins to choose theirs the next time they came in. But this plan did not suit Charity, who was bent upon giving immediate pleasure and at the same time wanted to give her own pompadour its first public airing, so, without staying for tea, or even to look at her geography questions, after choosing for herself an apron with tiny pink rosebuds sprinkled on a pale green ground, she wrapped the others in paper and set out for the farm.

She found her cousins in holiday mood. Their

father had gone for the day with the farmer to a distant cattle market and would not be home before evening, and, fond of him as his daughters were, they enjoyed an occasional day free from his sobering presence. Bess had baked a plate of hot cakes for tea and placed a dish of stewed cherries on the table, and these, together with the pompadour aprons, which had quickly been chosen and donned, gave quite a festive air to the tea-drinking. Bess looked particularly well in her new apron, with the bow at the back so arranged that its wide loops fell gracefully over the back fullness of her grey alpaca afternoon dress. 'Bess is to choose first, because she's the eldest,' Charity's mother had said. 'But you mark my words, this is Bess's apron,' and she had held up one with a pretty all-over design in soft pinks and mauves. Bess had taken up that apron as soon as the parcel was opened and held it up to her face before the big Alice-in-Wonderland mirror over the parlour mantelshelf, and Charity then had realized for the first time that Bess's eyes were not grey or blue, but a greyish violet. Bess herself must have been satisfied with what she saw in the mirror, for she tied the apron around her with no more than a casual glance at the one remaining. That left Mercy no choice, but she was very well pleased with the poppy and cornflower pattern.

Stella Pocock was with them. She had for the past nine months been apprenticed to a dressmaker at Mixlow, walking the three miles to and from her work daily, but that day she had stayed at home with what was then called a summer cold. Summer and winter, Stella was subject to colds, and the long walk to Mixlow in all weathers could not have been good for her. She had, as they said, shot up suddenly, and was then a tall, thin girl of eighteen. As she had grown up her features had sharpened slightly and her complexion, always pale, had become almost transparent; but, although more fragile-looking than formerly, she was still the same lovely, graceful creature Charity had adored when a child.

Of course, there was no pompadour apron for Stella, and as she did not happen to possess one she looked upon those of the others disparagingly. They were getting common, she said; the last time she and her mother were at Banbury they had seen a gipsy selling clothes-pegs in an apron very like Bess's. Bess laughed; she had heard of that gipsy before; then she had been wearing a hat the very image of the one Miss Fowkes had brought back from her holiday at Oxford. But allowances had to be made for Stella. She was not strong; her nerves were unstrung, her mother said so, and, of course, it must have been vexing for her to be wearing a red flannel bandage round her throat and having continually to mop her eyes with her handkerchief while the other girls were trying on their new aprons.

At tea she cheered up and told them about a servants' ball she had been to at one of the big houses where her mother worked. She had danced every dance and completely worn out the soles of a nearly new pair of white satin slippers which had been given to her for the occasion. Her frock had been given her, too, for the lady of the house was her godmother and she had rummaged the young ladies' wardrobe and found a really lovely white silk and given it to Mrs. Pocock for Stella, saying, 'It's quite a nice frock, though it has never suited Lady Margot. Her complexion won't bear a pure white. Stella will look well in it, she will certainly be the belle of the ball,' and the ball had been lovely; they should have heard the music, the schoolroom piano and two violins. . . .

'I wish I could dance,' sighed Charity, and Bess sprang up from her seat behind the teapot, saying, 'Well, why shouldn't you? We'll soon teach her, won't we, Stella? Let's go into the empty front parlour and give her her first lesson while Mercy's washing up. You come, too, Polly. You'll soon pick up the steps, being so tuney,' and they all ran down the long passage to one of the unused rooms at the front of the house. Although the only piece of furniture there was the heavy oak settle left behind by the farmer, the room was a pleasant one, with its bare floor-boards, wide-open windows, and white muslin curtains billowing inward in the breeze.

It was great fun, learning the steps. Polly, light-footed and sharp as a needle in grasping the rhythm, was guided by Bess. Charity, with Stella's arm round her waist, less quick and graceful, but doing her conscientious best. As they had no musical instrument of any kind, Stella and Bess took turns at chanting: *One, two, three, hop! One, two, three, hop! One, hop! Two hop! One, two, three, hop!*, breaking off occasionally to laugh at the mistakes of the beginners, or to fan their own faces and exclaim on the heat. Then Bess and Stella footed it together to show the others how it should be done. Bess was a good natural dancer, but she had not had the advantages of Stella, who had actually been to a real ball in a real ballroom. Bess's dancing had been done on the greensward on such rustic occasions as the Feast and the Flower Show. However, Stella was generous enough to praise her dancing and to offer to teach her one of the new waltzes. Then Mercy came in, caught Polly round the shoulders and clumped around the room with her, and Charity retired to a seat on the settle and became what Stella called a wallflower.

'What we want is some gentlemen partners,' panted Bess, stopping to fan her hot face and to tuck back the little curls from her forehead. 'Call in Luke,' suggested Polly mischievously. 'I'll bet he's not far away.' And, sure enough, the next moment, Luke's full moon face appeared between the window curtains. It had popped up from nowhere, like the head of a Jack-in-the-box, and was greeted by bursts of laughter. 'Am I wanted?' he asked, gazing into the faces of one after another of the girls, who were too overcome by mirth to answer. 'I thought I heard somebody call me,' he continued rather aggrievedly, 'and I thought as how you wanted me to dance.'

'Well, can you dance?' asked Bess tauntingly, and he said he expected he could if he tried. 'So could an elephant,' laughed Bess, 'but its partner'd be likely to get her feet squashed.'

'Let him come in for a bit,' urged Mercy, but Bess shook her head and said, no, she'd never dream of asking any man into the house while her father was away, no matter if it was the Prince of Wales himself.

While they were whispering together, Luke had thrust his head and shoulders inside the window and was watching their faces with an imploring expression on his own which might have softened Bess's heart towards him if Polly had not called pertly, 'You go back to your work, Luke. You know very well you've no business to go pushing yourself in where you're not wanted.' At that Luke's face flamed with mortification. 'All right, Miss Meddlesome,' he retorted. 'If you'd like to know, I have finished me work, and was just gooin' home to me supper when I heard me own name spoken. A pretty fine godchild you are! I'll see that you don't have that turnip lantern I've bin makin' for you. I'll go back and give it to th' pigs; they've got better manners than you, any day,' and off he went.

'What a country bumpkin! I can't think how you put up with him,' said Stella to Bess. 'Oh, he's rough and ready, of course,' said Bess, 'but he's not a bad sort, really.' With which opinion Polly did not at all agree. 'I think he's awful,' she said. 'How could Dad and Mother let him stand godfather to me? I never own him. If anybody asks me who my godfather is, I say Mr. Nobody,' and she looked ready to cry.

After they had rested they went at it again, *La, la, tumpity ta!* until the floor shook and the window-panes rattled. Mercy slipped out to begin cooking her father's supper. She was followed by Polly, whose evening it was for choir practice. Bess and Stella went on dancing. It seemed that they never would tire. Stella's cold had disappeared suddenly, as her colds were apt to do, and she had snatched the flannel bandage off her throat and flung it into the fireplace. She was in her element, teaching Bess, who, though far from an awkward learner, needed much instruction, and the exercise had brought a little colour into her cheeks. Bess also was flushed, and so absorbed in her effort to master the waltz that she no longer tried to control her troublesome curls, which had escaped in little bunches of whorls and tendrils at her nape and forehead; she panted a little and her eyes had gone dark, almost purple.

Charity watched them from her seat on the settle, trying to pick up a little instruction for herself from Stella's orders and explanations, but hopeless of ever becoming efficient in so difficult an art. It was Charity who first saw the new face at the window.

'Is Truman about?' asked the new comer, and the dancing came to a full stop. The speaker was the young squire, Roger Maitland, a visitor so unusual and unexpected that his sudden appearance caused a flutter of not unpleasant embarrassment. Bess

hastily pushed back her curls, pulled down her apron, and went to the window. Her father, she said, had gone out for the day, but was expected home shortly.

'Ah-h-h!' said the young man. 'I see! While the cat's away, etcetera? But go on with your dancing. I don't think you've got that waltz step quite right. Perhaps I had better come in and show you how it should go. Example is better than precept any day,' and, taking Bess's permission for granted, he vaulted over the window-sill. 'May I have the pleasure?' he asked.

'My father will be in any moment now,' demurred Bess, but he had already his arm round her waist and was humming his version of the dance tune. Round and round the room they floated, Bess's expression at first a little troubled, but soon one of perfect enjoyment, he gazing down into her mauve eyes and flushed, freckled face, as one might who looked for the first time on a new flower. His own eyes were dark and expressive, his face and neck were sun-tanned, and he wore his easy country clothes

with a grace that was captivating, especially to eyes accustomed to the stolid ungainliness of ploughmen.

The wide, sashlike ends of Bess's apron strings floated out behind her, one plait of hair escaped from its pins and fell on her shoulder, but she did not seem to tire. *Tum, tum, tumpity-ta!* Now and again Roger would whisper a word of direction, but there was little need of these, for Bess was an apt pupil. It may have been, too, that her teacher was not exacting, or they may have moved to a rhythm of their own.

Stella stood, lovely as a statue, and as cold and expressionless, one elbow resting upon the mantelpiece, one slippered foot tapping out the tune. After his first long waltz with Bess had ended, Mr. Roger approached her. 'May I have the pleasure!' he asked, and they danced together. When their dance was over, he returned to Bess, and Stella to her former position by the fireplace. Although Mr. Roger danced with Stella again and paid her such attentions as were proper, it could plainly be seen by an onlooker that his interest was centred upon Bess. Stella must have noticed and may have resented this. Bess's good looks were modest indeed compared to her own beauty; she herself was a more finished dancer than Bess, and, in her own estimation, was more versed in the ways of polite society, and it could not have pleased her to see Bess preferred to herself. But if she felt any resentment she gave no sign; she stood, cold and silent, one elbow upon the mantelshelf, her hand supporting her chin, until Mercy looked in at the door to say that her father was coming along the footpath, and Roger went out to meet him. Not by way of the window, as he had come in, but properly shown out of the front door by Bess, who, when she had seen him off, ran upstairs to tidy her hair, humming the waltz tune

Charity, hurrying home conscience-stricken to her neglected geography paper, found her uncle and Mr. Roger standing face to face in the lane, talking. 'No, Mr. Roger, I wouldn't advise it, not on that damp, heavy land, no!' Reuben was saying as she passed them. 'You keep it for grazing, as it's always been kept. It might be worth your while to get another good milking cow. But there's that other piece of yourn, Dun Plack, 'ud be better ploughed up and planted—'

So the village rumours had been true. Mr. Roger had come home for good and intended farming his own few acres.

When a popular fashion reached Restharrow it usually had a very long run. The bustle, for instance, survived in that village for at least five years after it had disappeared from the haunts of fashion, and the pompadour apron might have been expected to remain even longer in favour, being a bright and attractive adornment and

easy to come by; yet its vogue lasted no more than a year. And, when it came to an end, the aprons did not disappear gradually, the more fashionably inclined discarding theirs for something

newer and the less fashion-minded clinging to theirs to the last shred. One day, at Restharrow, pompadour aprons abounded; the next, there were none to be seen, and, oddly enough, the fashion was snuffed out by a man.

The old doctor at Mixlow, who attended the country people for miles around that town and to quite half his patients sent in no bill because he knew they were too poor to pay one, about the time when the pompadour aprons first appeared instituted what was known as a Doctor's Club, the members of which paid twopence weekly and, for that, when ill, were entitled to free attendance. When this club had been long enough in existence for the members to claim benefits, there was such an outbreak of minor ailments that he had to engage as assistant a young man, newly qualified, or perhaps partly qualified, for there was more of the medical student than the doctor about him. This Dr. Frewin was to the Restharrow folk a novelty in the way of doctors, used as they were to the aged, dignified and kindly, though somewhat stern, Dr. Fisher. He was a large young man with a fair, innocent-looking, almost babyish face, who, when in attendance at the cottage front room which served as a surgery at Restharrow, had an alarming habit of throwing himself back and balancing his weight on the back legs of the ordinary kitchen chair which served for surgery uses. In that position he would hold with some of the older and coarser women long, bantering conversations which covered the more modest and sedate with confusion. Many, perhaps most, country doctors of that day were outspoken, even coarse, in their language when dealing with the older country women. To some extent they had to be, for the use of scientific names for the parts of the body would only have caused confusion. Dr. Frewin went farther than these – much farther. The surgery became the favourite resort of a few choice spirits of the place, and on Monday and Thursday mornings the room was crowded.

It happened that one day at the surgery Dr. Frewin noticed two women patients jostling for precedence, one of whom was wearing an old fashioned white, the other a pompadour apron. 'Here! Come along, you with the decent white apron,' he called jocundly, and, after she had been dealt with, he called to the other, 'Now, you with the figleaf!'

'Figleaf' was not the word he used, but it is the nearest printable approach to it; his term was such that, within a week, three-fourths of the pompadour aprons in Restharrow had been converted into antimacassars. People laughed. How they laughed! But it was a pity about the aprons.

V

THE FLOWER SHOW

IF AN inhabitant of one of the neighbouring villages spoke of Restharrow to its detriment, nine times out of ten the retort of a native would be; 'Very like! That's as it may be; but after all we do have our own Flower Show,' implying by his tone: 'And that's more than you can say.' No other village of its size in the district could make such a boast, though some might be able to claim a share in a Flower Show which served for three or four villages and was held at the largest of these. The Restharrow Flower Show had been instituted by the late squire, Roger Maitland's father, in one of his generous moods. He had lent the meadow in which it was held, provided the marquee, and given and presented the prizes. After he had died no other such patron had offered, but the farmer, the innkeeper, and two or three head gardeners on neighbouring estates had formed a committee and kept the Show going. Mrs. Maitland still lent the meadow and formally presented the prizes provided by the committee. The fees paid by the owners of the various amusements were calculated to cover the necessary expenses.

By the villagers the Flower Show was regarded as the crowning event of the Restharrow year. It was always arranged to take place between haytime and harvest, so that the men of the village could be spared for a day from their fieldwork. The schoolchildren were given a holiday, and their mothers on that day did as little work as possible. On Flower Show day no washing flapped on the clothes lines, very few chimneys smoked, for no cooking was done, and between mealtimes the cottage doors were closed and the village street deserted, for all except a few poor bedridden souls had gone to the Flower Show.

After noon the place woke up for an hour. Those families that were pig-keepers always reserved a ham to be cooked and stand cold for that day; those who had no ham got in a tin of salmon, or cooked a piece of bacon to eat with fresh lettuce and green onions, soaked in vinegar. Those who could run to the expense, got in a nine-gallon

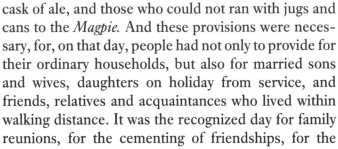

cask of ale, and those who could not ran with jugs and cans to the *Magpie*. And these provisions were necessary, for, on that day, people had not only to provide for their ordinary households, but also for married sons and wives, daughters on holiday from service, and friends, relatives and acquaintances who lived within walking distance. It was the recognized day for family reunions, for the cementing of friendships, for the wearing of new clothes and for general jollity. Compared to the Flower Show, Christmas was but a minor festivity.

The Show was held in a large, wooded meadow of park-like appearance adjoining the Manor House gardens. From ten o'clock in the morning onward a stream of villagers and their friends, thin at first, but steadily increasing in volume, might have been seen making its way over the greensward towards the big marquee flying the Union Jack and the smaller, but no less exciting, cluster of show booths, coconut shies, and gingerbread stalls by which it was surrounded. A brass band was engaged for the day, and the steam roundabout had an organ attached which was permitted to play by arrangement at such times as the bandsmen felt in need of refreshment. Hours before the general public began to arrive, in the cool, misty dawn, had come cottage gardeners, carrying such of their produce as they had deemed too valuable, or too delicate, to be delivered the previous evening. Flowers and fruit with the dew still upon them, lettuce and spinach and other tender things. They carried them lovingly, as a mother might carry a young infant, an absorbed expression upon their faces, intent upon preserving the unbruised freshness of their produce. If one of them met a tried friend, he would open his arms or raise the lid of his basket with the air of one conferring a great favour. From the rest of the world these exhibits were jealously guarded and any questions were met by a pretendedly jocular 'Wait and see!'

At ten o'clock the judges assembled to affix to the prize-winning entries the coveted cards, red, blue, and yellow, which denoted 'First', 'Second', and 'Third'. During their session within the closed marquee a throng would gather outside, anxious to know who had won the prizes and to decide if they had been won fairly. Often it was thought that they had not been fairly won. One prize-winner, for instance, had made for himself a cold frame from a couple of disused windows; another kept three pigs, instead of the more usual one, or two, and so had what some thought an unfair advantage in his manure supply, while it was the general opinion that a man who worked himself or had a son working in a subordinate position in one of the big house gardens should be permanently disqualified. However, after Mrs. Maitland, handsomely attired and seated on a high-backed, carved oak chair, brought from her house for the ceremony, had presented the prizes – ten shillings, seven and sixpence, and, thirds, five shillings – all disputes were suspended and the rest of the day was devoted to pleasure.

Charity's father was a keen gardener, and she and her mother always accompanied him to the prize-giving ceremony. Twice, Charity herself figured as a prize-winner. One year for the greatest variety of wild flowers, and, another year, when her entry was a close runner-up, with a special unscheduled prize for tasteful arrangement. After she had passed the schoolgirls' competition age-limit, she still loved to walk with her parents through the cool, moist, flower-scented aisles of the tent, stopping every few feet to admire the exhibits – stocks and asters, runner beans and vegetable marrows and well-scrubbed carrots and turnips from the cottage gardens, and, on the head gardeners' stall, great bunches of purple grapes, melons the colour of the harvest moon, and strange, exotic flowers from hothouse and garden. The rich colours, seen in the soft, mellow light filtering down through the yellow tent fabric, the moist, flower- and fruit-scented air, the greetings of neighbours, all dressed in their best and with their cares cast aside for the moment, the strains of the band music, softened by distance, all held for her such charm that, when younger, she had imagined Heaven as something like a perpetual Flower Show.

A few days after the dance in the pompadour aprons, she made the round of the exhibits with her parents as usual. Her father had been awarded the first prize for his onions and, after he had received the bright half-sovereign from Mrs. Maitland, he intended to go back to his workshop. Her mother would go with him and remain indoors for the rest of the day, ostensibly in case friends should happen to drop in for tea, but really because, like her husband, she did not care for crowded amusements. For Charity the day was only beginning, for Bess and Mercy and she were to spend the afternoon and evening enjoying the fun of the fair. Polly would be with the schoolchildren, adding to her laurels of former years at their sports, and Stella, after her day's work at Mixlow, could only hope to arrive in time for a dance or two.

Until her cousins arrived, Charity found pleasure enough in dawdling with her parents around the stalls, admiring and appraising the exhibits and observing the reactions of her fellows. Most of the women who walked through the show tent would exclaim with delight when they came to a fine or an uncommon bloom. 'There! ain't that a beauty!' they would cry to their companions; 'They sells such roses as that for sixpence apiece for gentlemen's buttonholes in towns'; or 'You can see that's a head gardener's flower. I wager its root cost a pound'; or they would jokingly wish for a dress of silk or velvet 'just that colour', or a bottle of scent made of its

perfume. The men, too, would admire some flower of outstanding beauty or rarity; but they, as gardeners themselves, would chiefly be concerned with the method of its production. To have a bit of glass and a stableful of manure was their ambition.

Only two of all the people there appeared to value the flowers entirely for their own loveliness. One of these was the Vicar, who on Flower Show day would tear himself away from his books and studies for the prize-giving. Charity had seen him sauntering alone round the banked-up show benches in his old greenish-black cassock, his short-sighted eyes peering into the very hearts of the roses, lilies and carnations, sniffing their scent, stroking their petals, and sometimes cupping a bloom in his hand;  for, although a notice board forbade touching the exhibits, he, as the Vicar, might do as he pleased, and it pleased him to look long into the golden pollen-dusted heart of a lily with a look on his face approaching adoration.

That, Charity thought, might have been expected of one whose business it was to preach the Rose of Sharon and the Lily of the Valley; but Mrs. Burdett was but a poor and presumably ignorant old country woman, and it was surprising to find her bending over a cluster of deep crimson roses with tears in her eyes. When she saw Charity beside her she smiled and said: 'I know I'm making a silly of myself, but whenever I see a perfect rose it makes me feel a sort of unworthiness. What have we menkind done to deserve such a sight!'

At one end of the marquee, a little apart from the show benches, beneath a placard marked PETS' SECTION, stood an array of rabbit hutches, birdcages, and wire-netting-faced boxes. These last were the extemporized abodes of cats. The Restharrow people were fond of cats – practically every household included one – and there were tabby cats, white cats, all black and black-and-white cats, and one immense long-haired tortoiseshell tom, the property of the innkeeper, and in former years a frequent prize-winner. In the birdcages were canaries and siskins. No other birds, for, although many caged wild birds were kept in the village, they were never shown because one year Mr. Virtue, who judged the pet entries, had carried outside and released a skylark, and when its owner had complained had thrown the empty cage at him, swearing with many oaths unfitting for a Flower Show that a man who was capable of robbing a little singing bird of its liberty should be sent to gaol for six months' hard.

That day, before the hutches and cages, stood Mr. Virtue himself, studying the exhibits with a whimsical look, then making little ticks or crosses in his note-book. As sole judge in that section, he had not to attend the general assessment, but could come and affix the prize labels when convenient to himself, a latitude due to an expert who also furnished the money for the prizes in his section. His was a thankless task, for the exhibits were a plebeian lot, and yet every owner was convinced that his or her own pet possessed more beauty, grace and intelligence than the more highly bred of its species.

'Just noting their points, Mr. Virtue?' asked Charity's father quizzingly, and Mr. Virtue retorted: 'Yes. Can you lend me a microscope?' Which, between the two, passed as an excellent joke.

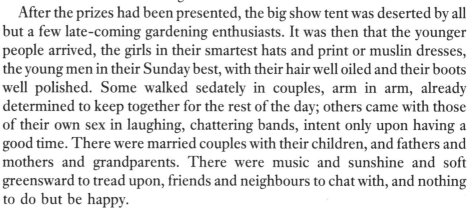

However, in the Cats' Class that year Mr. Virtue's work was lightened by the first appearance of a fine young tom in the very pink of perfect health and glossiness, his blackest of coats relieved by a white vest and leg-stripes, and with wide, candid-looking eyes of the greenest. 'Not your lucky day this time, old boy,' said the judge, poking the big yellow cat in the ribs. 'We all have our turn, then have to make way for the young and virile,' and he affixed the prize label to the temporary abode of the black-and-white tom and reached down a birdcage.

After the prizes had been presented, the big show tent was deserted by all but a few late-coming gardening enthusiasts. It was then that the younger people arrived, the girls in their smartest hats and print or muslin dresses, the young men in their Sunday best, with their hair well oiled and their boots well polished. Some walked sedately in couples, arm in arm, already determined to keep together for the rest of the day; others came with those of their own sex in laughing, chattering bands, intent only upon having a good time. There were married couples with their children, and fathers and mothers and grandparents. There were music and sunshine and soft greensward to tread upon, friends and neighbours to chat with, and nothing to do but be happy.

Charity and her cousins met at the gate of the meadow and made their way leisurely towards the tents, Bess's frilled muslin dress trailing a little on the grass and her sunshade held delicately over her shoulder to shield her always sensitive skin from the burning rays of the midsummer sun. Almost the first person they saw as they neared the edge of the crowd was Roger Maitland, starting the schoolchildren's races. When he caught sight of them, he already had the whistle to his lips, but he withdrew it for a moment to smile at Bess and to say to her in a low voice, 'Please keep me some dances.'

Flags were flying, the band was playing, swingboats soared higher and higher, till feet seemed to touch the blue; Aunt Sallies and coconut shies did good business, but, until the dancing began, the chief attraction was the roundabout. How deliciously luxurious it seemed to riders accustomed on other days to kitchenwork or hard field labour to float around without effort on the fiery-nostrilled, dapple-grey steeds to the strains of *Sweet Belle Mahone* or of *Jenny, my Own True Loved One*. Soon, someone began singing:

Jenny, my own true loved one, I'm going far from thee,
Over the raging billows, over the deep blue sea,

and others joined in:

Wait till the clouds roll by, Jenny,
Wait till the clouds roll by,

or the song may have been *Sweet Belle Mahone*: 'Wait for me at Heaven's gate, Sweet Belle Mahone', or 'Bring back to memory, days of long ago'. Whatever song was chosen, its burden would be patience and resignation, for patience and resignation were qualities born and bred in the countryfolk of that day, and such popular songs as expressed them were dear to their hearts, even in their moments of exhilaration. To the slow, dreamy music of such songs, they circled around, clinging to the upright brass supporting rods in a state of trancelike beatitude.

'Bring back to memory,' Bess hummed the air below her breath as the three girls drifted around the show tents watching the coconut shiers and the men and youths aiming with balls at the hideous old woman's figure with a pipe in its mouth, known as Aunt Sally. Those who succeeded in knocking the pipe from its mouth were given the choice of a prize from a stall in the background, loaded with mugs and jugs, pottery figures, witch balls and silvered vases; but so few succeeded that, at closing time, the stall was still loaded, as it is to be supposed was also the proprietor's pence bag. Then Luke came up to them carrying a coconut and offered to crack it if anybody fancied a bit. When they each in turn refused, he looked so disappointed that Mercy told him they would like some tomorrow; but Bess was disdainful and said that he ought to have known that she at any rate was not one of those persons who went about chewing.

From the tea tent came whiffs of hot tea steam and a tempting aroma of spiced dough cake. Tea with bread and butter and cake or buns was priced at sixpence a head, and though many considered that charge was excessive and declared that they only wished they themselves had the chance of providing a slap-up Sunday dinner at that price, their criticism usually ended with, 'But, oh! my poor feet! Sit down I must! And, arter all, there's no limit. We must do our best to eat and drink our sixpen'orth,' which worthy endeavour occupied them so long that the tea tent

was crowded to suffocation point.

One couple, it was said, one year had spent the whole holiday in the tea tent. Not because the weather was wet – it was a lovely day – but because on their arrival on the field they had happened to drop in for refreshment and the lady had found the atmosphere of the tent so much to her taste that she had said to her husband: 'If we're here to enjoy ourselves, why not stay where we are and enjoy ourselves? We've got good seats and plenty to eat and drink, so why go trapesing around?' and there they had stayed, sipping tea and talking to friends, the whole afternoon and evening. Fortunately, most people preferred to share in the fun outside, or the poor, perspiring ladies who worked like galley slaves filling tea urns, cutting huge piles of bread and butter and cake, and running from table to table with more hot water or milk, or to give change or to settle disputes, would, as they sometimes foretold, have dropped down dead from heat and exhaustion.

Near the tea tent, on a grassy knoll shaded by trees, a little removed from the throng, the wives of the committee-men sat on garden chairs and sipped the tea which had been specially brought out for them. Most of them were important, matronly looking persons, dressed in the dark, rich stuffs then considered proper to their age, with large gold lockets upon their bosoms and upon their heads little dark bonnets adorned with artificial flowers of the more modest varieties – violets, forget-me-nots, or love-in-a-mist. With them was Miss Fowkes, wearing her famous Oxford hat and a dress of the new cornflower blue; fashionable, but not her colour; indeed, as someone remarked at Charity's elbow, it made her face look as yellow as a duck's foot, though, fortunately, this was unsuspected by the wearer, who smiled happily as she waved and beckoned to Charity to join her. She found her surrounded by bats and balls, shuttlecocks and battledores, pocket-knives, work-boxes and writing-cases, prizes won by the children in their sports and brought to her for safe keeping. 'As you see, I can't move with all these valuables to guard, so do come and talk to me,' she cried gaily, and, after Charity had becomingly replied to the greetings of the other ladies present, she cleared for herself a space on the turf and, like the devoted disciple she was, sat down at the feet of her mistress.

But little conversation with Miss Fowkes was possible. Her seat was on the edge of the group, slightly below those of the other ladies, and overlooking a path along which people were constantly passing. 'Nice day, ain't it? Real Flower Show weather!' one and another would call to her as they passed, and she would respond with, 'Glorious! Glorious! And what a splendid gathering!' The rest of the privileged little party had more leisure to chat. Their position was such that they could see all that passed without themselves being too conspicuous, and Charity soon gathered that they were taking a lively interest in the scene. 'There! Did you ever!' exclaimed one of the matrons. 'If there isn't that young Maudie Dynes actually arm in arm with Bob Taverner! And her with a child still under a year! 'Tis to be hoped the poor silly thing's not going to make a fool of herself a second time!' and Mrs. Mercer, the farmer's wife, said in her deep, quiet voice: No, she didn't think so. Poor Maudie had had her lesson and they mustn't forget, for all her one slip, she was still but a young thing and wanted a bit of pleasure. She had heard, she added, though she couldn't say whether it was true or not, that Bob and Maudie were going to be married, and criticism was silenced.

Mrs. Mercer herself, it appeared, had once been young and fond of pleasure. She recalled for the benefit of one of the head gardeners' wives, a comparative newcomer to the district, some Flower Shows of earlier years. The year when the roundabout first

appeared had been a landmark in the progress and importance of the festivity. Before there had been but a few gingerbread and sweet stalls and a coconut shy, and, of course, no band, only old Jeff Tuffrey and his fiddle for the dancing. 'But the old times were good times and we all enjoyed them. I know I did. You may not believe it, but I actually danced my hair down one of those years. The old squire persuaded me. 'May I have the pleasure, Mrs. Mercer?' he said, and, before I could say knife, he had me by the waist, and me the mother of three children! After that, of course, I had to dance with Mercer. Then others we knew came up— Well, well, I was still in my twenties.'

Mrs. Mercer's reminiscences were cut short by a voice exclaiming: 'Well, I never! If my eyes don't deceive me, that's young Mr. Maitland over there, talking to one of the Truman girls,' and all eyes were turned in the direction of one of the less frequented paths, a little apart from the throng and lightly screened by bushes, but clearly visible from the eminence occupied by the tea-drinkers, where Mr. Roger and Bess could be

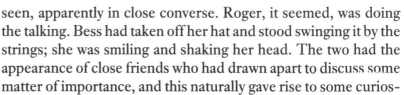

seen, apparently in close converse. Roger, it seemed, was doing the talking. Bess had taken off her hat and stood swinging it by the strings; she was smiling and shaking her head. The two had the appearance of close friends who had drawn apart to discuss some matter of importance, and this naturally gave rise to some curiosity among the ladies seated on the knoll. 'By the look of it, they've plenty to say to each other,' said one of the ladies. And another: 'If you ask me, I'll say they look as thick as thieves.' Then spoke a severe-looking dame in an aggrieved tone: 'I'm surprised, I really am, at his stopping at all for the amusements, and no other gentry present, for his mother went home, as she always does, after she'd handed out the prizes; and why he should be talking in a corner to Bess Truman is hard to say; you'd've thought he'd've come over to us for a cup of tea. He must have seen us.'

'Tish! Tish!' said Mrs. Mercer. 'What does he want at his age with a lot of old women like us! The young fly to the young like a needle to the loadstone; and Bess Truman's a nice-looking girl, and a good girl, too, and, besides, isn't she Reuben's daughter? What more natural than that the young squire show her some attention for her father's sake? And, for all we know, he may be giving her a message to take to Reuben.'

If so, the message had by that time been given, for the two had parted, Bess to stroll back to the main path, Roger to go on his way in the other direction, he with several backward glances, she never once looking back. Either because Mrs. Mercer, who, as the wife of the largest employer of labour in the place, was a lady second only to Mrs. Maitland in importance, had again silenced criticism, or because the company had suddenly recollected that Charity and Bess were cousins, the conversation turned to another subject. 'Isn't it delightful to see everybody happy?' asked Miss Fowkes, who had observed nothing of the little by-play. 'But I think I see your cousins waving to you,' she continued. 'How charming Bess is looking to-day!' And Bess was, indeed, looking charming. She looked, as they said, as if butter would not melt in her mouth, and not one word did she say about having seen Mr. Roger. Instead, she fairly rated Mercy for getting lost in the throng.

When the dancing began, the moment the band struck up, Roger appeared and claimed the dance, which he said had been promised him by Bess. 'No! No! Mr. Roger, I didn't say I would dance with you. I only said I might,' Bess protested; but, even as she was speaking, she took the arm he offered, and a moment later they were floating around to the strains of *The Blue Danube*.

Charity danced with a young soldier home on furlough, the son of a neighbour, a grave, quiet young man who seemed anxious to impress upon her that the private soldier was no longer looked upon as the scum of the earth by his superiors, as in the bad old days. For picked men, he said, there were now all sorts of advantages; he himself was attending classes with a view to bettering his school education sufficiently to stand a good chance of promotion. 'And let's see,' he said, 'you've got a cousin in the Army, corporal or something, isn't he, out in India?' And Charity, after explaining that Oliver was not really her cousin, but a cousin of her cousins, said Oliver was now a sergeant-major. 'Crikey!' ejaculated the young soldier, much impressed. 'You'll hardly know him when he comes home; they let you know who they are all right, those S.M.s!' Charity laughed, she was unable to imagine Oliver as other than the thin, gawky boy in uniform who had tossed her over the stile. Then the spur worn by her partner got entangled in the frilled muslin skirt of another dancer and Charity went down on her knees to help in releasing it, and for some time she saw little of what was going on. Afterwards, she danced an old country dance with Luke, because he looked so neglected and forlorn that she felt sorry for him, and all her faculties were involved in piloting him around. When, at last she had a breathing space, Bess was again dancing with Roger. Apparently there had been some dispute as to their partnership, for, as Bess floated off on Roger's arm, she heard one of Reuben's younger ploughmen say in a lugubrious tone, 'But she promised me! She promised me!' and another voice asking him acidly, 'Ain't you larned yet that a gal's promises be but piecrust, made to be broke?' ''Specially when t'other chap's richer and handsomer,' added another voice.

People, she could see and hear, were looking at and talking about Bess, and it made her feel uncomfortable. However, she told herself, Bess was older than she was and probably knew better what was right and proper, and she made a determined effort to put the whole affair out of her mind. That was not difficult when the band was playing and the dancers were gliding around on the trampled greensward and the fairy lights upon bushes and trees were twinkling in the twilight, red, yellow, and green and blue. Presently, the older people who had ringed around as spectators drifted off in twos and threes and families, towards their suppers and beds; but the dancers still circled, the girls in their light frocks like moths flitting hither and thither, their partners invisible, save for a face here and there, picked out for an instant, red or yellow or blue, by the flickering light of a lamp. Even when the candles within the fairy lamps, one by one, flickered and went out, and, but for the bandsmen's light and the naphtha flares on the booths farther down the field, all was in darkness, the dancing continued. 'You're tired, my pretty. Let's go and sit down under the trees a while,' said a man's voice tenderly; but the girl said no, they could sit down under trees any night of the year. At least he could, if he could get anybody to sit down with him; she was for the dance. Stars came out over the elm tops; bats dashed and tumbled over the heads of the dancers and night moths brushed their cheeks, but the couples only clung together more closely and the dance went on, for all there were determined to drain to the last drop the cup of that day's pleasure.

But even a Flower Show day must come to an end, and punctually on the stroke of eleven the band gave the signal that all was over by playing *God save the Queen.*

Bess, Mercy, and Charity ran like so many Cinderellas over the greensward, under the trees and out on the road. They had never before stayed till the end of the dancing, but, other years, had walked quietly and sedately away between nine and ten with Charity's mother, stopping now and again to exchange remarks with other home-going parties. Although their time of return had been left that year to their own discretion – for weren't they now all grown-up girls, or, in Charity's case, as good as? – they knew they must have long been expected at their homes. 'Oh, what a day! What a

glorious day! I've enjoyed every moment of it,' they panted as they ran. They had neither the breath nor the time to say more.

When Charity got indoors her father had already gone to bed and her mother soon followed him, leaving her to finish her supper and put out the light. Charity, helping herself hugely to stewed plums and custard, felt vaguely uneasy about Bess's behaviour; but, after a night's sleep, she decided that she had made much of little. Why should not Bess dance with Mr. Roger? There was no harm in her doing so, and it was only natural that he should have asked her to dance with him after what had happened a few days before at the farm. There was no other public holiday before the Feast in April, and probably by that time he would have found someone else to interest him. Bess herself made nothing of the occurrence. When, a few days later, Charity was at Waterside, the dancing, the band, and the state of the turf were all discussed, but all Bess said about Roger was that he danced so well that it spoilt anybody for other partners, and this she said in such a light, matter-of-fact tone that Charity felt ashamed of ever having thought twice about the incident. She was

glad she had not mentioned it to her mother. Her mother was a darling, but she was very old-fashioned in her ideas.

Perhaps Charity should have spoken. Had she done so, it might have prevented some after-trouble. But, again, it might not have done. Bess hated and scorned what she called 'prunes and prisms and don'ts and mustn't', and well-intended advice from her aunt might have driven her to further lengths than she actually reached. Her fault, if fault it could be called, was no more than the flouting of the country convention which decreed that an unmarried girl must on no account do anything, however innocent, to make herself conspicuous. She must not get herself talked about. That, most unreasonably, was considered an unforgivable offence by the very persons who did, and thoroughly enjoyed doing, the talking.

Whether Bess was much talked about at that time cannot be said. There was probably some gossip about her dancing and appearing to be on friendly terms with the young squire, though none of it reached the ears of her relatives; or it may have been that less interest than might have been expected was taken in her affairs, for it happened that, that same week, a more urgent and exciting event occurred. The poor-box inside the church door was found broken open and empty. There was no mystery as to the identity of the thief; a tramp had that morning begged his way from house to house through the village and had last been seen sitting on the church stile, examining the blade of a pocket-knife. 'As good as caught red-handed,' people said, 'an' might've been collared and popped in quod within a couple of hours if it hadn't a-bin f'r this maggot our parson's got in his head.' For what caused the excitement and the endless discussion was less the actual theft than the Vicar's attitude towards the thief. When told of the crime and dragged almost forcibly to the church to inspect the evidence, he had flatly refused to have the tramp followed and prosecuted.

'The money in the box,' he had said, 'if money it contained, which it frequently does not, was intended by the almsgivers to relieve the needs of the poor, and who could be poorer or more in need than the man you describe! Hand him over to the police? No, that might be giving him a final thrust downward. Let us pray for him as an erring brother whose need and temptations we have no means of knowing.'

'Pray for him, my elbow!' growled Clerk Savings, on guard for the day beside the rifled alms-box. 'I'd pray for him to get six months' hard, as he 'uld do if any justice wer' left in this country. At one time 't'ud' a bin a hangin' job, an' ought to be now, breakin' into th' house o' God an' stealin' the alms of th' faithful! What beats me is to know why I wasn't fetched. I wus the one to be sent for, and if I had bin I should 'a' dealt with it proper. Might as well 'a' fetched a babby in arms as our reverend!'

The church robbery was altogether an unsatisfactory affair. To begin with, nobody knew what money, if any, there was in the box. Some said the fellow had made off with a pound; others, 'more like twopence ha'penny'; the general estimate, quite unfounded, was five or six shillings. The parishioners thought that the Vicar had failed in his duty; the Vicar was distressed by the uncharitable attitude of his parishioners towards the sinner, and Clerk Savings was furious because, as he expressed it, the Vicar had been called in over his own head. There was no Court case and not a word about Restharrow's loss in the local newspaper. What, if properly dealt with, might have provided excitement for weeks had ended in a prayer in church for the poor and outcast with their grievous temptations, and the erring brother himself must speedily have realized the error of his ways, for even if he had found a few coppers in the alms-box they could not have sufficed to replace the pocket-knife which he left behind with its blade broken.

—— VI ——
NATURE STUDY

NATURE study was as yet an unheard of subject in village schools; but Miss Fowkes was in many of her ideas in advance of her time, and occasionally on an especially fine and sunny afternoon she would say to Charity: 'It seems a shame to keep these infants indoors on a day like this. They will learn nothing, for they will most of them fall asleep, face forward on the desk. I think you had better take them out in the sunshine for an hour or two. Take them for a walk, and, on the way, you might point out and tell them the names of any of the less common wild flowers you pass. It always seems a pity to me that, living in the country as they do, any flower which is not a buttercup or a daisy, or a cowslip or a bluebell, is to them no more than that red, yellow or blue flower.' And when Charity had marshalled her charges and marched them two and two through the village, she would allow them to scatter and explore the hedgerow in a meadow, those who had become interested searching for flowers, the others in their own way enjoying the outing. They were good, obedient children, especially on such an occasion, which they looked upon as one of their greatest treats; and Charity enjoyed the school walks as much as her charges.

Miss Fowkes was mistaken in thinking that the chidren had no names for the less familiar flowers. They had names which she had never heard for many. 'Goat's-beard! Tommy! Goat's-beard! I've told you a thousand times that the name of that flower is goat's-beard and that it has nothing *whatever* to do with the male fowl; so don't be rude!' But although already well in training for a schoolmarm, Charity was not devoid of taste and encouraged her infants to use such of the old flower-names as were not calculated to raise a blush. Wild arum was not insisted upon for lords and ladies; kiss-me-quick was accepted for tansy; angel's eyes passed current for speedwell; and why speak formally of toad-flax when butter-and-eggs described the flower more exactly? Nor had she any prejudice against wild foods. On their spring outings quantities of young green hawthorn leaves were devoured under the name of 'bread and cheese'. The leaves of sorrel, or sour grass, were a favourite refreshment; and of crab apples, sweet chestnuts, hips and haws and blackberries in their season the children ate pounds. The only stipulation made by their teacher was that they should not swallow the stones of the haws, because, she told them, a boy her mother had known had once swallowed so many of these that he afterwards became terribly ill and had to be dosed with a teacup of castor oil.

Some weeks after the Flower Show came a day of blue skies and moist autumn sunshine. It was well on in September, and the flowers which remained were mostly the coarse yellow flowers left over from late summer. But it was blackberry time and the time of ripe haws and streaked crab apples. There were late mushrooms to be found in the meadows and a new, tender growth of watercress in the brook, both eagerly sought by the children, who loved to take home something for tea. Very soon

the winter would come and the little ones would go to school muffled in scarves or their mothers' old shawls, their limbs and faces mottled with cold and with chilblains on their toes. 'We must make the most of such weather as we have to-day,' said Miss Fowkes. 'Take them out in the sunshine.' Then, when they were all in alinement, with Charity beside the last couple, Miss Fowkes brought out a little basket and handed it to Charity, saying: 'I wish you'd pick me a few blackberries. I should like to make one more pie, and Michaelmas will be here before we know where we are,' and she gave Charity a confidential little smile which said as plainly as words could have done, 'You and I know that the weather and not the date affects the condition of blackberries, but while we are in Rome I suppose we must respect the Roman customs.'

Nothing could have suited Charity better, for she knew that Bess, that afternoon, had gone blackberrying in the direction of Warren Pond, an unusual proceeding with Bess, who as a general rule hated to get her hands scratched and left the picking of blackberries when required to her younger sisters, who had only to run to the nearest hedge to fill a pie-dish. However, that day she had apparently a sudden fancy for blackberrying. Charity, on her way to afternoon school, had met her in the street, carrying a basket and a hooked stick, and she had said she was going blackberrying. She had been wearing her pink gingham dress and a shady, rush-plaited hat with a wreath of pink rose-buds; the frock, Charity had thought, too good to risk tearing; and when Charity had said, 'How stylish you look!' she had flourished her stick and replied, 'But you see I mean business!' Now Charity felt sure she would find her, picking industriously from the hedge surrounding a copse through which ran a path from the road to the pond, a large, rushy sheet of water, belonging to the Maitlands. It was one of the least frequented spots near the village and the blackberries there grew large and juicy and sweet as sugar and dropped off the briars, for no one went there to pick them; there were plenty nearer home.

In the copse, beneath the trees, were hillocks and dells and limestone cliffs, the workings of a long-disused quarry. The shell of an old limekiln beside one of the pathways was smothered in ivy and briars, and the cart-track on which horses had once sweated and strained with their loads was blocked with boulders and bracken. What had become a green solitude must at one time have been a busy and cheerful place. Men had earned their living there and, between accidents, had rejoiced in the high wages paid for their dangerous work. The ringing of their picks, the trundling of their barrows, the report of their charges and the thunder of subsidences must once have sounded there. Some there had suffered the anguish of injuries; some had died, for the moss-grown inscription on a tombstone in the churchyard stated that fact. Now the names on the stone were but names; those who had borne them were forgotten. Since the day of terror when a prematurely fired train had resulted in an explosion which had killed four men, in what had been the quarry-bed trees had sprung up and come to maturity, bracken and briars had formed an impenetr-able thicket, and the peculiarly deep silence of once populous places from which life has ebbed overhung the old workings.

Then came Charity with her infants, and for an hour the old place awoke. While she with a few willing helpers filled Miss Fowkes's basket, the other children amused themselves by shouting their own names, 'Jack!' 'Margaret!' 'Sally!', and listening for the echo thrown back by a cliff, 'J-a-a-ck!' 'Mar-g-r-e-t!' 'S-a-

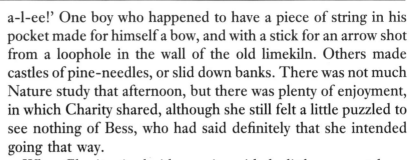

a-l-ee!' One boy who happened to have a piece of string in his pocket made for himself a bow, and with a stick for an arrow shot from a loophole in the wall of the old limekiln. Others made castles of pine-needles, or slid down banks. There was not much Nature study that afternoon, but there was plenty of enjoyment, in which Charity shared, although she still felt a little puzzled to see nothing of Bess, who had said definitely that she intended going that way.

When Charity, tired with romping with the little ones, sat down to rest, she gave some of the larger and more adventurous boys permission to play King of the Castle on a high but gently sloping mound left from the old workings. For a time all went well, and she sat with one of the babies asleep on her lap, breathing the sweet, pine-scented air and admiring the new autumn tints on birch and bracken. But, soon there were cries of alarm and, one after another, the boys came sliding down the mound on their bottoms, crying, 'Oh, Teacher! Teacher! There's a lion in the copse. Us heard him a-roarin'. Let's run! Let's run!' At first she laughed and told them not to be silly; there were no lions in England, except in wild beast shows; but they appeared to be really alarmed, one of the smallest was crying, and, to reassure them, she decided herself to climb to the top of the mound and investigate.

Taking with her one of the bigger and braver boys as a guide, and bidding the others to stay where they were and take care of the little ones, she climbed the slope, looking back often at her charges, who stood in a huddled group with faces turned up to watch her ascent. Although she had sometimes played in the copse when a child, she did not remember climbing that particular mound, which was higher than she had estimated. At the top she found a flattened space, a few feet wide, like a raised walk, between pine trees. The pines, towering above the green level of the rest of the wood, caught every breath of wind and filled the air with their sighing. That, and the subdued voices of the children below, were, at first, the only sounds she could distinguish. Then, gradually, she became aware of deep moaning or crooning, a soft murmur, more a throbbing of the air than a sound, rising now to a moan, now sinking to a concerted sighing. 'Listen! Is that what you heard?' she asked the child whose hot little hand she held, and he nodded. 'Oh, you silly children!' she cried. 'It's only a lot of wood-pigeons cooing! a sound you must have heard thousands of times, though perhaps not so many together,' and although at first the boy protested that he knew very well what them old wood-pigeons said – Take two cows, Taffy! Take two cows, Taffy! – and that rum row wasn't like them at all, and he was sartin sure 'twas an old lion, got out of a show, like that one got out at Towcester, he at last allowed himself to be convinced and slid down the slope on his buttocks as the quickest way of taking the good news to his companions.

Whether the children had really taken that most gentle of sounds, the cooing of doves, for the roar of a lion, or whether one of them more imaginative than the rest had first said it was in make-believe play and the others had taken him seriously, Charity was never to know. She did not question the children, for before she returned to the level, she had a surprise which turned her thoughts into another channel.

After seeing Dicky safely down and wondering if she might venture to follow him in a similar fashion, which she decided against as too undignified a mode of progression for a teacher, she remained for a few moments, looking around her. Standing high above the general level of the wood, she could see the pond. It was nearer than she had thought. So near, indeed, that it seemed that anyone wishing to bathe could have taken a flying leap over the few fringing tree-tops into the water. It was a narrow L-shaped stretch, banked by thick rush beds and islanded by accumulations of water weeds and clumps of water lilies. Like the copse, the pond was overgrown, neglected and seldom visited. A schoolboy bathing there the year before had become entangled in an under-water growth and been drowned, and the poles which had been used in the search for his body still lay on one of the banks, in company with the skeleton of an old toboggan, a relic of Mr. Roger's school holidays. Immediately beneath the mound where she stood was a wooden boathouse, its boarded roof and sides weathered to a silvery grey, which housed, she knew, a large, flat-bottomed boat which Roger's father had used for fishing and duck-shooting and which he, himself, had sometimes used when a boy. The old boat must be leaky by this time, she thought, and was turning to go, when, suddenly, that very vessel shot round the bend of the L and made for the boathouse. In it a tall, slender young man in white flannels stood poling it out from the rushes. It was Mr. Roger, of course, but who was the lady sitting in the stern, trailing one hand in the water? She was wearing a pink frock and the hat lying upon her lap had pink on it. It couldn't be Bess? But Bess it was. The sound of her voice came distinctly over the water. 'I could go on floating like this for ever,' she was saying, 'but I must go now, I must, really.'

The boat and its occupants disappeared beneath the boat-house arch and Charity descended, gathered together her infants and hurried them at such a rate out of the copse and away down the road that they had no energy left for noise-making. Charity was determined not to be seen by Bess and, to that end, instead of the way by which they had come, took another narrow byway, and, although no longer likely to be seen, so hurried the children that one of them asked, 'Teacher, have we been

117

naughty?' and when one of them said that he wanted to leave the room, she told him in a tone which, for her, was sarcastic, 'You'll have to wait till you get inside one.' Teacher was cross. The lovely outing was ending badly. It was a subdued little party which filed into the playground.

Charity was in an uncomfortable position. To know that she had secret knowledge of Bess's doings which Bess herself did not suspect made her feel sly and mean, and, to cleanse her own conscience, rather than as a warning to Bess, she decided to tell her that she had seen her with Roger.

But how? If she said, 'I saw you in the boat with Mr. Roger,' Bess would naturally ask, 'Where were you?' and whatever answer she gave she would appear as a despicable Peeping Tom, for had she not spied on the couple, herself unseen, and hurried off before they landed? Better lead up to it tactfully by saying, 'Where did you go for your blackberries after all?' or 'I took my class to Warren Copse on Thursday' and trust to luck to get further.

As it turned out, no such opening was necessary. The next time the two were alone together Bess said lightly, 'I went out in a boat on Thursday afternoon. It was lovely on the water,' and Charity asked with feigned astonishment, 'But how came you to be in a boat?' 'Oh, just by taking somebody's hand and stepping on board, first with one foot, then with the' other, and sitting down in the stern,' said Bess teasingly, and Charity could think of nothing better to say than: 'But who were you with? Not Mr. Roger?'

'Yes, with the great Roger Maitland, the Lord of the Manor himself! And – would you believe it? – I find he's just an ordinary human being, even as you and me. Can you believe that either? If so, I'm sure nobody else in the parish could. It makes me sick, and I expect it makes him sick, too, to see the way they set him up on a pedestal. The young squire this and the young squire that, they say in churchgoing voices. You girls mustn't look at or speak to him, not even if he looks at or speaks to you, but cast down your eyes and drop your curtsy – anything more would be unbecoming. And he, for his part, must keep to his own sort or the nation knows what might happen. You'd think folks about here were born in the year dot! But I'm not going to lie down and say, "Please wipe your feet on me" to anybody; not this little girl! I shall look at and talk to anybody I want to, if only to show that I think myself as good as anybody,' a revolutionary outpouring which so astonished Charity that she missed the opportunity of declaring herself an involuntary witness of the boating scene. Instead, she asked mildly, 'Do you like Mr. Roger, Bess?' and Bess laughed and said, 'Oh, he's all right. I like him very well to talk to, after talking to suet dumplings like Luke; but as to liking him more than that, I don't know that I do. Though he's of age, he's more like a boy than a man, and how can he help it, always waited upon, hand, foot, and finger, and

Isabel Naftel 1886

everything made easy for him? As Dad says, such ones don't know the nature of life. But Mr. Roger's jolly good company; you should have heard some of the tales he told me about their Oxford goings on! "God bless Marlborough and damn the dons" some of them chalked on the college doors when they were forbidden to go to the big ball at Blenheim. Other things, too; you cannot help laughing. But there it is, as I said before, he and his kind've all been brought up to believe the world was made on purpose for them.'

'Why, Bess, you're quite a socialist!' exclaimed Charity, and Bess said: 'I believe I am. It'd make anybody turn socialist to live at Restharrow.'

'Does Uncle Reuben know about your going out in the boat?' asked Charity timidly, and Bess gave her a searching look before she replied, 'Not that I know of. I haven't told him, and you needn't go telling your mother or anybody. I'm old enough to look after myself, and it's my business.' Charity felt a little offended. 'You need not be afraid,' she said. 'I'm no tell-tale.' But, though somewhat relieved, her conscience was still not easy. She was well aware that if her mother had known of Bess's association with the young squire she would not have approved. How many times had Charity heard her say when a girl in the village had made herself in any way conspicuous, 'It doesn't do! It doesn't do in a small place like this! You know what the Bible says, "abstain from the very appearance of evil"; and that's a good rule at Restharrow, if you want to live free of annoyances. Not but what, I must say, it's hard on the young, who mean no harm.'

After the day of Bess's outbreak, Charity saw less of her than usual for a fortnight. The time of the annual visit of Her Majesty's Inspector of Schools was drawing near and she had extra lessons of her own to prepare, as well as to help Miss Fowkes coach some of the backward pupils. At that time the Inspector's visit was regarded by teachers and pupils alike as an ordeal, which it seldom failed to prove. If anyone had told Charity then that she would live to see a successor of the ogre of her own childhood take a backward child upon his knee and prompt its answers to his questions she would have thought they were joking. That year, too, she had fears and apprehensions on her own behalf, for the time of her probation as monitress had expired and upon the decision of the great man her whole future depended. For it was he, and only he, who could accept or reject her application for the advanced post of pupil teacher. But for her personally all went well on the day of judgement.

Mr. Findlater was a learned man, an historian, with a leaning to the already becoming-less-popular Right. It happened that Charity's history paper dealt with the events leading up to the Civil War, and, unwittingly, she gained her examiner's favour by supporting the royal cause. At the end of her *viva voce*, he grunted, 'Very creditable,' and, instead of going away and leaving her in suspense, as he often did such candidates, he told her at once that the appointment was hers. After he had gone, Miss Fowkes kissed and congratulated her upon 'passing with honours', and she bounded home to tell her parents the good news with her head in the air. It was years later, when she came to read Mr. Findlater's *England in the Seventeenth Century* that she recognized the working of Chance.

The ordeal over, apprehension gave place to relief, and, to celebrate her success, Charity decided to do no lessons on the following Saturday morning, but go give herself a whole day's holiday. Miss Fowkes, she knew, intended to stay in bed all day and rest from her labours, with a well-cosied-down teapot on her bedside table and one of her Jane Austens to read. But such a programme, though all very well for fifty, appeared a mere waste of a day to fifteen. Charity was on pleasure bent. Accordingly, immediately after breakfast, she bounded across the meadow to Waterside, hoping to persuade Bess to go with her to Banbury. Her father had given her a sovereign to mark the occasion of her promotion to the full status of pupil teacher, and the coin was, as her mother said, burning a hole in her pocket. It would buy her a new winter coat, and to have Bess's advice when choosing one would, she knew, be a great advantage. Quality first, Bess would say, then cut, then colour, and, however attractive a thing may be, if it doesn't suit you or your purpose, better keep your money in your pocket. Bess was not likely to need much persuasion to come, for she dearly loved a trip into Banbury in the carrier's cart to see the shops and to enjoy a cup of tea at Betts's.

Very little cooking was done at Waterside on a Saturday morning. Saturday was the day for eating what was left in the larder, in view of the Sunday cooking, and Charity found Bess, as she had expected to find her, sitting on one of the window-seats in the living kitchen with a basket of mending on the table before her. Charity had often helped with the mending, which Bess was inclined to allow to accumulate, preferring to employ the needle she used deftly upon other, more decorative needle-work, and always before, Bess had said that she liked to have company when engaged upon such dull jobs as mending; but, on that Saturday morning, she did not even seem pleased to see Charity. Nor was she eager to join in the outing. When invited, she said that she did not think she could spare the time; and, as the carrier's cart was not due at the crossroads much before noon, Charity sat down, drew a stocking over her hand, and began darning.

For a few minutes they worked in silence, or, rather, Charity worked while Bess drooped over her sewing, putting in a stitch now and again and gazing idly at her work betweenwhiles. At last Charity could bear the silence no longer. 'I hope I have done nothing to offend you, Bess,' she said. Bess said, 'No. Nothing at all. If everybody minded their own business as you do, this world'd be a pleasanter place.' That was as far as they got at the moment, but, after putting in a few more stitches, Bess burst out with: 'I don't think I can stand this place much longer. Restharrow's full of interfering old women, a regular tabby cats' nest, you can't speak or move but one of 'em's got their claws into you. I'll tell Father I'm going to take a situation as sewing-maid or something. Mercy can very well manage here, and stand it I can't, so there!' And she flung her best scissors down on the table.

'Why, Bess, whatever's the matter?' asked the astonished Charity. 'You know you've always said that you'd hate to go out to service and have to scrape your hair back and wear a little black bonnet for church. And you always seemed to like Waterside and said that you'd never leave your father, not even to get married. Why have you changed your mind?' Bess folded her patched pillowcase and laid it on the pile of finished work and began darning a stocking before she spoke. 'Well, I may as well tell you,' she said, 'but for God's sake don't go telling anybody, not even Aunt Alice, or I shall die of shame. Dad's had a letter.'

'A letter? Who from? And why should it worry you?' were Charity's natural questions, and, for answer, Bess brought out from her apron pocket an envelope. 'You just read that!' she said, and Charity unfolded the letter and read:

REUBEN TRUMAN
'I advise you to keep an eye on that eldest daughter of yours. She's meeting the young squire secret. If you'd seen what I seen down by Warren pond yesterday you'd have taken your horsewhip to her. You know what they say, a word to the wise. This letter comes from

'A WELL WISHER.'

There was no other signature and no address was given. The communication was neatly written in script on such paper as was then sold in penny packets, six sheets of paper, six envelopes, and a slip of pink blotting paper. No clue there to the sender. Charity examined the postmark. It was that of Mixlow, their own post town. All the letters written at Restharrow and

handed to the postman bore that postmark, as well as those posted in the town and in other villages for miles around. The address on the envelope was also in script. Anyone above the level of absolute illiteracy might have written it. The names of several people she knew did not like Bess flashed through Charity's mind, but not one of them, she felt sure, was capable of such a mean action. 'Whoever can have done it!' she cried helplessly. But Bess had not as yet arrived at the point of trying to trace the sender. She held the whole village responsible and accused the population at large of envy, hatred and malice. Her cheeks flushed, and her eyes wet with anger and mortification, she cried, 'The hateful, hateful creatures! How I loathe them!' including many of her neighbours who had none but kindly feelings towards her and some whom she really liked.

'What does Uncle Reuben say about it?' asked Charity when she had recovered a little from her bewilderment and Bess's indignation had for the moment exhausted itself.

'He didn't say anything when he first read it. Just folded up the letter, put it in his pocket, and went out, and I thought it was one of his usual letters, from the corn-merchant or somebody. But, afterwards, when Polly had gone out and Mercy was scrubbing the courtyard, he came back and gave me the letter and said he'd thought at first he'd put it in the fire and say nothing about it to anybody; that was all such letters deserved; but, now, he thought that as it was about me I had better read it, and when I had read it, him standing by and looking on all the time, he said, "Is there any truth in what it says about you and Mr. Roger?" and of course I had to tell him that we had met once or twice by accident and that he had taken me for a row in his boat on the pond and shown himself friendly in other ways.

'At that, Dad looked a bit worried. You know the way he's got of shaking his head when things don't go just as he'd like? Well, he just stood there, sighing and shaking his head over me till I wanted to scream. "Seems there's more in it than I thought," he said at last. "Now, tell me the truth, my dear. Has there been any sweethearting between the two of you?" And I said, "Certainly not! Only a little ordinary fun, such as a girl might have with a cousin, if she'd got one." At that he looked a bit more satisfied and began talking about how careful a girl ought to be never to give a handle to gossip, and how, since our mother died, he'd tried to be father and mother, too, but he knew that the best man in the world, let alone such a one as himself, could never take the place of a mother, and he looked so sad that when he asked me to promise him never to be alone with Roger any more I just threw my arms round his neck and promised. And that's partly what's worrying me. I can trust you, can't I, Charity?'

Charity said, 'You know very well you can,' and, lowering her voice to a whisper, Bess continued: 'I wouldn't tell this to anybody else in the world but you. Though our other meetings were accidental, or nearly so, I had promised to meet Roger at the boathouse this afternoon, and I want you to help me. Will you?'

An unkind voice within whispered to Charity, 'Ah, she's told you all because she wants your help,' and she answered Bess a little coldly: 'I will if I can, but what do you want me to do?'

'I want you to go down to the pond this afternoon. You'll find Roger there. And I want you to tell him about the letter and the promise I've made Dad. Tell him I shan't be seeing him again, but I'll not forget the pleasant times we've had. You'll do this little thing for me, won't you, Charity?'

'And you really don't mean ever to see him again?'

'Of course not. I've given my word. And why should I want to? There's been enough fuss and bother about the few times we have met. He's good fun to talk to and it's nice to be taken notice of by a young gentleman like him, but I'd rather never set eyes on him again than vex Dad. But we're sure to see each other, living in the same place, and if I'm to pass him by with a plain "Good day to you, sir" – for I s'pose if I don't "sir" him there'll be another letter – perhaps, to be on the safe side, I'd better drop him a curtsy – I should like him to know the reason for the change. And I don't relish the idea of him waiting for hours and hours this afternoon and me not turning up. He doesn't deserve that, for the letter's not his fault. So please, Charity, dear, kind Charity, do do this one little thing to oblige me!'

To Charity it did not seem so small a thing. She was young and inexperienced and of a retiring disposition, and, could she have chosen, she would almost as soon have walked into a lion's den as carry such a message to Mr. Roger at his boathouse. And she was disappointed. All her plans for her one precious holiday were knocked on the head. That golden sovereign was still in her purse. She had not even been able to tell Bess about it, or about the examination, or anything. But there was no escaping her mission and she said that she would go if Bess was sure, quite, sure, that she would keep the promise she had made her father.

Bess sprung up from her chair, pretended to lick her finger, drew it across her throat, and swore she would by the old childish oath, *finger wet, finger dry*, and, Mercy coming in at that moment to lay the cloth for dinner, no more could be said.

Neither Mercy nor Polly had been told about the letter, and they chatted cheerfully about everyday matters at the table. Reuben's expression may have been somewhat more grave and thoughtful than ordinarily, but he appeared to enjoy the simple fare, and, when speech was required of him, spoke freely and naturally. Bess seemed to have completely regained her spirits. She chaffed Polly about one of her recent singing successes and Charity about her interview with the dread Inspector. Charity began to think she was heartless; but her father, who was a more experienced observer, no doubt attributed her flushed cheeks and raised voice to excitement, for his manner towards her was tender and soothing. After the meal was over, he asked her to come with him to the garden and see what last night's wind had done to the dahlias, adding that she'd be none the worse for a breath of fresh air and sunshine.

When she returned and found Charity alone in the living kitchen, she said, 'He's taken back the letter, and he says I'm not to worry about it any more, but to leave it to him to deal with. And now you'd better go. You know what you've got to say to Roger, don't you? Of course, you can't show him the letter now. You must tell him what was in

it, and be sure and notice how he takes it, so that you can tell me afterwards. When that's done and you get back, we'll try to put the horrid old business out of our minds. Father means to destroy the letter; he said so. And, Charity, I'm sorry you've been done out of your trip to Banbury. Next Saturday I'll go with you and we'll have such a day! We shall be able to laugh at this ridiculous fuss by that time.'

It had been decided between them that, in order to avoid the village street and the possibility of being seen and questioned by either of her parents, Charity should go by a roundabout way through the fields to the pond. In other circumstances she would have enjoyed this walk along narrow field paths, by berried hedgerows and always within sight, or at least sound, of the running brook; but that day her mind was so occupied with the coming interview that she was barely conscious of her surroundings. She had been late in starting, too, and had to run most of the way. On she went, stumbling over tussocks on little trodden paths, rough with molehills and overgrown with bindweed and briar, her mind no more at ease than her body. Her errand was not at all to her taste. She felt she was deceiving her uncle and her parents. If her mother were thinking of her at that moment, she would picture her with Bess, gazing into shop windows, or sipping tea and nibbling a Banbury cake in the Old Teashop; and here she was, quite close to her home, hot and dusty and bothered, panting and stumbling on an errand she knew in her own heart was likely to worsen rather than improve matters. She felt herself entangled in a web not of her own making. Still, there was Bess, proud, pretty, lovable Bess, to be thought of. She was entangled even more than herself and she must do what she could to help her.

She found Roger on the path which led through the copse, near the mound, scanning the way by which he expected Bess to come, and somehow, she could never remember how, she delivered her message. The young squire was not unnaturally indignant at what he considered unwarranted interference. 'It's come to a pretty pass,' he cried, 'if one cannot look at or speak to the daughter of an old neighbour without causing a scandal. One would think we were living in the bad old days of the villainous squire and the betrayed village maiden. I'm surprised at Reuben. He should know me better! And surprised that Bess should submit so meekly to her father's unreasonable decree. Tell her I thought she was a girl of more spirit. However, if I am not to see her again, I am not. It is her decision and I must abide by it, but tell her I never thought of her as one so ready to desert a friend.'

'It is really because of the letter,' said Charity timidly. 'Uncle Reuben does not like Bess to be talked about. Surely you can see his point of view?' And that started him off again. The anonymous letter-writer, he declared, must be found and brought to justice. He or she must be made to suffer by a prosecution for libel, for, if Charity had repeated the contents of the letter aright, libel it was to put such an interpretation upon an innocent friendship. And he made her repeat as nearly as she could remember what had been written, which repetition made him angrier than ever, although she had from the first left out the bit about the horsewhipping. She tried to implore him to let the matter drop and be forgotten, but he talked so hotly and angrily that she could not get in a word, and she stood before him miserably wondering what she ought to do. She had delivered her message, given all the explanation possible, and she longed to go; yet, though he seemed to be talking to himself, regardless of her presence, she felt she could not turn round and leave him talking alone in the wood.

He was still storming and she was still standing with bent head, like a guilty creature before him, when one appeared whom they had little expected to see there. It was Reuben, in his decent market-day suit and his low, square crowned market-day hat, who emerged from the winding path

through the bushes. 'Ah, young sir,' he said. 'I thought I might find you here, though Charity I did not expect to see. However, as she is here, she may as well stop and hear what I've got to say. I s'pose she's given you some idea of what I've come about. Read that letter.'

Roger read, then re-read the letter Reuben had handed to him. 'Damned impertinence!' he exclaimed, and he folded the letter and was about to put it in his own pocket when Reuben stretched out his hand. 'I'll take that, if you please,' he said. ''Tis addressed to me and I'm the one to deal with it,' and he stooped down, scooped out a shallow hole in the earth with his hand, tore the letter to fragments and put a lighted match to it. Over the shrivelling tinder the two men eyed each other. The one young, handsome, and endowed with the privileges of class and education; the other but an old countryman with only his ingrained integrity and common sense to support him, but rich in experience. 'Now, just a few words,' said Reuben, 'and as far as I'm concerned the whole dirty business is finished. You and Bess are better apart. I think she sees that herself now, for I've got her word there shall be no more of these unseemly meetings. Of course, if you should meet in the ordinary way, in the street, or going into church, with other folks about, you'll naturally be civil to each other. I don't need to teach either of you your manners. It's these meetings in out-of-the-way places I don't like. They're not for her good, nor for your good, and, by God, sir, I won't have 'em!'

Roger had not listened to this speech, probably one of the longest Reuben had ever made, without signs of impatience. Flushed with anger and outraged pride, he had muttered interjections of dissent, and there was a note of sarcasm in his tone when he said, 'Surely, Mr. Truman, you do not suspect me of trying to seduce your daughter?'

'No, I do not,' was Reuben's reply. 'I've got too good an opinion of you to suspect anything of that sort; and, if I hadn't, I know my own daughter. You won't find our Bess giving way to any shady practices; she's got too much pride. But she's young and maybe a bit giddy, and flattery from anybody in your position might set her against her own proper way of life; and, above all, I'm not goin' to have her talked about. So now you know.'

'Well, Mr. Truman,' said Roger haughtily, 'if you feel like that about a few innocent civilities, there's no more to be said. Good day to you,' and he turned and went back to his boathouse.

Reuben took off his hat, brought out a clean white handkerchief and mopped his brow. 'Well, that's it and that's all about it,' he said. When they were out of the wood he asked Charity which way she had come and when she said by the field way, he said,

'We'd better go back that way then.' Afterwards he spoke only of ordinary everyday things. He did not then or ever afterwards ask how she came to be in the wood with Roger, or explain his own presence there. He may have suspected that Bess and Roger had arranged to meet there that afternoon; or he may have gone there as to the most likely place to find Roger alone. That the young squire had painted up his father's old boat and meant to go in for some duck-shooting was village talk at the moment.

What Reuben's thoughts and feelings were cannot be said; but Charity's feeling was one of relief. Neither Bess nor Roger appeared to have been deeply involved, or they would not have been so ready to sever their intimacy. It had, as Bess had said, been but a bit of fun, and, except that her father had had a hot, tiring walk and a disagreeable interview, nobody was any the worse for it. The whole puzzling business had ended happily, and, as she tripped before or beside her uncle, according to the width of the field path, she felt she had escaped from a tangle in the affairs of others and might again live her own life. She had still to learn that life is not so simple or so detached, that the threads of human destiny intertwine, and that one thread pulled roughly may get the whole skein in a tangle.

VII

SNAKE IN THE GRASS

OFTEN, at Restharrow, when one neighbour remarked that that day things had turned out better than she had expected, another would say quenchingly, 'Ah, you're up and dressed, but you haven't gone to bed yet!' A dreary hint that not one of those gathered around the tea-table at Waterside Farm that Saturday evening thought of applying to themselves and their own affairs. Bess talked brightly, every now and then casting a questioning glance at Charity, who, when she came in, had told her that all was satisfactorily concluded, but as yet had had no opportunity of telling the whole story. Polly had brought indoors three small kittens, the progeny of the stable cat, and their laughable antics did much to enliven the meal.

When Reuben went out, saying, 'Saturday evening or no Saturday evening, the stock's got to be seen to,' Bess almost dragged Charity to the empty room where they had danced. 'Now tell me everything,' she demanded. 'How did he take it? Did he seem sorry he was not to see me any more?'

Charity began her story and had just come to the point where Reuben had appeared when Bess grasped her by the shoulder. 'Look! Look who's coming,' she whispered, and Charity saw through the window a majestic figure in dove-grey silk, half covered by a transparent black lace mantle, hurrying as much as a lady of importance could permit herself to hurry towards the front gate. It was Mrs. Maitland. She had with her on a leash her two little Skye terriers, and, as she entered the gate the little creatures, unused to such hurried progress, got their leashes entangled and tumbled over each other. 'Order! Order!' commanded their mistress, and her tone when speaking to her cherished pets did not augur well for whomsoever she had come to interview. 'Oh, I can't see her! I can't!' whispered Bess hoarsely, apparently as near to being afraid as Charity had ever seen her; and, as leaving the room they were in would have necessitated passing the front door, the two girls crouched behind the window-curtains, Charity's arm round Bess's trembling shoulders.

Mrs. Maitland's sharp rat-tat was answered by Mercy. 'Is your father within?' asked that lady, wasting no time on preliminary greetings. 'Oh, you will please fetch him. Tell him I wish to speak to him immediately. No thank you, I will not come in. My little dogs do not like strange houses.'

In their position, near the open window, Bess and Charity heard all that was said. Bess, shivering like a guilty thing, whispered, 'Oh, don't! Pray don't!' when Charity made a slight noise with her feet.

Soon, Reuben, having doffed his old yard smock, came to the door and invited Mrs. Maitland to enter, which invitation she again refused. 'I wish to speak to you about your eldest daughter. Her name I believe is Elizabeth,' she said haughtily. 'For her own good, I advise you to get her a place in service, away from home.'

'But, ma'am,' said Reuben, still courteously, 'will you not come in and sit down? I am not used to discussing my family affairs on the doorstep. You would rather not? Then, with all due respect, I must tell you that whether my daughter leaves home or not is none of your business. What right have you to take upon yourself to interfere?'

'I have a perfect right. I have to-day received a letter, giving me certain information—'

'I know, or can guess, what that letter said. I had the fellow to it myself this morning. But, let me remind you, ma'am, that I didn't come to your house and order you to send your son away. After I'd made proper inquiries, as I had a right to do, I burnt it, as I've always been told's the right way to deal with such muck; but it seems you think otherwise, and if you won't come in and sit down, ma'am, I've no more to say, for it goes against the grain with me to keep a lady standing.'

'But you will send Elizabeth away? If I can be of any assistance in getting her a superior situation, as sewing-maid, or something of that kind—'

'I thank you, ma'am, but, no,' said Reuben sternly. 'My daughter's done no wrong and she's not going to be packed off to service in disgrace. But, although I've no need to, just to ease your mind like, I'll tell you here and now that she's no wish in the world to see your son any more. She's had more than enough annoyance already over a bit of light chat with one who, after all, is but a young thing like herself. There's been no harm whatever in anything that's passed between them, not the least bit in the world; the worst you can say is 'twas thoughtless, and, as far as me and mine's concerned, 'tis all over. Good day to you, ma'am.' But Mrs. Maitland was in no humour for leave-taking; she was already at the gate.

There was no longer any possibility of keeping the matter secret. Mrs. Maitland's voice, loud and clear at all times, had been raised in anger, and everyone in the house or in the nearer portion of the farmyard must have heard the conversation. Polly had gone to her choir practice before Mrs. Maitland's arrival, but Mercy had heard enough for Charity to find her in tears. When the situation had been explained to her, she passed instantaneously from tearful bewilderment to indignation. 'How dare she! How dare she!' she cried, and declared she would go herself that very moment to the Manor House and tell Mrs. Maitland to mind her own business. The idea of Mercy, usually retiring and shy to the point of speechlessness, telling the great Mrs. Maitland to mind her own business brought a wan smile to poor Bess's woebegone face. Her father laughed heartily. 'You'll do no such thing,' he said. 'You couldn't if you tried to; and when you come to think on't you'll see that she thought it was her own business. The poor soul was only trying to do her best for her own, same as I was doing what I thought was best for my

own, and it grieved me to see her, tired and upset, standing there on the doorstep, too proud to come in and rest herself. I've got nothing against her, nor against her son, for the matter of that, beyond his being young and thoughtless; but, whether I liked it or not, I had to stand firm, or she'd've been riding over me roughshod. And the best thing you can do, Mercy, is to make a good strong cup of tea for yourselves, and you, Bess, my dear, go and lie down on your bed. You've had a hard lesson. Now I'll go and finish what I was doing. There's no sense or reason on letting the poor animals suffer for our ups and downs.'

Even in the midst of their distress, while Mrs. Maitland had been speaking, one thought had occurred to both Charity and Bess. Were the Pococks in, and were they listening? Now, when Mercy was questioned, she said she did not know, she had not seen or heard them all the afternoon, and they hoped they were to escape the humiliation of having to discuss what had happened with Stella. But they were not to

be spared. As Charity followed Bess upstairs, she happened to glance upward, and there, leaning over the banister, she beheld Stella Pocock. Stella was smiling; but, as their eyes met, she drew a long face and exclaimed, 'Oh, Bess, what is the matter? I didn't mean to listen, I didn't really, but Mrs. Maitland shouted so and I couldn't help hearing. Why is she so angry, and with you above all people? I'm sure you've never done anything to offend her!'

While the story was unfolded, or as much of it as was thought impossible to hide, Stella was unusually sympathetic. 'Poor Bess! What a shame!' she ejaculated repeatedly. 'I can't see that you've done anything at all to be blamed for. Anybody in your place'd been pleased to go out with young Mr. Maitland. I'm sure, if he'd asked me, I'd have gone like a shot. So'd any girl, and why that old tabby's making all this fuss about it beats me!' and she ran off to her own room and came back with a little bottle of *eau de Cologne* to sponge Bess's forehead.

'Oh, those miserable letters! It's them that have worked the mischief,' sighed Bess miserably, and Mercy, coming in at that moment with the tea, flared up again. 'I only wish I could lay hands on whoever it was who wrote them,' she cried. 'I'd wring their neck for them, that I would!'

'I wonder who did write them,' said Stella ponderingly, and she went on to suggest the names of several most unlikely people, including those of the Vicar and Mr. Virtue. But although her suggestions as to the possible writer of the letters were stupid, Stella showed the best side of her nature that evening. 'Poor Bess! I am so sorry!' she said again and again as she lavishly sprinkled her *eau de Cologne* on Bess's pillow. 'Stella is not such a bad sort,' said Charity when Stella had gone downstairs for a moment, and Bess said, 'Well, perhaps not,' though she added that it was vexing to be treated as an invalid, and that she wished they had not other people living in the house, for, try as you might, they were bound to know everything. 'But Stella is really sympathetic, isn't she?' urged Charity. 'Well, she seems so,' Bess admitted;  'but I don't know! I really don't! You never do know where you are with Stella, and, if you ask me, I think she's being a bit too kind,' and Charity, remembering the look of exultation on Stella's face as they had mounted the staircase, herself felt uncertain.

When Charity reached home and told her mother of the day's doings, as she had been bidden to tell her by Reuben, her mother was angry. Angry with Charity for having become what she called mixed up in the affair, angry with Bess for her frivolous conduct, and, above all, angry with Mrs. Maitland for having taken up the attitude she had. 'Who does she think she is?' she cried. 'The Queen of England, and that son of hers a prince of the realm? I only wish I had been at Waterside this afternoon. I'd have told her a few home truths! Reuben's too mild and kindly for anything when it comes to being at grips with a woman. I'll lay any money he said afterwards that he was sorry he'd had to vex her. Ah, if I didn't think so! Not but what that letter was a dirty trick on her, as well as on us, and I shan't rest till I find out who sent it. One of the men on the farm, I'll bet! One of them Reuben's had to find fault with at some time. But we must go quietly to work; 'tis not the sort of thing to be shouted from the house-tops. And a fine holiday you've had, trapesing about the fields as a go-between! I hope it'll be a lesson to you, and one you won't forget in a hurry!' and Charity went to bed thinking how hard it was to know what to do for the best.

Of course everyone in the village must have heard one version or another of what had happened. In those days, in a small place like Restharrow, where very little of first-rate interest occurred, such a titbit of news was a godsend to the gossips. For a few weeks, when Bess appeared in the village, she was stared at, and, once or twice, she saw, or thought she saw, one neighbour nudge another as she passed them in the street. But, as usually happened when one belonging to a respected family was implicated, whatever gossip circulated, circulated below the surface. Mr. Penpethy called at the farm and stayed to tea, which he had never done before. He was very kind and gentle when speaking to Bess, and, as he was taking his leave, he said to her, 'We must try to forgive our enemies, my dear, and pray for those who despitefully use us,' which seemed to signify that he was not as oblivious as some thought him to what went on among his parishioners.

At the farm, the letters and the events which had led up to them were seldom mentioned. As Reuben said one day when he was told that Stella had brought up the subject, such matters were best put out of mind. 'Do you remember all that fuss and bother about those nasty old letters?' she had said, as though Bess were likely to forget. 'I wonder who sent them,' she had continued. 'Whoever did ought to be well punished. But I don't s'pose we shall ever find out now.' And Bess, who was retrimming her best hat, had held it at arm's length to judge the effect before she replied, 'Let's leave them, whoever they are, to their own conscience.' Then, after a few minutes' silence, Stella had said meditatively, 'I wonder if there'll be any more and who'll get the next,' a speculation which the others present regarded as too far-fetched to require enlarging upon. The next! What an idea! Of course no more would be sent. Why should there be? The two already sent and received had surely caused annoyance enough to satisfy that unknown enemy, that snake in the grass.

Roger Maitland had disappeared from the place. According to the maids at the Manor House, he had sailed for the West Indies and would be away for at least six months. Perhaps longer; it all depended upon what he found when he got there. The Maitlands, it appeared, had a small estate on one of the islands, which had been bought as an investment by Roger's father, from which for some time no dividends had been received, and his mother had sent Roger to look into the matter. It was said afterwards that he found their plantation gone to rack and ruin and the manager gone native; but the blow, if the disappointment amounted to a blow, was softened for him by his meeting on the voyage out the lady he afterwards married. His promised bride was to some modest extent an heiress, and later the whole village benefited by her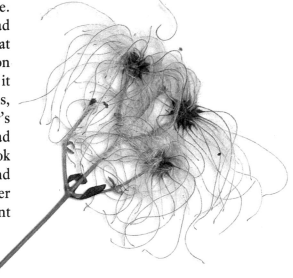
presence; but theirs was another story, ripening in time, to provide future entertainment for the Restharrow villagers. Exciting events, in which many of themselves were to be involved, were close upon them.

The winter had come. The footpath over the meadow was slippery with mud; the stream ran in spate, and the trees stood bare. Except for a few nipped blooms on the monthly rose, the Waterside garden was flowerless. In the village people were making their Christmas puddings and mincemeat; there were fires in the grates and the curtains were drawn and toast was made for five o'clock tea by lamplight. The weather was too cold and cheerless for out-of-door gossip. After water had been fetched from the well, the women seldom left their own firesides. Everybody and everything seemed to have settled down until the spring.

Then came 'the next'. One morning in the middle of December a young man in the village whose wife was away from home nursing her sick mother was advised by the anonymous writer to 'Keep an eye on that wife of yours. She's having high jinks at Wallingham. Ask her who it is she meets every night after dark in Lover's Lane.' The young man was of a jealous disposition, as, no doubt, was known to his anonymous correspondent, and, without saying a word to anybody, he took french leave from his work, locked up his house, and trudged the six miles across country on a day of thaw and rain and bitter wind to his wife's maiden home at Wallingham; to find when he reached there a house of mourning and his wife in the state any other young woman might be who, a few hours before, had lost a dearly loved parent. Without any inquiry on his part, the young husband's doubts were dispersed, for almost the first words of his father-in-law were, 'And there's Alice here, she hasn't had her clothes off at night or been over the doorstep for a breath of fresh air since she came. Not left her poor mother for ten minutes, she hasn't. It's a good job you've come, for maybe you can persuade her to lie down for an hour.' After the young man had done what he could to help, he trudged back the six cold, wet, weary miles, to be ready for his work in the morning. 'Cussin' an' swearin' an' stumblin' over furrows an' gettin' wetshod by steppin' into puddles,' he said afterwards; 'it'd bin a bad look out for the bloke what wrote that letter if I'd come across him!' When he reached Restharrow, before facing his dark, fireless home, he turned into the *Magpie* for a mug of hot ale and handed the letter round.

The habitués of that establishment had a few weeks before heard about and discussed the letter received by Reuben; but that they had not taken very seriously, regarding it as part of Bess's little escapade and a matter for mirth, rather than indignation. But that such a letter should have been sent to one of themselves and have cost the poor chap a day's pay, and, over and above that, a twelve-mile hommock, over ploughed fields part of the way, and in unked weather, was, as one of them said, carrying the thing beyond a joke.

All present agreed that something must be done about it. But what? Someone suggested calling in the police, but he was talked down. The less a man had to do with the law the better was an old Restharrow maxim. After a good deal of discussion, they decided to take Old Postie into their confidence and to get him to note the addresses of all letters handed to him for posting, and to try to remember and tell them the names of the senders. At the same time the young men and lads might be told to keep a watch on the cottages; they might just as well be doing that as lounging outside under the signpost of an evening, hollerin' and wrestlin' and strikin' these 'ere Bengal lights and throwin' 'em about and makin' 'emselves a general nuisance. Ducking in the pond was mentioned as a suitable punishment for the offender, when found.

Indignation and the desire for vengeance grew when other such letters began to arrive, addressed to different people in the village and all apparently from the same source. For a week or two they appeared regularly at intervals of a few days, and they were horrible letters. Husbands were informed that one or other of their numerous progeny had another father than themselves; wives that their husbands were 'carrying on' with the dairymaid at such and such a farmhouse; parents that their sons had stolen money, or been seen poaching, or that their daughters were on the road to ruin. The farmer was told that his workmen were robbing his corn-bin; workers that there was a tale-bearer trying to oust them from their employment. One leading cottage gardener

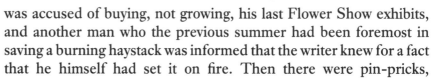

was accused of buying, not growing, his last Flower Show exhibits, and another man who the previous summer had been foremost in saving a burning haystack was informed that the writer knew for a fact that he himself had set it on fire. Then there were pin-pricks, reminders of some slight physical deformity, splay feet, a red nose, or an impediment in the speech. Whoever the writer might be, it was evident that he or she knew the village folk and the village affairs intimately. The letters all bore the Mixlow postmark, all were written in neat script on identical paper and ironically signed 'Well Wisher'.

Over Bess's affair the village had been divided. Some folks had said there was no smoke without fire and they themselves had always thought Bess Truman a stuck-up little bit of goods who'd get all she deserved before she'd finished. Others, and those the greater number, had been more indulgent. Bess might be a bit flighty, they said, and inclined to dress above her station; but, after all, the girl was young and not bad-looking, and there was no harm in her, only high spirits; and, anyhow, sending that letter to Reuben was a dirty old trick. The two sides had agreed to differ amicably; what had happened did not touch them personally, beyond providing matter for speculation which had helped to relieve the tedium of village life. Now practically every household was involved, for the families were so interrelated that those who had themselves escaped had at heart the cause of some relative. Members of those families which had so far escaped were apprehensive. Nobody knew what was going to turn up by post any morning. The postman was watched from one end of the village to the other and every house where he had been seen to hand in a letter was soon crowded with callers, some of whom seemed to be disappointed when told that the letter was but from 'my poor old mother' or 'our young Jenny' or Bill or Arthur.

Indignation rose to fever heat. 'Us've got to find out who's a doin' on't, and punish 'em ourselves if the law can't do nothin',' men said to each other, and one man who considered himself an authority on the law on the strength of having once been tried in a court and sentenced to fourteen days' imprisonment for poaching, roared out: 'The law, my elbow! We ain't a-goin' to bring any bobbies into it, nor yet no beaks, with the duckpond handy. It's a clear case for ducking!' And ducked the offender would certainly have been if he could have laid hands on him.

At the *Magpie* an informal committee sat every evening to investigate possible clues to the mystery. They had secured as many as they could of the letters and examined them again and again beneath an

140

old reading glass someone had produced, shaking their heads wisely. The postman who delivered the Restharrow letters each morning and, on his return journey, carried back those handed to him for posting at Mixlow, though willing enough, could throw no light on the matter. He recorded the addresses of all letters given to him to post and submitted the list to the landlord daily, but not one of the anonymous letters appeared to have passed through his hands before they were given to him for the morning delivery. When it had been concluded that the writer must post them in the Post Office letter-box at Mixlow, people began to be afraid to go there for their Saturday night shopping, lest they should fall under suspicion.

Almost everybody had a pet theory as to the originator of the letters, which they would expound at great length whenever they could find a listener. So-and-So, one said, had a shifty, hang-dog sort of look and they for their part had never trusted him; or they knew for a fact that somebody else had been the best writer in her class at school. Of course, she couldn't have had much practice lately with that tribe of small children, but the speaker would not be surprised if the letters were her handiwork. 'You know how artful and cunning them clever ones be.' Or, there was that Madge Price, now in service with the baker's wife at Mixlow, only two doors off the Post Office. All she'd have to do would be to slip out after dark to the post-box and be seen by nobody. At that point the listener, with some suspect of her own in view, would *pooh-pooh* the idea of clean, tidy, good-humoured Madge Price having anything to do with the letters. And, she would add, why go as far afield as Mixlow? Or even to t'other end of Restharrow? She knew what she knew and was only waiting till the time was ripe to declare it.

Even Charity's name was mentioned. One man was reported to have said at the *Magpie*, 'And there's that little wench o' George Finch's. She's always walkin' about wi' books and papers under her arm. S'pose she ain't had no hand in it?' 'Charity? Charity Finch? No, no!' said another. 'You've only got to look at the child to know she'd never get up to such tricks.' And the first speaker said, 'Well, no, she don't look as if she'd got the sense,' which, when repeated to her, amused Bess mightily.

There were more direct approaches. One evening, at the *Magpie*, a mild-mannered little man who had a big, raw-boned, rough-tongued wife was cornered. 'Now, Andrew, my lad,' said the spokesman kindly, 'we all know that you've had the luck to pluck a bitter weed in matrimony, for haven't us heard times out of number your Liddy a-hollerin' out to you to wipe y'r gret hommickin' feet on the mat, or to leave y'r filthy old coat in th' wash'us, and not come muckin' up her clean house. It's no good y'r denyin' y'r henpecked, because us all knows you be, and sorry enough we are for you, and that your 'ooman ain't exactly a lover of her kind, that we know also. So, now, tell us th' truth. Has your Liddy had any hand in them letters? Have 'ee seen any signs, such as th' inkpot standin' about?'

All through the speech Andrew had been fretting and fuming. At the end of it he boiled over. 'My Liddy have any hand in them letters?' he shouted. 'I tell you my Lydia's as straight as a die. She wouldn't demean herself to touch such muck with a pair of tongs. And as to me being henpecked, that's as may be, though I can't say that I've noticed it. If any man's got a good wife, it's Andrew Walker. Why should a chap be let to go messing up a floor that his wife's just been down on her marrows to clean? It don't seem right to me, somehow! And if being warned off sometimes is being henpecked, well, then, I be henpecked, but you needn't trouble yourselves to be sorry for me, 'cos I like it!' And he got up and went out without finishing his beer.

Then, one evening, a band of youths who were acting as spies burst into the inn

taproom. In the course of their prowling they had peeped through a crack in a shutter and seen Mrs. Burdett writing away, as they said, for dear life. One of them said she seemed to be writing a letter; another, that when his turn came to peep she was writing in a book. 'Writin' down the addresses where she means to work mischief, I'll lay,' said one of the men. 'And now's the time. Let's go and catch the old witch red-handed.' ''Ere! 'ere!' said another. 'I allus thought there wer' summat underhanded about that old party, or why should she go strolling the country like she do, and at her age!' 'To post them letters, to be sure!' came in chorus. 'What fools we've a-bin not to think of her before! We'll larn her to go writin' nonnymous letters and stealin' off to post 'em at Mixlow! Come on, boys! There's plenty of water in th' duckpond!'

A few of the older, steadier men held back. 'Arter all, we don't know as she done it,' they said, 'or that she's a-doin' it now; she might be writin' to her relations, or adding up her bits of expenses; and even if she has done it, we can't go duckin' her in this weather at her age; it might do her a mischief and we should have to answer for it, and sarve us right for setting ourselves up as judge, jury and constable,' and they drew in a closer circle round the fire. Some of them blamed themselves afterwards for, as they said, not going to see fair play. From all accounts, the play at Mrs. Burdett's house that night was far from fair.

When the party of youths and young men reached her cottage and peeped through the hole in the shutter Mrs. Burdett was seen, still seated at her table, writing slowly and carefully with a quill pen upon a blank page of an old ledger, and the sight so infuriated them that they burst into the room without knocking. 'Now, then! We've caught you! Hand over that book, you crafty old devil, or 't will be the worse for you!' shouted one of the ringleaders. 'Hand it over, I say!' and he tried to wrench the book from her. 'No! No! It is mine! What business have you to demand it,' cried Mrs. Burdett, much alarmed, but determined to retain her property, and she held on to the ledger so tenaciously that she was dragged round the table to the doorway. Nobody actually struck her, but, during the struggle, one sleeve of her dress was torn out, her feet were trodden on, her ankles kicked and her shins badly bruised against some article of furniture. And worse was to come, for when a sudden wrench tore the ledger from her grasp, she fell back and her head was cut on the edge of the table. She fell to the floor senseless. Without staying to see if she were seriously hurt, the excited gang rushed off towards the inn, shouting, 'Let's go and show it 'em, then come back and duck her. We'll put an end to her tricks. The witch! The damned old witch! To the pub! To the pub! Come along, boys!'

They did not come back, for, when examined, the book was found to contain nothing of an incriminating nature, and had not some neighbours, disturbed by the shouting, run to her house to see what was the matter, Mrs. Burdett might have lain on the floor all night. As it was, the doctor had to be fetched from Mixlow. After he had examined her, he said that though her injury was not likely to be fatal, she had sustained a shock which at her age might prove more serious. She was carefully tended by neighbours that night, the next day she was taken away to the hospital, where those in authority advised her to prosecute her assailants. This she refused to do, saying, 'You don't know the Restharrow folks as I do, sir. If I set the police on them, I can never go back there, for I should have no more peace, and all I want is peace and quiet and to be let to go my own way, and maybe they are sorry for what they have done by this time.'

All her assailants were sorry and a few were deeply ashamed when they found that the entries in the book, written in her old-fashioned spidery handwriting, with long 'f'-like s's, had no connexion whatever with the anonymous letters. It was, they said, just a lot of drooling nonsense she had written, about birds and flowers and things, which, though harmless enough, showed that the poor old soul had gone a bit queer in the headpiece; but, if she liked to waste pen, paper and ink, and wear out what she had left of her eyesight, that was her own lookout, and the shattered ledger was returned to her house and placed on the table, together with a half-pound packet of tea as a peace offering.

Some of the leaves of the ledger had been scattered and lay the next morning in the roadside gutter, and Charity, on her way to school, secured one of these. It may have been the very leaf upon which Mrs. Burdett was writing at the time of her disturbance, for the entry ended abruptly and a few spots of blood showed through the mudstains. What Mrs. Burdett had written was puzzling. Miss Fowkes thought she had been keeping a kind of diary, Mrs. Finch that she had been copying from a book, but both advised Charity to put the leaf in the fire and have done with it, for Mrs. Burdett, they said, would not want to see anything likely to remind her of her ordeal. Charity read it over and over, then put it away in a drawer and kept it for years. It ran as follows:

'The aconites under my blenheim orange apple out early this year, but pale and peaky as if the sun was not strong enough to colour a flower a right yellow, but they look nice with their little green frills round their necks and I was glad when I saw them for when the aconites open I know that the snowdrops will soon be here and then we shall have the daffies and the wallflowers and know that its spring.

'A great big missel thrush, spotted like a toad, was eating the last of the ivy berries over my little house down the garden, and afterwards, my! didn't he sing. I looked at him and he looked at me out of his great round eyes and I said you've got more than I've got, you've got a thankful heart to be singing like that for a few dried up old ivy berries. My tom pussy that I've had these ten years very poorly with a nasty cut on his foreleg. Been caught in a trap I fancy. Those who set traps for poor animals ought to spend a night caught by the leg in one. I remember when mantraps were set for poachers. Then folks used to say . . .'

Charity would have liked to learn more about the mantraps and what people said about them, but she never had an opportunity to ask Mrs. Burdett to tell her more, for she never returned to her cottage at Restharrow. Before she was due to leave the hospital, a brother of hers appeared in the village and said he was taking his sister back with him to their old home in Westmorland. He and his wife had long wanted her to share their home; he had a good farm and money enough for them all; but Avis, as he called his sister, had clung to her own cottage and independence. She had always been like that. When a girl she had loved to wander alone, watching the birds and searching for flowers, and he found that she liked to do that still. At Overshaw, she could do as much of it as she liked and had strength for, but he had managed to persuade her that now, at her age, she needed a comfortable hearth-place to come back to, and her own folks to look after her if she should fall ill, and she had decided to go back with him to the home of their childhood. Restharrow, he thought, seemed a roughish place for a widow woman to live alone in, but he'd say no more of that, for he'd promised his sister not to, and, rough as it might be, it seemed there were some good Christian people living there. All this he said with such a strong Northern burr in his voice that to hear him talk was like listening to a foreign language when he came to thank Charity's mother for caring for his sister on the night she received her injuries and for visiting her in the hospital after- wards. Mr. Finch said that he seemed a good, substantial sort of fellow, and Mrs. Finch that it was as good as a tonic to her to know that Mrs. Burdett would be in good hands.

Mrs. Burdett's cottage was bespoken by a soon-to-be-married young couple. And Charity's father held a Dutch auction and sold what she did not wish to take with her of her furniture. The Dutch auction was great fun; everybody in the village attended it, everything was sold, and all vowed afterwards that it had been as good entertainment, if not better, than one of those Dutch auctions at fairs, where they sold solid gold watches for five shillings and threw in a silver chain, free, gratis, and for nothing. 'Who'd've thought that Carpenter Finch had had it in him to make folks laugh till they busted their sides-a-most, and him generally that prim and proper that you'd think butter 'uldn't melt in his mouth?'

The Dutch auction helped to distract public attention from the anonymous letters, and, apart from that, village interest was waning. Indignation had burnt itself out, and no more letters came to revive it. There were two or three ill-natured persons who said that, of course, there were no more, now old Mother Burdett had been laid by the heels; but they usually got the answer, 'The less we says about that poor old soul the better. Knockin' a poor old 'ooman about ain't nothin' to boast of, and us Restharrow folks ain't thought none the better of for it, either. Only the other day a Burmile man says to me . . .'

Mr. Virtue, looking in at the *Magpie* one evening for a glass of brandy and water, said the final word. 'Don't let me hear another word about those letters,' he said, dropping water into his brandy as sparingly as he measured out his medicines. 'You don't know who sent 'em, and I can't tell you, for I don't know myself; but this I will say, whoever it was he's had a fine run for his money. He meant to annoy and he has annoyed. My God, hasn't he! It must have been as good as a play to him to hear all your arguing and suspecting and quarrelling and all but fighting over 'em! I advised you at the start to ignore the letters. Always ignore 'em myself, and I've had scores in my time. According to my unknown correspondents, I've been a champion smasher of the Ten Commandments. But think that I ever lost any sleep over 'em? Not I! Here's to 'em, every one of 'em, who've wasted their penny stamps on me!' and he threw back his head and swallowed the contents of his glass. Then, in a more mellow tone, he continued: 'Take my advice and let the matter rest. You say the letters have stopped coming? Nobody's had one for a fortnight? Then don't let a word cross your lips about them in public and I'll lay ten to one there won't be any more.'

Thenceforth, if anyone tried to bring up the subject of the letters, another would say, 'Oh, cheese it, old lad! Us've heard more than enough about they,' or, more gravely, 'Let's take Dog Virtue's advice and let them things bide. Arter all, 't ain't a matter f'r our boasting.'

No more anonymous letters were delivered at Restharrow at that time, or, as far as Charity knew, ever afterwards, and gradually the story of them took its place as one to be told by the winter fireside as that of an unsolved mystery. But, though the discovery was never made public, the identity of the writer became known to a few, and how this came about shall be told in the next chapter.

VIII

ST. VALENTINE'S EVE

ON the eve of St. Valentine's, Bess and Charity sat with their feet on the fender in the warm, bright living kitchen at Waterside, Bess stitching industriously, Charity gazing into the glowing coals, thinking. Every door and window in the place was closed, for the weather was as bad as it can be in February. For a week there had been night frosts, followed by days of the damp, creeping cold which rises from damp pastures and ploughed fields and seems to seep into the very marrow. Upon the hedgerow thorns the melted hoar frost hung in drops of moisture at the point of each twig and the lowering grey sky threatened snow, or very cold rain. 'Tarrible weather!' 'Just about unkid!' people called to each other and passed on hurriedly, fearing to be detained. Washing hung to dry around cottage fires and filled the rooms with steam and the smell of soapsuds. The old and poor who went to pick up sticks in the copses were hard put to it to dry them for burning, and, if they found their fires out when they returned, went to bed to get themselves warm.

On winter afternoons school was dismissed at three to allow those children who lived at a distance to get home before dark, and, that day, the moment she was free, Charity had hurried to Waterside to see what the girls were doing about valentines.

Stella stood at the living kitchen table, cutting out a garment. The cold weather, as Mrs. Pocock said, had got on her chest again, and she had not gone that day to her dressmaking. She was wearing a pale blue knitted scarf twisted round her delicate throat, her feet were thrust into red felt slippers, and she carried about with her a strong smell of camphorated oil; but she was in one of her sociable moods, and when Mercy in a clean starched white apron and with her face shining from her afternoon toilet brought in cups of tea and a plate of hot cakes they all drew round the fire in a circle and discussed the one topic of the day.

That, of course, was valentines, for the next day was Valentine's Day and Old Postie would go his round no matter what the weather. Would he bring anything for those

there assembled? That was the first question. He might, or he might not, for the custom of sending valentines was in its decline. It was said to have gone out of fashion altogether in the upper circles of society and in towns, but in such places as Restharrow valentines were still sent and received. Lovers, as a matter of course, expected to receive from the one and only a valentine of the elaborate boxed kind, with the coloured vignette of a bouquet, or a pair of billing and cooing doves, or a human heart, stuck through with a skewer-like arrow, frilled round with white paper lace and inscribed with appropriate verses. Others than lovers  who cared to keep up the old custom sent to each other pretty trifles. The year before Charity had on St. Valentine's morning received by post a mysterious package which, when opened, was found to contain a pair of scarlet silk garters with gilt clasps. She had known very well that the handwriting of the address was Bess's, but she had at first pretended not to recognize it; that was part of the fun. Her father's valentine had not been so pleasant a surprise. It was one of the ugly kind, coarsely printed on a sheet of thin paper, and showing a carpenter at his bench, exclaiming, according to the balloon of speech which issued from his lips, 'I can't get it to join, nohow!' which was not to be wondered at when it was seen that the glue pot beside him was labelled 'Water'. He had not known who had sent it and he had not troubled to guess, for he had known that no reflection on his craftsmanship was intended. The sender had simply walked into the stationer's shop at Mixlow and purchased the first valentine which came to hand in the box marked 'Carpenters'. 'Well, it's Valentine's Day, and I s'pose they must have their joke,' he had said, and left it at that. Charity's mother had found her valentine on her dressing-table, an oval cardboard box of candied fruit with a picture on the lid, and she had called to Charity, dressing in the next room, 'You extravagant young puss! You know my weakness!' and Charity had run and kissed and thanked her for her lovely new nightgown.

But such gifts of love were not those under discussion in the Waterside kitchen. At that moment the girls were concerned with the unexpected, exciting kind, sent by some unknown admirer of the opposite sex. Though affecting to despise such communications as silly, each of the girls secretly hoped to receive one or more of such valentines the next morning. After all, thought Charity, they were a kind of tribute and showed that the receiver was not without attractions. Bess often got three or four, but Charity so far had received none. Neither, as far as was known, had Stella.

It was Stella who said, 'Let *us* send somebody a valentine!' 'But who can we send it to?' asked the others. 'Somebody who'll be shocked, or it'll be no fun,' she replied, and a search began for pens, ink and paper. 'I know what we'll do! We'll all send one!' said Stella when these were collected, and the others agreed that it would be fun, but to whom could they send them?

'I think I'll send mine to Mr. Onders,' said Stella meditatively, and the idea was greeted with laughter, for Mr. Onders was the new curate, a shy, pink-faced, very young man in spectacles, lately engaged to help Mr. Penpethy on account of his failing health. The laughter was rather shocked laughter. 'Oh, Stella! you can't!' remonstrated Bess. 'He's only been here a month and we hardly know him. Besides, he might tell Mr. Penpethy.'

'The more fool he if he does,' laughed Stella, 'and it doesn't matter if he does, for he won't know who sent it. How will this do!' and she recited the old Valentine rhyme:

> *Roses are red and violets blue,*
> *Carnations sweet, and so are you,*
> *And so's the one who sends you this,*
> *And when we meet we'll have a kiss.*

It was a stock valentine and familiar to all of them, but when applied to the shy, prim, almost coy-looking curate, it seemed outrageously funny, and, although she again protested, 'But you can't! You really can't!' Bess laughed as much as the other two.

'Oh, can't I? You'll see!' said Stella and forthwith sat down at the table and began writing. Bess went on sewing. As she said to Charity afterwards, she had had enough of anonymous communications to last her a lifetime. Mercy said she would like to send her valentine to Luke. She didn't suppose the poor fellow had had one in his life and it might give him pleasure. But what could she write? Could Charity think of anything? And Charity suggested, 'This is the morn':

> *This is the morn, the blessed morn,*
> *A little bird sat on a thorn,*
> *Choosing its mate for all the year,*
> *As I have chosen you, my dear.*

Although Mercy objected to the last line as not quite suitable, she was charmed with the rhyme as a whole, the only remaining difficulty was that she could not remember the words long enough to get them down on paper, so Charity wrote them in pencil for her to copy and she, too, sat down at the table.

Charity had decided to take her valentine to Miss Fowkes. A few snowdrops were out in a sheltered spot near the brook at her home and these she would take with her to school the next morning. 'My valentine, Miss Fowkes,' she would say; or perhaps she might say 'my *dear* Miss Fowkes' upon such an occasion; she would decide that later. If they were to be given as a valentine, she must write something to go with them. What should it be?

> *When these you see,*
> *Pray think of me.*

Appropriate, she thought, but scarcely sufficient, and she wondered if it would appear too familiar if she added as another line, 'Your Charity'. If she afterwards thought that might appear too forthcoming, she could alter it when she reached home.

Her short valentine was soon written, and she had nothing to do but to sit watching the others writing. Mercy, sitting square at the table, her tongue slightly protruding, was laboriously copying the sheet supplied by Charity. Stella, who was ordinarily what was then known as slap-dash penwoman, making large, queerly shaped letters which soon filled a page, seemed, that day, to be taking unusual pains with her handwriting. Her head bent over the sheet, her bright hair falling over her face, she was forming small, delicate strokes with her pen, slowly and carefully. Charity, who already knew what she had intended to write, thought it no harm to look over her shoulder.

'Oh Stella, how beautifully you can print!' she exclaimed.

The effect of that innocently intended remark was such that, for the rest of her life, Charity's memory retained the impression of Stella, her head thrown back, her usually pale cheeks crimson, and, in her eyes, an expression of mingled guilt, fear, and defiance. For an instant the eyes of the two met. Not a word was spoken by either, but something more subtle than words passed between them, and Charity realized in a flash why Stella's delicate script had seemed to her vaguely familiar. She had seen it before, several times, for it was the script of the anonymous letter-writer.

For an instant the two gazed into each other's faces; then Stella sprung up from her seat at the table, crumpled her sheet and flung it into the fire. 'Oh, I can't bother! Too much trouble!' she said. 'And I'd better go now. Mother will be in,' and, without any further leave-taking she went, banging the door behind her. Bess looked up from her needlework, 'There's manners for you!' she said. 'Anybody'd think she was doing it to please us, instead of its being her own idea,' but it was the abruptness of Stella's departure she referred to; as to the cause of that sudden exit she had no suspicion. Mercy had not looked up from her writing: 'c-h-o-s-e-n' she was murmuring aloud as she formed the letters. Neither of them had noticed anything unusual.

The revelation of Stella's treachery had so shocked and wounded Charity that it was as much as she could do to talk naturally to her cousins for the ten minutes before, pleading the darkness and cold, she left them earlier than she would otherwise have done. They suspected nothing; she felt sure of that, for they both of them pressed her to stay longer, saying that Luke would be going home soon and would be only too pleased to escort her; and, when they had found her determined to go, Bess, holding a candle in the doorway to light her across the dark courtyard, had called after her: 'Mind you bring all your valentines in a bushel basket to show us to-morrow.'

Alone on the footpath, Charity's mind cleared a little. She asked herself if it might not be possible that Stella's expression had been one of annoyance at her own bad manners in looking over her shoulder while she was writing. How she wished she could think so! But it was no good trying to deceive herself. She had once before seen that expression in Stella's eyes. A long time ago, when she had caught her cheating at their game in the orchard. Then, as to-day, there had been that angry, sly, cornered look, with something in it of pleading, and perhaps a little of shame. A horribly revealing look, made still more horrible by coming from one of Stella's loveliness.

As she neared her home and saw the cheerfully lighted window, she paused and stood leaning on the handrail of the plank bridge, trying to decide what she ought to do. She was as sure as if Stella had confessed in words that she had written the anonymous letters. But not a word had passed between them, and how could she describe a look? And she did not want to describe it. She did not want anyone but herself to know. She did not want Stella punished. And why should she mention to anyone her suspicion. After all, it was but a suspicion, or so it would appear to others, though she herself was only too sure.

The brook babbled coldly beneath the plank bridge, the trees sighed in the night wind, and Charity shivered. She looked up to the few stars showing through the scudding storm clouds: they could not help her; nothing could. Within that lighted window she knew there were those she could trust and whose advice she could rely upon; but, in case she was

mistaken, would it be fair to Stella to say anything? Full of conflicting thoughts and desires, and remembering her father's maxim, when in doubt or difficulty, sleep upon it, she went indoors and to bed as quickly as she might.

The next morning she carried the snowdrops to Miss Fowkes, but they were accompanied by no valentine. The one she had written had ended, as Stella's had, in the fire; and not until afterwards did she realize that the 'dear' she had meditated had been applied, not to Miss Fowkes, but to herself. 'How lovely!' Miss Fowkes had exclaimed as she took the snowdrops, 'Thank you! Thank you, Charity dear!'

That evening Charity and her mother were alone in the house. The fourteenth of each month was her father's club night, when he walked into Mixlow to pay his subscription to the Oddfellows Benefit Club, and usually, as he said, made a night of it, meaning that he might not be home before eleven o'clock, a late hour at Restharrow. When he came home he would be gay and animated, not from what he had drunk, for he seldom took more than one pint of ale, but because the talk at the club had been stimulating. Members of other, more conventional fraternities used at that time to say that the Oddfellows were no better than a lot of freemasons, and this idea was not discouraged by the Oddfellows themselves. Though their mysteries probably consisted of no more than a password to gain admittance to their clubroom, the addressing of each other as 'Brother' while there, and the possession of an elected member known as 'our almoner', whose office it was to visit the sick and dispense benefits, they liked to think of their own as a secret society. In politics, the majority of the brethren were Liberals with a Radical tinge; many of them were less strict churchgoers than their neighbours – one man belonging to the Mixlow branch professed to be an atheist – and, altogether, the Oddfellows were regarded as a daring lot; though, strange as it may have appeared to some people, their lives were generally exemplary.

On Mr. Finch's club night, his wife would often say after he had gone, 'Talk about women gossiping! Nobody knows what gossip is until they've heard a lot of men together. But there! who'd begrudge them their little treat, playing with their passwords and three knocks on the door, like a lot of children, bless them! I've laid out his best suit, got his back collar-stud through, put a clean handkerchief in his breast pocket and seen that he took his umbrella, and now I must look round for something for supper, for he'll come back as hungry as a hawk!' and she would put on something tasty to cook for supper, which she and Charity would, of course, share. That night, no rabbit or tripe or pig's fry being available, she had cut three thick slices of ham and put them in the oven, meaning, later, to top each slice with a poached duck's egg.

Charity had taken the opportunity to wash her hair, and her mother was towelling it briskly in front of the fire when she suddenly suspended her action and said, 'You don't think Mrs. Pocock had anything to do with those letters, do you?'

Charity started. She had the moment before been thinking: 'She's rubbing the outside of my head, but she little knows what's going on inside it'; but all she said was, 'No, I don't think so. Not Mrs. Pocock.' She may have laid unconscious stress on the 'Mrs.', for her mother exclaimed instantly, 'You don't think it was Stella?' and, gradually, led on by one question after another, Charity told her all she surmised. And what a relief it was to unburden her mind to the one of all the world whose judgement she knew she could trust.

Her mother did not appear as astonished as she had expected. She had had, or now imagined that she had had, glimmerings of the truth, and really

the wonder was that general suspicion had never for a moment fallen upon one who went daily to Mixlow, where the letters were posted. 'We've all been as blind as bats!' declared Mrs. Finch. 'We'd ought to have known that anybody can look like an angel and yet have a heart as black as my hat!'

After they had talked the matter over, both deeply shocked and Charity still grieved, though no longer without some enjoyment of the situation, the two of them knowing what no one else in the village knew, and discussing it at night in their quiet cottage before a roaring fire and with an appetizing smell of frizzled ham coming from the oven, Charity said: 'And now, Mother, what ought I to do?'

'Do?' said her mother. 'Do nothing! What can you do? You can't tell them at the farm. 'Twould make things very awkward, them having to live together. And you can't go crying it from the housetops without them knowing. Besides, there's been bad feeling enough about it in the place already, and it just won't do to start it all off again. You do nothing and say nothing; we won't let it go beyond these four walls for the present. When you're with Stella, you be a bit cold to her, but not so as anybody else notices it. She knows that you know and she'll see by your manner you haven't forgotten, and that'll give her something to think about for the time being. Then leave her to me. I'll deal with her!' and with such a sense of relief as she had never before experienced, Charity promised to follow her mother's advice. When the time came for their share of the ham and eggs to be brought out of the oven, she was surprised to find herself not only hungry, but also moderately cheerful.

Mrs. Finch's opportunity to deal with Stella did not occur immediately. After St. Valentine's Day Stella became seriously unwell and was at home for weeks. Her state so alarmed her mother that she procured the loan of a little governess car belonging to the nursery party at one of the houses where she worked to take her to consult the doctor at Mixlow. After examining Stella, Dr. Fisher said he could find nothing definitely wrong with her health. As her mother already knew, she had a chest which needed care, but that she would probably outgrow. 'Let her have good food and plenty of milk and eggs and get her out in the fresh air whenever the sun shines, and the roses will soon be blooming here again,' and he playfully pinched Stella's cheek and sent her out to keep watch over the pony he saw browsing on his new quickset hedge.

'Um-er-er. She's got nothing on her mind, I suppose?' he asked after Stella had gone, and when Mrs. Pocock had assured him that the child had not a care in the world, he rose from his chair and said in his blunt, old-fashioned way, 'That may be at the root of the trouble. Too much time in which to imagine troubles which do not exist. If you take my advice, you will get her married as soon as possible. A husband and half a dozen thumping great babies are a grand cure in such cases. Eh, Mrs. Pocock?' And he dispensed with his own hands a tonic for the one he spoke of as our interesting invalid, and refused to accept any fee, for was not Mrs. Pocock a widow, and an uncommonly nice-spoken little widow, too, and Stella a young and pretty orphan to boot? To advise them, he said, was a privilege.

When the warmer days came, Stella was better and able to return to her dressmaking, and an evening came when, returning from her work at Mixlow, she met Mrs. Finch in the street. Hearing that, though she was really quite well now, Stella's cough still troubled her at night, Mrs. Finch offered to give her a bottle of her own homemade raspberry vinegar, if she would step indoors. When her mother and Stella came into the parlour, Charity was sitting at the table, doing her home lessons. A moment before she had buried her face in the bowl of wallflowers which stood before her and thought as she drank in the scent how delightful it was to know that the winter with all its worries and excitements was over. When she saw them come in her heart sank, for she knew by her mother's resolute expression that the time had come for Stella to be dealt with, and there was nothing she so much disliked as a scene. She need not have been afraid. Her mother, too, disliked what she called an upset, and her voice and manner were kindly matter of fact when she said, 'And here's Charity, busy with her books as usual,' and invited Stella to be seated. Then she crossed the room to the corner cupboard and reached down from a shelf a half-pint bottle of the raspberry vinegar. 'Slip this in your satchel,' she said. 'You'll find a sip or two comforting when your cough bothers you, and you needn't be afraid to take it. Dr. Fisher won't mind. I send him a pint bottle for his own use every year; though, would you believe it, he has it on his suet puddings. Says it won't keep till he gets his winter touches of bronchitis.'

Stella thanked her prettily and slipped the bottle into the satchel in which she took her dinner to Mixlow, keeping her eyes all the time on Mrs. Finch's face, as Charity thought, apprehensively. Mrs. Finch continued to face her. 'Stella,' she said, 'I hear you can print very nicely.'

Stella laughed a nervous little laugh. 'What if I can?' she said. 'As far as I know, printing's no crime.'

'That all depends on what's printed. I've heard of folks who've found themselves in the lock-up through printing too well. And you don't want to go to gaol, do you, Stella? And you don't want to be disgraced and have the finger of scorn pointed at you at home here in Restharrow? So take my advice – and I mean this seriously – don't ever do any printing any more.'

Stella's head drooped like the head of a lovely flower on its stem. ''Twas only done for a joke,' she murmured almost inaudibly. Which feeble excuse so vexed Mrs. Finch that she exclaimed sharply, 'Joke, forsooth! Our ideas of a joke differ! Think of all the trouble you've made. You did ought by rights to be put where you'd learn better judgement; and if ever you get up to any such tricks again, you will. That I promise you! Howsoever, you're young and not well, and this time I'll spare you if, here and now, you'll give me your solemn word never, in all your life, to play such a prank again. Now

promise!' And Stella, her expression still more aggrieved than ashamed, said, 'I promise.'

Charity felt Stella's humiliation keenly and wished more than once during the interview that she had kept her discovery entirely to herself. When she went out to see her off at the gate she picked for her a large bunch of purple and white lilac, and, as she held the cool, fragrant flowers against Stella's face for her to smell, she could not help saying: 'Don't be angry, Stella. Nobody knows you sent the letters but Mother and me, and we shall never, never tell anybody.' Then Stella looked back at her more kindly than she had done for years and there were tears in her eyes when she said, 'I was sorry myself about poor old Mrs. Burdett, though it wasn't my fault, really. I didn't mean to hurt anybody.'

'Stupid creature!' exclaimed Mrs. Finch when, hoping to mollify her, Charity repeated those parting words. 'I s'pose she hasn't the sense to know there are other ways of hurting than the breaking of bones! Such ones as her only learn by suffering themselves. But we've done what we can and there we must leave it. Go back to your sums, child, if your brains aren't too scattered, and I'll see about supper.'

The summer following the events narrated was one of the most glorious within their living memory. For weeks at a time the weather was flawless, with cloudless skies and brilliant sunshine by day, followed by gentle, dew-dropping nights. What rain fell, fell at appropriate times, by night, and between haytime and harvest. Even the farmer was heard to say, not too grudgingly, 'Wonderful weather, for sure!' At Waterside there were picnic meals in the hayfields and orchard; and outings to Banbury and to neighbouring villages; to feasts and clubs, and to dance on the green in the lightest of muslin dresses. For the young in such weather it was joy enough to be alive. All that summer Bess was eagerly courted by young Ted Furlonger, the son of the blacksmith in the neighbouring village of Embley. No matter where she went, to feast or club, Ted followed her, and, at other times, he was often at the farm, ostensibly to see Reuben on his father's business, though most of his time there was spent in following Bess about the garden and orchard, or sitting at gaze in the kitchen while she did her needlework. The blacksmith's trade was then at its most flourishing. Horses were still in use for all agricultural purposes, making much shoeing, and to this had been added of late years the upkeep of the new agricultural machinery. The Furlongers had one of those fine old family businesses which had descended from father to son for generations, and, according to country standards of that day, they were exceedingly well to do, and Ted was no ignorant country youth, such as poor old Luke;

he had been educated at the local grammar school, and was himself a fine, well-set-up young fellow with modern ideas. But, except to keep him dangling after her as a handy partner for dances, Bess would have none of him, and she told him plainly, more than once, she had no intention of marrying. Even Reuben, for all his tolerance, seemed a little grieved at this; it would have been an ideal match from his point of view. Bess so near home, just that pleasant walk through fields; he could have seen her almost daily; and to know her well provided for would have been a comfort. However, as he told Mrs. Finch, it was Bess's business; he should say nothing to persuade her; the best marriage in the world was a bad one if either of the couple had not got just the man or the woman they wanted, and that only they could decide. Mrs. Finch was furious. Throwing away her chances, she called Bess's behaviour. 'You mark my words,' she said to her husband, 'that girl'll go round and round the wood and bring out a crooked stick in the end!' In the autumn Roger Maitland returned to his home and on Sunday mornings was seen by all coming into church by the chancel door with the brim of his glossy top hat pressed to his breast. When they met, as they were bound to do, in the village, he bowed politely to Bess, Bess acknowledged his salutation becomingly, and that was all that passed between them. None of the neighbours troubled to watch their movements; there were newer and more rewarding subjects for gossip afoot, and their brief association was no more remembered than last year's flowers.

When there was talk of Roger's engagement, Bess merely said, 'Let's hope they'll be happy!' as she might have said of any other newly engaged couple. As far as outsiders could judge, that couple were quite happy.

Life at the Manor House was certainly more comfortable. The whole house was renovated and re-furnished, new servants were engaged and a carriage and horses were purchased. On the estate a small but model home farm was established; broken-down fences were mended, and old gates, dragging on the hinges, were replaced by new ones.

'Lord!' said an old labourer on the estate, 'just see what a bit o' money can do! They tells us in church that 'tis the root of all evil, but, seems to me, that from it all blessin's do flow!'

The only imaginable drawback to the bride's felicity may at first have been a resident mother-in-law. It was said in the village that the two ladies did not hit it off, and perhaps they did not, for in less than a year

Mrs. Maitland senior left the Manor House for an establishment of her own at Harrogate. 'Far enough off! They don't mean to have any runnin' in and out of one another's houses!' was the village comment. '*And* I don't blame our new young lady,' said those who were already experiencing the benefits of the new régime in the shape of school treats and Christmas trees, half-tons of coal and flannel waistcoats and petticoats.

One activity of the young bride which was not dependent upon her fortune should be recorded. After Mr. Penpethy had called upon her, as in duty bound, she sought him out in his own dreary abode and so charmed him by her gentle manner and her intelligent interest in his own pursuits that she became a welcome visitor at the house where no woman had entered for years. Gradually, she introduced at the Vicarage many improvements which added to the comfort of the Vicar, and eventually per-

suaded him to allow her to find for him a good working housekeeper, the kind of woman who would cook and care for him without making any demands on his time or attention.

Clerk Savings, thus deposed, hated the housekeeper and never forgave the squire's lady. 'That 'ooman's fair starvin' the master,' he told people. 'In my time we got a good leg o' mutton or a round o' beef and I roast 'en on Saturday to last th' week, cut an' come again, and there wer' allus a bit o' good wholesome victuals in the place, and ready whenever he might fancy a cut. But what do I see now when I goes into the kitchen wi' my vegetables? That graven image of a housekeeper stirrin' little messes in saucepans, or a beatin' up what she calls a homelit, or doin' summat to a bundle o' sparrer grass that 'tother beauty 'ave sent in from her garden, and I've seen her takin' little tinny winny puddens out of th' oven, not big enough to feed a fly. And th' Reverend's vest and pants airin' on a 'oss round the fire, and her a single 'ooman; but she's as bold as brass, that one! I did make it my business to go to Madge Perks, as have allus washed for his Reverence, and I telled 'er "That one up there at th' Vicarage don't trust 'ee; she's a airin' your washing," I says. But, Lord! what wer' th' good? Women all hold together like a hank o' wool, and Madge laughed and said that another turn by th' fire 'udn't do the things no harm; 'twas rather damp weather. And her badgers th' poor ole gent fair out of his life. When he's a mind to go out, it's "Sir, won't you change yer shoes? I've cleaned 'em an' put 'em to warm by yer study fire," an' "Sir, won't yer do this, or won't yer do that?" I've seen wi' me own eyes that 'ooman run arter the man wi' a clothes brush! 'Twasn't so in my time. No! No! Things be changed up there. 'Tis shockin'! 'Tis shockin'! You mark my words, our Reverend won't be long for this world!'

As Clerk Savings had foretold, Mr. Penpethy was not much longer for our world, but it is good to know that his last few years here were spent in comparative comfort and brightened by friendship.

IX

THE SWEETBRIAR HEDGE

AT the very best time of the year, when the meadows were yellow with buttercups and the hedges were white with may and the cuckoo was calling from five in the morning till twilight, it became known that the Pococks were to have a young man visitor. Not a relative, either, though from words that Mrs. Pocock let fall it seemed probable that he would soon become one. Arnold Milton was the brother of a lady's maid employed at one of the houses where Mrs. Pocock went sewing. Their parents were dead and they had no settled home or near relatives at whose house they could meet for their holidays, and when Miss Milton had said in Mrs. Pocock's hearing that her brother would like to spend a few weeks in her neighbourhood if she could find him accommodation, Mrs. Pocock had, as she expressed it, taken pity on them and invited him to stay at her own home.

But, far from being an object for pity, the young man appeared to be in what most people would have considered an enviable position. He was a schoolmaster, who, after some years as assistant, had recently been appointed to a school of his own in a large village near Northampton. As was then usual, a partly furnished house was provided by the school managers for the headmaster. A very nice house, his sister had said, with three bedrooms and water laid on to the kitchen sink, and the village where the school was situated was large and lively, with something going on all the time. The retiring headmaster had been much respected; he and his wife had often been invited to tea or supper at the Vicarage, no stand-offishness; people were more friendly in those parts. The school managers had probably taken for granted that, at twenty-eight, Arnold was married. But he was not, he had been too taken up with his work and studies to think about marrying, and the running of a house of his own was going to be a bit of a puzzle. She herself would have loved to have gone and kept house for him, but she could not possibly leave her ladyship now she was ailing; perhaps better, too, to stick to her independence; he might marry later, you never knew. She had advised him to engage a housekeeper, some elderly person, of course, whose presence could give rise to no scandal. But all that could be arranged; the great thing was that he had actually got a school of his own. His house would be her own home in future; she should spend all her holidays there. Was it not splendid?

The housekeeper, whom Miss Milton was addressing, laughed the sardonic laugh of middle-aged experience and said, 'Splendid as long as its lasts! Marriage alters all things! A wife seems at present his most pressing need, and a young man with a good house and salary won't have to look far for one.'

That speech of the housekeeper's may have given Mrs. Pocock, down on her knees, mending the carpet in a corner of the room, the idea of securing for herself so desirable a guest, for she lost no time in getting Miss Milton alone with herself and proposing that her brother should spend his holiday at Waterside. There were only herself and her little girl in their part of the house, so he would have the rest and quiet he needed, and she'd see that he was well looked after, even if she had to sacrifice a day's work here and there. Not as a paying guest, as Miss Milton suggested. Oh no! she could not agree to that when Miss Milton had been such a kind friend to her in the past; her brother must come as one of the family. 'You trust him to me, Miss Milton,' she said, 'and I'll see that he has a holiday that he'll long remember,' and Miss Milton, relieved to have the matter so easily settled, for accommodation was scarce in the neighbourhood, unconsciously used one of Mrs. Pocock's favourite expressions, 'You shan't be the loser,' she said, and pressed into her hand a sovereign towards getting in provisions.

To those who knew Mrs. Pocock, it seemed likely that, far from being a loser, she would gain a successful and, according to country standards, a well-to-do husband for her daughter. 'Miss Milton says her brother's not much of a one for girls, but you wait till he sees our Stella!' she said in an unguarded moment to Bess. Stella appeared to be, and probably was, unconscious of her mother's design, though it was noticeable that her health improved and that she took even more pains than ordinarily with the new spring outfit she was making. 'I don't think I've ever seen Stella look so well,' said Charity to Bess a few days before Arnold Milton's arrival at Waterside. 'Getting ready to be fallen in love with,' responded Bess with her nose in the air.

Charity and her cousins could not help being interested in the Pocock's prospective visitor. They wondered what he would be like and if they would see much of him. Something, of course, they were bound to see, as he would be staying in the same house as themselves; but would he be permitted to talk to them, or to go out in the stables

and about the farm with Reuben, as other summer visitors had done, or would the Pococks monopolize him as Stella's exclusive property? They pictured him as a lean, pale, spectacled young man, worn out with much study, and it amused them to think of him, innocent and unsuspecting as a lamb, walking straight into the trap of matrimony. But although they laughed at Mrs. Pocock's transparent wiles, and pitied, or pretended to pity, her predestined victim, they were all of them so touched with the freemasonry of sex that they felt themselves in honour bound to further in any way they might the scheme of the matchmaker.

For some days after Arnold's arrival at the farm, Bess and Mercy kept strictly to their own part of the house and only caught brief glimpses of him as he passed their windows, though in those brief glimpses they saw sufficient to know that he was not in the least like they had imagined. Arnold Milton was what was then called a presentable young fellow. He was a good height and muscular and healthy-looking; he wore good clothes, parted his hair in the middle, and the ends of his straw-coloured moustache were carefully waxed. Bess pronounced him at first sight civilized-looking. Charity, whose favourite type he was not, thought he had rather a towny appearance; and Mercy, as usual, expressed no opinion, but said that she hoped the Pococks were giving him good food. That hope may have been prompted by the knowledge that cooking was not Stella's strong point, for it had turned out that, instead of sacrificing here and there a day's pay for her own work, as she had at first suggested, Mrs. Pocock had arranged that Stella, who was an unpaid apprentice, should take her summer holidays and keep house while her mother was otherwise engaged. She would be company for Mr. Milton, said her mother, young company, and that was what he needed after his long years of study. Stella, who hated housework, looked discontented. 'I don't think I care for men much. At any rate, not schoolmasters,' she said to Bess one day. That, and the fact that no sound of the youthful mirth which Mrs. Pocock had prescribed for Arnold ever reached ears which, if not exactly listening, were not closed, looked as if matters were not progressing according to plan.

Then, one afternoon, Reuben, who had had some conversation with the young man and found him interested in old country relics, brought him indoors to see his collection of horse brasses. The best of his collection hung in a glass case on the wall of the parlour, and as they passed through the living kitchen where Bess was polishing the candlesticks, Reuben introduced the two to each other in what he called proper form – 'Mr. Milton, meet my daughter' – and they exchanged a few remarks on the weather. Very little was said, but, as Bess said long afterwards, she took to the man at once, and when they passed through the kitchen again on their way out and Reuben said, 'I've got a lot more brasses lying loose about the house, but I couldn't put my hand on 'em at the moment. You must come in and have a cup of tea with us one of these days. Mustn't he, Bess?' Bess, who usually objected to visitors at short notice because, she said, it didn't give you time to do full justice, said impulsively, 'What about to-morrow? Ask Stella to bring you.'

The next morning Charity received a little note, folded in the cocked-hat shape and addressed to her at the school, charging her, without fail, to be at Waterside by four o'clock at the latest, as Stella was bringing her young man to tea. 'He doesn't seem at all a bad sort and I think we shall like him,' Bess had added; then, as a postscript, she had written beneath, 'Be sure and burn this', which instruction Charity faithfully carried out, though she saw no reason whatever for doing so and had no excuse to offer when, seeing her thrust it between the bars at her home, her mother reproved her for wasting good paper which would have made a couple of spills for candle-lighting.

They had a pleasant time at Waterside that afternoon. Bess was especially lively and entertaining and, as always when animated, she was looking her best. After Reuben had gone back to his work, she and Arnold did most of the talking, discussing all manner of subjects, some of which had certainly never been discussed in that kitchen before. Arnold, like Bess, it appeared, was a bit of a rebel against convention, and, far from being shocked when Bess expressed some of her daring opinions, he encouraged and led her on. His last school had been in the poor quarter of a town, and it had aroused his indignation that some of the less fortunate children should come to school cold, hungry, and barefooted. 'And you should see their homes,' he said; 'like pigsties, no warmth, no comfort, no cleanliness! They fall asleep in class for want of proper rest in proper beds,' and Bess, always quickly aroused to indignation, called such a state of affairs a sin and a shame and a disgrace to the nation.

'There are some very poor cottages in Restharrow,' put in Charity mildly. 'But they're mostly kept clean and the children don't have to go to school barefoot,' snapped Bess, and Charity did not like to point out before a stranger that although the Restharrow children had shoes and stockings, such as they were, many came to school wet-footed. Perhaps it was as well that she did not, for, according to the views of their new acquaintance, the making the best of things and the seeming content of country people was largely to blame for bad cottages and low wages. He seemed positively to hate the creep-er-covered walls and diamond-paned windows of some of the older cottages; such houses, he said, were damp and dark within and a trap for disease germs. Charity ventured to say that although no doubt some old cottages were unhealthy, others had large, light rooms and were snug, for which speech she was rewarded by Bess with a look which bade her beware of airing her ignorance. Stella, who had been quite talkative at the tea-table, began to look bored and rose readily when Charity proposed a turn in the walled garden. 'Did you ever hear such talk?' she said as they stood looking up at the sky through the blossoming apple tree. 'Why should they go exciting themselves about what's no business of theirs?' Charity was not so sure it was none of their business. She thought something ought to be done to put an end to the state of affairs described by Arnold, though she agreed that the discussing of it was dampening at a friendly tea party. 'Let's go in and get them to play snakes and ladders,' she proposed.

Bess and Arnold were still seated at table, but the subject of conversation had

changed. Bess was reading the visitor's teacup, swirling the dregs around, turning it upside down to drain, then gazing at the tea-leaf formations with the intent, witchlike expression assumed on such occasions. 'I see wedding bells in your cup,' she said, 'and they are near the rim. That means a speedy wedding.' 'But not mine! Not mine!' protested Arnold, 'I mean to live and die a bachelor.' The seer's lips trembled with amusement and Charity smiled openly. 'Man proposes—' said Bess. 'Have I not told you that that is just what I do *not* intend to do!' retorted Arnold. His protest must have shaken Bess's conviction, for, the next time Charity spoke of Arnold as Stella's young man, she said quite snappishly, 'Don't make too sure! He may have more sense than we credited!'

That conversation between the two was the first of many. It seemed to Charity that whenever she went to Waterside she found Bess and Arnold discussing some wrong which they declared ought to be righted. Workhouses, prisons, poverty, wealth, workmen's long hours, and women's rights, all had their turn. Bess nodded agreement to all Arnold said, and Arnold, when Bess was speaking, listened as to an oracle. No doubt Arnold was better informed on all these subjects than Bess, though even he could have had little first-hand knowledge of some of them, and many of the solutions put forward struck Charity as far-fetched, for they were inclined to go to extremes which could never have been workable. Still, their warm championship of much-needed reforms did their hearts credit. 'What you two want is a little heaven on earth,' said Reuben one day, but neither retorted, 'And we mean to have it,' as young people in such circumstances would do to-day, for ordinary people had not as yet realized their power, or their responsibility.

But the two now close friends were not always discussing social wrongs; between-whiles they took their pleasure as became their ages. Although they did not go out together for formal walks, they might often be seen out in the orchard or down by the brook, and could be heard laughing and talking as gaily together as though all was right with the world.

On Whit-Monday Charity and her cousins, with Stella and Arnold and Arnold's sister, were to go to Embley Feast, and Charity had risen early to bath and dress before breakfast. It was a perfect morning with bright sunshine and little warm, wandering winds which stirred the tulips in the garden beneath her window and brought to her as she stood pulling on her best grey dress the delicious scent of early blooming stocks and gilly-flowers. She was to join the rest of the party at Waterside, for they had arranged to go to the neighbouring village through the fields, which would not only shorten the way by a mile, but would also, as Bess had said, be a treat, with the grass fresh and green and the may blossom out. And Arnold's sister Rose would be with them; she had one whole day off a month, and this was the day. Charity had already met her several times at Waterside and found her interesting – to her mind, far more interesting than Arnold – and this would be an opportunity to get to know her better. It would be quite a large party. They could not walk in a drove. Bess and Mercy would go on in front, she supposed, then Rose and herself, followed, perhaps at a little distance by Arnold and Stella. So she arranged it in her own mind while she stood before her looking-glass adjusting the white collar and the little black bow at her throat and drawing the two thick plaits of hair over her shoulders. The face which looked back at her from the glass was, in its quiet way, not unattractive, with its broad white forehead, serious-looking grey eyes, and cheeks faintly tinged with pink. A thoughtful face, people said when describing it, or a sensitive face. But Charity at sixteen took no account of her own expression; she had long before decided that she had no personal attractions, and it was her feeling of freshness after her bath and her clean clothes that she rejoiced in at that moment; that, and the prospect of the outing with merry companions.

It was half-past nine when Charity reached Waterside and walked into the living kitchen without having seen anyone. They were to start at ten, and Rose had evidently not yet arrived, but she could hear Mercy's firm footfall upstairs and knew she was making her father's bed. Bess might be with her, or dressing. The housework downstairs was finished and everything was in order for leaving for the day. She walked up and down the kitchen for a few minutes, too unsettled in mind to sit down and read; then thought she would go upstairs and see what Bess was doing.

As she came out of the kitchen into the hall she noticed that the glass-panelled door which led to the walled garden was open. Never had the little enclosed plot looked more lovely. In the morning light and morning freshness, against the young, tender green of leaf and blade, the brighter tints of the old-fashioned flowers, peony, tulip, and crown imperial, stood out with almost startling clearness. In their dewy perfection they seemed, not flowers that had grown, but flowers newly created. Charity stepped into the doorway to breathe the sweet air, and saw, quite close to her, though invisible from within, Bess standing with Arnold.

They stood with a low sweetbriar hedge between them. Bess had evidently come out to shake the breakfast crumbs for the birds, for she had a folded tablecloth over one arm; in the other hand she held a few bruised sweetbriar leaves and was inhaling the scent; but absent-mindedly, for her whole attention seemed fixed on the face but a yard or so from her own. Arnold must have been to meet the postman, for he held a wrappered newspaper in his hand. They had probably been chatting over the hedge, but, at the moment, neither was speaking, they were gazing into each other's eyes.

Theirs was a tender, absorbed, yet at the same time triumphant look, so fixed and deep-drinking that it seemed some urgent message was passing between them. Charity had never before seen that expression in human eyes, but she recognized it instinctively: the two were in love with each other. They had evidently not heard her light footstep, and, blushing with shame for her involuntary intrusion, she withdrew.

A few minutes later Bess came in from the garden and whisked Charity upstairs to help her dress for their outing. 'What a day! What a heavenly day!' she exclaimed again and again. 'I don't think I've ever known such weather in May. The flowers in the walled garden are coming out lovely and the sweetbriar hedge is in leaf, I've just been out looking at everything, and it's made me feel so happy! As the day is so warm I think I might wear my mauve muslin. I could wear my little black jacket over it and take it off for the dancing. You're ready and Mercy's ready and Stella's been togged up for hours. Rose'll be here directly. I must hurry! I must hurry! I must hurry!' but, for all that, she did not appear to hurry herself in making an even more than usually fastidious toilet. Never were plaits more carefully woven, curls more exactly placed, or bows more tastefully tied and pulled out than by Bess on that Whitsuntide morning.

But at last they were off, over the fields and the stiles and the brooks to Embley. They set out in much the same order as Charity had imagined, but soon Arnold's group merged in Bess's and he walked beside her the rest of the way. They were, for them, unusually silent. That day no abstract ideas were discussed and no plans were made for world reformation; it appeared to suffice them to walk side by side, their elbows touching, and to glance shyly now and then at each other's faces.

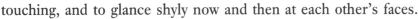

Charity walked staidly with Rose behind the main group, and presently Stella joined them; then, finding their conversation no more exciting than that of her former companions, she hovered between the two groups, now with one, now with the other. Once she stopped to break from the hedge a branch of blossoming may, then carried it with her, held aloft, like a may garland. In her white frock and blue sash, with the blossoming bough, she might have stepped straight out of a picture by Botticelli, and that day she did not disgrace her angelic appearance. When she joined in the conversation her remarks were agreeable and her tone was pleasant, but, for the greater part of the way she walked a few paces apart, flourishing her may bough and humming softly one of the old may songs. If she knew what was going on between Bess and Arnold, the knowledge left her unruffled. After all, she had never been what the country folks called a dog in the manger. If she wanted a thing, it was war with the knife for it; if not, it could go to whomsoever it might; she was indifferent. And that morning her mind may have been occupied with her own projects; for, as they were crossing the last bridge over the stream, she said to Charity, 'Do you think Bess and Arnold would mind if I go with Jane Elliott when we get to Embley? She has asked me to meet her and to go round the shows together, and her two brothers are coming in time for the dancing,' and Arnold, who had heard what she said, called, rather too heartily, 'Not in the least!' 'And you won't mention at home that I was not with you all the time? And if I'm not home before you, you might say that I had stopped to talk to somebody. I dare say one of the Elliott boys'll see me home, so you needn't trouble to wait about for me.' At that moment Jane Elliott approached, strolling along the footpath to meet her friend, and, nobody having raised the slightest objection, the two went off together.

Mercy had all along intended to go straight to the house of the Furlongers, who had asked the whole party to dinner, and on their arrival at Embley she went at once to the Forge. Rose and Charity were getting on so well together that they decided on partnership for the day. So, as soon as the booths and stalls came in sight, they all went their different ways, leaving Arnold and Bess to take their pleasure alone together, to Bess's professed amazement, though almost certainly not to her dissatisfaction.

Neither Rose nor Charity cared for noisy crowds, and when they found that the Vicarage garden was for that one day thrown open to the public they paid their sixpence for the local hospital and passed through wrought-iron gates into an oasis of peaceful beauty. The garden with its lawns, shrubberies and flower borders, all at their freshest and fairest, appeared to have less attraction for the holiday crowd than the fun of the fair. A few couples sauntered on the pathways, pausing to admire the Vicar's peonies, for which the garden was famous; others had established themselves on garden seats and were lunching out of paper bags, but, altogether, these numbered too few to disturb the serenity of the extensive grounds. Rose and Charity seated themselves in a leafy recess in a small sunk garden where irises bloomed around a basin of goldfish. Over their heads drooped the gold-ladened boughs of a laburnum and other laburnums closed the little garden around. 'If we've come here to 'joy ourselves, why not stay here and 'joy ourselves?' asked Charity, quoting the old couple in the Flower Show tea tent, and Rose declared she could stay there for ever. They did stay for at least an hour; until, in fact, the Vicar himself appeared and offered to show them some of his treasures, which was in itself a most enjoyable experience, though Charity's chief enjoyment that day was getting to know Rose better.

Rose Milton was five years older than her brother. She was a small, pale, rather serious-looking young woman, always tastefully dressed and self-possessed. At first Charity had thought her reserved, but on closer acquaintance she found her ready enough to talk to an interested listener. And she talked entertainingly, for she had a sense of humour and she had travelled abroad a good deal with a former employer, spending one winter in Rome and another in Paris, besides making visits of shorter duration to other famous places. When travelling with her mistress, Rose had made good use of her opportunities, visiting in her off-duty time famous buildings and picture galleries and observing the customs of the

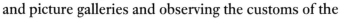

countries. For Rose was an intelligent girl; she had read a good deal, as she had had many opportunities of doing in the long evenings when waiting up for her ladies to return from their balls and parties. She had often had the run of the family library, a privilege, she told Charity, that was readily conceded to a lady's own maid who was fond of reading. Altogether, Rose Milton was as unlike as possible to the stage or the novelist's conception of a lady's maid, as indeed were the generality of lady's maids of that date, when no fastidious woman of fashion would have tolerated near her person the noisy, slap-dash Abigail of fiction.

For the position some education was needed, and, before entering her first situation the would-be maid had to serve a five-year apprenticeship to dressmaking, followed by a course in hairdressing at some establishment of repute. Ladies of that day relied in the ordinary way on their own maids for the care and dressing of their long hair. Only on special occasions, such as a Court function, an important ball, or a fashionable wedding, was it thought necessary to call in outside professional aid. Then the hairdresser, always a man and more often than not a foreigner, came to the house carrying a mysterious-looking black bag, and was conducted upstairs to the lady's bed- or dressing-room, where he practised his art with the lady's maid in close attendance to hand him his implements and to gather as much of his method as possible for her own future use. In times of any but serious illness, the maid turned sick nurse, and at all times her relation to her mistress was a close personal relation. She had to be one who could be thoroughly trusted, and such a one was Rose.

Rose had been fortunate in those she had served; all appeared to have been worthy of her devotion. After she had been telling Charity about her winter in Rome with all its wonders of fountains and flowers and pictures and statues, Charity exclaimed, 'How lucky you were! How lucky!' Rose gazed up at the golden chains of the laburnums for a moment in silence, and then said, 'Well, yes, in a way; but I would not go through that time again for anything. It was the saddest time in my life, for it was there that my darling Miss Sybil's cough that had long been troublesome got worse, and my heart was torn by anxiety. When at last she consented to see the English doctor, he sent her straight back to London to a specialist, and, after that, it was but a question of time. Her father – she had no mother – tried everything money could buy, and the next winter came with us himself to the Riviera; but it was no good; nothing could save her; she died. . . . But this is fine talk for a Bank Holiday outing! I don't know what made me begin it, unless perhaps Stella reminded me of Miss Sybil; she has the same lovely fairness, with more colour though; Miss Sybil had a lovely colour, and her expression just like a light shining through! But this is sad talk for this lovely day. Let us go and see what the others are doing.' And they were about to go when the Vicar appeared and took such pleasure in showing his flowers, as they did in viewing them, that they were still gazing and admiring when the church clock struck twelve.

When they reached the forge house, they found old Mr. Furlonger stretched out on two chairs, resting. As a senior member of the Club and one of its founders, he had with a few other elders headed the procession to and from the church service which preceded the festivities, and he still wore, pinned to his coat, a huge rosette of the Club colours, Oxford blue and yellow. He was a tall, stout old man, swarthy as a gipsy, who had had immense physical strength in his day. Now his place at the anvil had been taken by his son, and he was doing his best to resign himself to what he described as pottering around – a situation which suited ill a man who had been for the best part of his life at the head of a thriving business and had prided himself on his feats of strength; but, as he said, it had to be borne, and bear it he did, though since his retirement he was apt to be silent and grumpy. However, that day he was in better spirits, and welcomed Charity and her friend with old-fashioned compliments. An appetizing smell of cooking pervaded the house, and Charity was not surprised to hear that Mercy was out in the kitchen, helping Mrs. Furlonger and the maid with the dishing-up of the dinner. Soon Mercy came into the room with a tablecloth and began laying out the best silver, heavy solid ware which tired the hands when in use. Everything there was on the same scale: furniture, clock, and the few ornaments, though not in the taste of the day, were all good and solid. Almost every article had a history: this had belonged to Mr. Furlonger's parents, that to his grandparents, another had been in the house since no one knew when; perhaps it had been brought there when the house was first furnished by the Furlonger family towards the end of the eighteenth century. They were the possessions of a hardy and a hard-working race which had given its best to its craft and for which, in return, only the best had been good enough.

Soon Ted Furlonger came in. He was dressed in his best and wore a wide sash of the Club colours over his shoulder, but, judging by his expression, he was in anything but a holiday mood. When asked where he had been, he said glumly that, as a Club member, he had had to attend the church service, but that in his opinion it had been a waste of time, with the shop chock-a-block with jobs and both journeymen holiday-making. When Charity asked him if he had seen Bess, there was concentrated venom in his tone when he answered, 'Oh, aye,

I've *seen* her!' and she gathered that the sight of Bess with another than himself, and that other one he had supposed to be but a mere acquaintance of hers, accounted for his depression.

Bess and Arnold came in soon after Ted, Bess full of reproaches for those who, she said, had deserted her all the morning, but apparently not much cast down in spirits by their so-called desertion. Then huge dishes of roast fowls and ham and vegetables were brought in and they all sat down to a substantial meal, talking and laughing happily, with the exception of Ted, who declared that he did not feel hungry, but afterwards cleared an enormous plateful of food in the absent-minded manner of one who had more important matters on his mind. Before the meal was over, he asked to be excused, saying that there was work waiting that must be done, and somebody had to see to it. It didn't do for all to be idle! Which caused his father to say, after he had gone upstairs to change, 'Don't tell me any more that the age of miracles is over! Our young Ted's a good enough boy, and well on the way to making a fine smith, but never what you might call a glutton for hard work, especially at holiday time, and he's been talking for days about your coming and saying that he'd do this and that and the other. I can't think what ails the chap!' But his mother knew what ailed Ted. 'Leave the boy alone,' she said. 'He'll come round presently. Just another teeny-weeny shaving of ham, Mr. Milton? As I always say, a fowl's not worth eating without it; and, Bess, my dear, you're not getting on at all well. Let me give you another slice off the breast and a spoonful of stuffing? Yes, Mercy, thank you, you may fetch the rhubarb tart out of the oven, if you'll be so kind, and you'll fill a jug of cream on the slab in the larder. Perhaps you wouldn't mind taking the girl's dinner with you? I'd like her to have it good and hot, though she little deserves it after smashing one of my best wineglasses this morning. Now, come along, all of you! You're all pecking at your plates like sparrows, and you'll not get another meal till tea-time, so up with your plates!'

As his mother had foretold, Ted 'came round'. He squired Rose and Charity round the club amusements, though still with a joyless look in his eyes, especially when they happened to light upon Bess with Arnold. But he got over it all in time, and later transferred his affections to Charity, which caused her much trouble with her mother, who had difficulty in comprehending that a daughter of hers could be so blind to her own interests as to prefer teaching other people's children to having a husband and children of her own, 'and all of the best and money in the bank' to boot.

On the homeward journey over the misty meadows in the moonlight there were but two groups. Stella had her own escort, and Rose had been driven off by road to Marston Place in the conveyance sent for her, as arranged. As dusk was falling, Arnold insisted that Charity and Mercy should keep close behind him and Bess, 'for we don't want to lose the only two virtues we possess,' he declared, which mild joke caused much merriment. So, with Bess's arm tightly drawn through his own and with Mercy and Charity as rearguard, they passed beneath glimmering hawthorn hedges and over meadows, stiles and bridges in the peaceful twilight. Once, when they crossed a plank bridge, Arnold ex- claimed, 'Did you hear that frog jump?' and it was Bess 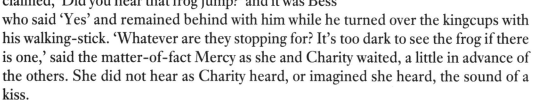 who said 'Yes' and remained behind with him while he turned over the kingcups with his walking-stick. 'Whatever are they stopping for? It's too dark to see the frog if there is one,' said the matter-of-fact Mercy as she and Charity waited, a little in advance of the others. She did not hear as Charity heard, or imagined she heard, the sound of a kiss.

Kiss or no kiss, there's no more hiding of love nor there's hiding of measles, as the saying went at Restharrow, and, before that week was out, Mrs. Sykes, ironing at the table beneath the window in Mrs. Finch's kitchen, said suddenly, 'I see Reuben's Bess's got a sweetheart at last.' She spoke with one eye on Mrs. Finch while taking up an iron from the fire and spitting upon it to try its heat, and either because she hated the dirty habit of spitting upon an iron or to discourage what she thought baseless gossip, Mrs. Finch frowned. 'That's the first I've heard of anything of the kind,' she said coldly.

The old woman, her withered-apple cheeks and small inquisitive eyes framed in a white cap-frill, pursed up her lips and nodded. 'Aye, she's a sly puss, that Bess!' she said, and thumped on a sheet with her iron. 'Well, seein's believin' and feelin's the naked truth, as they say, an' if you'd seed what I seed at the church stile last night you'd know as much as I do meself. Holdin' of hands wi' that young schoolmaster, an' him helpin' her over the stile as careful as countin' gold; and her holdin' her skirts close down to her ankles, as prim as me lady! Ho! Ho! I thinks to meself, you wasn't always so choice, me gal! I've seed 'ee lop over that stile with yer drawers showin' many a time. The case is altered! The case is altered! thinks I!' Before the old woman had finished *tee-heeing*, Mrs. Finch said in her grandest manner, 'Staying in the same house, as he is, I s'pose Mr. Milton feels bound to show my niece some civility.'

'Civility! Civility, forsooth!' tittered Mrs. Sykes, 'I med be a poor ig'orant ole washer'ooman as 'aven't seen much, but what I do know I do know, an' if them two wasn't lookin' babies into one another's eyes call me a fool and a-done w'it!' And, displeased with the reception of her toothsome morsel of gossip, she turned sulky and soon went home.

'What a curious expression, "looking babies into each other's eyes",' said Charity after Mrs. Sykes had departed. 'What did she mean by it? No scandal, I hope?' And her mother said rather abstractedly, 'Oh, no, no. She meant nothing scandalous. It's just an old country saying about any courtin' couple who seem more than ordinary wrapped up in each other. I once heard a clergyman who took an interest in such sayings tell somebody that it meant the little picture of yourself you can see when you look hard into anybody else's eyes; but, myself, I've always understood that it meant that when sweethearts look like that at one another there's bound to be babies sooner or later. After marriage, of course; I don't think it means anything vulgar.' 'I see,' said Charity. 'The look is the beginning of the story and the babies come in the last chapter,' and her mother agreed that things did usually happen like that. 'For, after all,' she sighed, 'in love or not in love, we're all of us human. But do you think there is anything in what she said about Bess?' Charity said she should not be surprised if there were something in it; she thought Bess and Mr. Milton liked each other; and her mother said, well, things will be as they will be, though she had always thought that in the end Bess would have taken young Furlonger. She didn't know what ailed young people in these days; no sooner full grown than they must be off to the ends of the earth. 'There's you with your training college, and God knows where afterwards, and our young Oliver in heathen lands, and now Bess! The others'll go too, and in fifty years' time, you mark my words, there won't be a Finch or a Truman left in Restharrow parish. Still, as I say, things will be as they will be, and there's no denying that Bess was never cut out for country life in the rough, and maybe she'd be happier as a schoolmaster's wife, if such is to be her lot in life,' and she soon talked herself into approval.

That evening, when Charity was unpicking the seams of a skirt her mother was going to wash and turn for her and thinking how dull was the job which had kept her indoors, Bess, all blown by the wind and with little sparkling raindrops on her hair and scarf, burst into the cottage, exclaiming, 'I can't stay a moment, Aunt Alice, but I feel I must tell you and Charity. Such news! You'd never guess it in a month of Sundays, and nobody else has got any idea! I'm engaged, engaged to Arnold! and Dad knows and he says that all he wants is for me to be happy. Kiss me! Kiss me!' and there were kisses and hugs all round. Then Mr. Finch, finding that Arnold had been left outside in the rain, had to fetch him in, and a bottle of home-made wine was opened and healths were drunk to the radiant pair.

'Whew! what a tornado! And what a surprise! I wonder you

weren't both of you flabbergasted. I had enough to do to keep my own head,' cried Mr. Finch afterwards, stretching himself out in mock prostration in his chair; and his wife rejoined with an air of superiority that she had seen it coming for some time, which meant for exactly two hours.

There was nothing to delay the wedding. A house stood waiting, a small, but sufficient income was assured, and Bess's modest outfit was soon prepared. It had already been partly provided by her own skill at needlework. Like other girls of her day, she had made and laid by underwear in half-dozens. This was done with no definite idea of marriage, but rather from a love of acquiring pretty things and the need for congenial employment in leisure hours in the days before there were outside amusements. 'You never know what you'll need,' a girl would remark when showing her laid-by treasures to a friend; or she might say, 'I've made these in case,' which, though it might possibly include marriage, was supposed to refer as well to any other contingency.

For the wedding ceremony a new dress was considered desirable, though not absolutely necessary, and Bess was thinking of wearing her new summer frock when, one day, her father came to her in the kitchen with the bag which contained his savings and counted ten golden sovereigns into her palm. 'There, my dear,' he said. 'That is for you to buy your wedding gown and anything else you may fancy. But don't spend every penny, my dearie; keep something back; you don't want to have to go running to Arnold for money the moment you're married. A bride ought by rights to have her purse-penny when she leaves home, and there was a time when even poor folks had too much pride to let their daughter go empty-handed. A father'd see that his girl had something in her pocket, if only half a crown, for her purse-penny; but things are sadly altered now in the way of self-respect,' and he drew back into place the brass ring

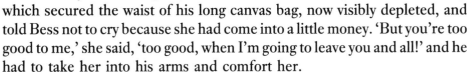

which secured the waist of his long canvas bag, now visibly depleted, and told Bess not to cry because she had come into a little money. 'But you're too good to me,' she said, 'too good, when I'm going to leave you and all!' and he had to take her into his arms and comfort her.

Bess's was an old-fashioned country wedding, without white-be-ribboned carriages, or anything which could afterwards be described as a reception. One August morning, before the early freshness had gone from the fields, the little procession came winding along the footpath. First came the bride on her father's arm, all in white to outward appearance, but wearing the traditional 'something blue' in the shape of blue ribbon garters, made and presented by Mrs. Finch, who, determined that the marriage should be a lucky one, had also provided the 'something old', a lace and net veil, the work of her own great-aunt. The very veil, indeed, that had once disappeared when spread to dry on a lavender bush, and had been found

three months afterwards in the nest of a thieving mag-
pie. This veil, thrown back over her hat and floating
slightly, gave the happy, laughing bride a hurrying,
eager look as she stepped lightly over the greensward.
Mercy and Charity, in their new summer dresses, pink
and mauve respectively, followed as bridesmaids.
They carried huge home-made bouquets of mixed
summer garden flowers, of all colours and delicious
scent. A similar bouquet had been made for Bess, but,
at the last moment before they started, a head gardener
friend of her father had sent her one of white carnations and maidenhair, and the more homely posy had
been handed to Mrs. Finch to enliven her sober grey gown and black silk mantle.

After the wedding party proper, strung out in twos and threes and groups along the
footpath, came relatives, invited guests, and neighbours who had chosen to cross the
meadow to escort the bride from her home. All were in their Sunday best and all
carried flowers, which they intended to strew before the bridal pair after the ceremony.
The Pococks had gone to visit some relatives. The bridegroom had gone on to the
church, as was proper; Polly was already in her place in the choir, and Luke, at his own
request, had been left behind to help his mother and Mrs. Sykes with the cooking.

The school holidays had begun and girls in clean pinafores and boys with clean
faces, all carrying flowers, lined the way from the stile to the church porch. Clerk
Savings stood with Arnold at the door to make sure that his own peculiar rules of
precedence were observed. 'Here 'em come,' he said as the bride's party appeared;
'an' I see 'em be bringin' two vartues along wi' 'em, Charity an' Mercy. Pity you ain't
got no Patience! That'd bin the one to stand by 'ee in Holy Matrimony.' Miss Fowkes
at the harmonium struck up a wedding march which, though somewhat wheezy and
halting, added to the impressiveness of the ceremony. Mr. Penpethy on that occasion
had not forgotten his engagement. Bess and Arnold were the last couple he married,
and afterwards people said that he had looked like a saint at the altar. 'An' that thin and
pale you could a'most see through the poor old gentleman.' Afterwards, in the vestry,
he said, patting Arnold's wrist, 'Your gain is our loss, my lad; but cherish her as she
deserves and we'll forgive you.' Then he took Bess's hand and said, 'Bless you, my
dear!' and they all trooped out to face the rice- and flower-throwing.

The guests previously invited and others picked up on the way filled the big barn,
where two long tables were spread. Hot roast beef and plum pudding were then not
considered too heavy fare for a hot August noon, and the guests passed their plates
again and again. Jugs of foaming ale circulated and the old traditional toasts were
honoured.

Only Mercy noticed that Luke was missing. When she questioned him afterwards, he said he had gone to look for a lost whetstone in a recently mown field, and, being Mercy, she did not reproach him for not being at hand to help swell the chorus of cheers when the newly married pair had been driven off to the station in Farmer Mercer's best dog-cart; but, instead, sat him down at the back kitchen table to cold beef and ale. She wished she could have told him that Bess had missed and inquired for him when she had made her final adieux; but, of course, she had not given him a thought. How could it have been expected of her? She had her own life to live, and her life that day was at its apex of happiness. How should she know that her sunshine was Luke's shadow?

Bess found her new home all she had hoped for, and her letters reflected her satisfaction. She was making such-and-such improvements in the house; she had been with Arnold to tea at the Vicarage; she was teaching needlework to the girls in school, and had engaged a young maid to do the rough housework. She was as happy as a lark, but there was nowhere like dear Waterside and she longed for the Christmas holidays. Mrs. Finch had come to take such a pleasure and pride in the match that she had almost persuaded herself it was one of her own making. 'What did I tell you?' she would say after reading one of Bess's letters. 'Bess was never cut out for our rough life. She needed a little refinement and gaiety and a man she could look up to, not one who, however thriving, 'ud be coming in grimy from his work, like that Ted Furlonger. No! as I said from the first, 't'ud never have done, though the lad's well enough in his way.'

Yet, a year or so later, she and Charity came as near to quarrelling as they ever did in their lives over that same lad! The situation was saved at the last moment by Mrs. Finch laughing and saying, 'Don't take any notice of what I say. I s'pose it's the waste of a good husband I can't bear. Waste always goes against the grain with me, as you know. Well, well, well! If you won't have Ted, you won't. You know your own mind best and I won't try to persuade you. But I don't like him going out of the family. Do you think he might by any chance fancy Mercy?'

—— X ——

FIELD FIRES

ONE October Saturday afternoon Charity had gone to the more distant Waterside fields to pick sloes, or slans, as the fruit was called locally, intending, when she had filled her basket, to call at the farm. It had been a good year for sloes; never had the bushes been so loaded or the fruit larger and juicier, each sloe like a small plum, misted with pale purple bloom. Her mother had already filled a nine-gallon cask with the wine she had made, but this she had determined to keep for some special occasion, as it had been a kind of vintage year. 'Not a tap shall be knocked into that barrel till the day of Charity's wedding, or the day she gets her own school,' she had declared. But now she had said that if Charity would go round the hedgerows and fill the basket she gave her she would make another quart or two for what she called common use. 'It's a bit late for them, I know,' she said, 'but there must be pecks still hanging on the boughs, and the wine won't be any the worse for a touch of frost. Better, according to some folks' opinion. 'Twas always said when I was a child that celery, sloes and savoy cabbage wasn't worth a tinker's cuss till they'd been frosted.' And Charity had taken the basket and strolled along the hedgerows, picking the finest.

By the time her basket was full she was a long way from home. The fields she had come to were large arable fields, lying bare beneath a grey sky, some still stubble, others ribbed like brown corduroy from ploughing, or levelled and sown with winter wheat. The only bright colour was provided by the hedgerows, still washed with the crimson of haws and brightened by the sunset tints of the sprinkling of leaves still left on the quickset. Moisture rose from the ploughed fields and drifted in thin veil-like clouds low down over the earth's surface, bearing with it the strong earthy scents of charlock and stubble and freshly turned clods, with a flavour of smoke from some invisible field fire.

No footpath ran in that direction, for no cottage or farm building was anywhere near. Except for the birds which scoured the stubble in flocks, or sank twittering into some hedgerow tree where they loaded the branches like feathered fruit, Charity for some time passed from field to field without seeing a living creature. Then there came to her, faintly at first, then loud and insistent, the bleating of sheep, and she skirted the field where they were folded and called a greeting to old Shepherd Moss. He was driving in stakes to extend his fold, his white beard bobbing in time to the strokes of his mallet, and did not hear or see her; but, a little further on, crouching down on the damp earth at the open end of a turnip clamp, she found his son Clem. He had apparently been sent to fetch turnips to be ground in the cutter and fed to the sheep, for a bushel scuttle lay near him, empty and on its side; but Clem was otherwise engaged. He was carving a turnip with his pocket-knife with minute, delicate strokes, and when he became aware of Charity standing over him he opened his palm and showed her his handiwork. He had fashioned a flower, a rose, quite recognizably a wild

rose, though the petals were an eighth of an inch in thickness and the one leaf, of similar thickness, had been pinned to the stalk with a thorn. Charity praised it loudly, as she would have done whatever its degree of excellence, but in this instance sincerely, shouting a little, as one does instinctively when speaking to one slow of comprehension.

Poor Clem! He was Shepherd Moss's Lammas lamb, the last of a long family and, as sometimes happens with the child of ageing parents, he was defective, having a cleft palate which impaired his articulation. The village children called him a looney and teased him. His intellect was not of the brightest; but at that moment the expression in his pale eyes of pure joy in his handiwork was not unintelligent.

'It's lovely, Clem! A real dog-rose! How clever of you to cut it!' 'F'oo! F'oo!' mouthed the lad, rising and offering her his rose. To please him, she took it and carried it on her own palm, as one might carry a gem. When she reached the next field gate she turned. The shepherd had finished driving his stakes and was banging hurdles about, the ewes all the time keeping up their loud, plaintive cries. As yet Clem had evidently not been missed by his father and had again crouched down by the clamp and was using his penknife. Poor Clem! she thought, slipping his rose in her pocket. If he had had a chance, he might have made a good stonemason, or something; now all he could be sure of was a hiding for laziness, and that in the near future.

Charity plodded on beside the hedgerows, the stiff, clayey soil clinging to her boot soles and the mist wrapping her around. The cries of the ewes followed her for a time, then became fainter, and soon there was no sound to be heard but the occasional flapping of a wing. She had come to the highest point of the farmland. These were the fields she had seen every day from the footpath. Seen from that distance, they had an everyday, cheerful look, now they seemed strange and mysterious. Rough stone walls, falling in places to ruins, supported the hedgerow banks. These, she had been told, had been built as relief work by starving men during the agricultural depression of the forties, and she thought of them sighing and groaning as they lifted the stones into position. But that was long ago. The thorn bushes in the hedges which had been planted above the walls had had time to become old and gnarled and hung with lichen, and the bad time for farm workers had passed from the memory of all but a few old people who at the time had been chidren. Since that time many a harvest had been carried from the fields by the starving men's descendants with cheers for the merry, merry harvest home to come; and their children's children had walked entwined in couples along the field margins and loitered in the gateways, with no thought of the earlier toilers. Yet in the brooding grey silence it seemed to her that something remained of the tears and the cheers and the kisses that lonely upland had known. She stood in a massive stone-built gateway to take her bearings. Restharrow lay hidden somewhere below in the distance, but she saw the stackyard and farm buildings of Waterside and smoke rising from one of the house chimneys. She was nearing the field fire, wreaths of aromatic smoke drifted around her, and she thought she would go to the fire and ask the man or boy in attendance to tell her the nearest way down to Waterside.

She had not far to go. The next gateway opened on to a newly harrowed field with, in two long lines down its whole length, small smoking heaps of couch grass. A man in earth-coloured clothes stood prodding one of the smoking heaps with a pitchfork and, when that was burning to his satisfaction, he shambled heavily down the line, attending to those fires which needed attention. Earth-coloured, heavy-footed, with hunched-up shoulders, to one to whom he was a stranger he might have appeared little more than an animated clod, but Charity recognized in him a very human individual. It was Luke.

'Hullo, Luke!' she called cheerfully. 'What are you doing up here? I thought Saturday was your afternoon for cleaning the stables,' and Luke said he had finished his work 'down yonder' and, having an hour to spare, he had thought he would come up and see how the fires were burning. But it was hard going, he said, hommicking over the wet land, and he brought out his clasp knife and, standing first on one foot, then on the other, slowly and deliberately scraped the soil from his boot soles. Charity thought he looked unusually thoughtful and a little downcast, and she wondered if he was grieving for Bess's lost presence. Now she came to think of it, he had been looking downcast lately; his broad red face had still its kindly expression, but it had lost its old beaming smile.

'This wet squitch is a caution to keep alight,' said Luke, squatting down beside a sulking fire and taking matches and paper from his pocket. Then he leaned forward, puffed out his cheeks, and blew on the feeble flame he had lighted. No more was said until it was burning to his satisfaction, then, sitting back on his heels, he looked up into Charity's face and said, 'You be lonesome these days, seemingly?' and Charity said, yes, she was lonesome in a way since her cousin was married, but added brightly that she had enjoyed her walk; the fields up there were so quiet and old-seeming, sort of enchanted, she thought.

'They be lonesome, right 'nuff,' said Luke, 'and they be the best place for lonesome people. Nobody 'ud come here if they wasn't lonesome; they'd go and enjoy 'emselves where other folks wer'.'

'Are you lonely, Luke?' asked Charity, and at that a look of real suffering came into his china-blue eyes. He rose and shook himself. The smoke from the rekindled fire rose in a spiral, then mingled with the smoke of other fires to float in a pale blue haze over the newly-raked acres, but Luke made no attempt to answer her question. Instead, he burst out with more spirit than she had ever seen in him before, 'I can't stand this life much longer! Come day, go day, one day's the same as t'other; same old 'osses, same old fields! You ploughs and you harrows an' you gets in th' seed corn; then comes haytime an' harvest an' you starts all over again! I be just about sick an' sated of it all, an' I've a gert mind to take th' Queen's shillin'.'

'You go for a soldier!' exclaimed the amazed Charity. 'I can't imagine you as one somehow; and I thought you liked the farm work. You have always seemed to like the

horses and things, and you are Uncle's right-hand man, you know you are! Besides, what would your mother do without you? It would break her heart if you enlisted, but you can't mean to!'

Luke smiled rather shamefacedly. 'No, I don't s'pose I do mean it,' he said, 'an' if I did I don't reckon any recruiting sergeant'd look at me; but everybody gets a bit unkid at times and then they sez anything. Talks as their belly guides 'em, as the sayin' goes. Don't take any notice of me, I sh'll be as bright as a button come mornin'. You get along down to a good fire an' y'r tea,' and Charity, seeing that he had rather be alone, left him.

She knew very well what was the matter with Luke. He must always have known that Bess would never marry him; probably he had never dreamed that she would; but while she had remained at the farm he had had opportunities of seeing and serving her, and with her going the sunshine had gone from his life. At the gateway she turned and looked back. Luke was still standing leaning on his pitchfork where she had left him. She waved to him, but he did not see her waving and she turned sadly away. By the time she reached Waterside dusk was falling.

After the mist and the dripping hedgerows, the living kitchen at Waterside looked a picture of homely comfort. Polly was toasting muffins before a huge fire. She had been on her favourite Sunday-afternoon errand to waylay the muffin man, who once a week on that day at that season came through the village with his wares in a flat oil-cloth-covered tray on his head, ringing his bell and calling, *Muffins and crumpets! Who'll buy! Who'll buy! Muffins and crumpets and S-a-a-l-l-y L-u-n-n-s!* A covered soup-plate containing those she had toasted stood to keep hot on the high steel fender. Firelight gleamed on the walls and ceiling and picked out with its flickering light the brass candlesticks and the crockery on the dresser.

'Hullo! Here you are, you old owl!' she cried when Charity came blinking into the firelit room. 'Wherever have you been? We've been just bursting to tell you the news. You'd never guess! Dad's had a letter, Mrs. Harper brought it from the post office at Mixlow and Cousin Oliver's coming home from India!' And she danced excitedly around the room, waving her toasting-fork with a crumpet impaled upon it, singing, 'He's coming home! He's coming home! Our Cousin Oliver's coming home as soon as a ship can carry him!'

Charity was almost as excited as Polly, and the next few minutes were spent in discussing what they would do to welcome the wanderer when he arrived. Polly thought of ringing the long row of room-bells over the back kitchen mantelpiece. She thought she could just manage to produce on them *Home, sweet Home*, or *Hail the Conquering*, and, indeed, if she could not it would not have been for want of practice, for, as her father had said, she had 'terrified' those bells from the time when she could first climb on a chair and reach them with a walking-stick. Charity was for some more quiet ways of welcoming their cousin. She thought a wreath of snowdrops round his plate would give him more pleasure, and the snowdrops would be out by the time he arrived, as he had said in his letter that he had to wait for a ship. Polly buttered her crumpets lavishly and returned to her toasting. She had never seen Oliver; he had left the country before she had been born, and now she asked what he was like. Mercy, who had just come into the room, said he was just a nice boy, full of mischief and fun. Polly would find him a tease. Charity suggested that Oliver might have changed during all those years away; he had been a boy when he left home, now he must be a man; but the man Oliver she could not visualize; she still thought of him as the long-limbed country youth in uniform who had played with and teased her twelve years before.

Then Reuben came in and the lamp was lighted and they gathered around the tea-table. 'Oh, Polly! I do wish you'd go easier with the butter!' said Mercy reprovingly, as she uncovered the dish. 'Those crumpets are swimming, regularly swimming, and you know Bess always told you it was vulgar to spread butter too thick!' 'Um-m, um-m! Perhaps she did say so, but for all that I noticed that when we had crumpets she liked the bottom layer,' was Polly's retort, and for once neither her father nor Mercy checked her pertness. Polly's manners was a stock subject; that of Oliver's return was new and absorbing.

'Let's see,' said Reuben reflectively, 'young Oliver'll be thirty by this time. Time he married and settled down. We must see if we can't find him a wife.' 'What about Sally Price?' asked pert little Polly, and the idea of Sally Price as a wife for a smart young soldier made them all laugh, for Sall was a queer, old-fashioned little body of forty whose youth had been spent in caring for her aged and invalid parents and who had only recently appeared to have awakened to the danger of old-maidhood. Then all she could do, poor maid, was to purchase a spray of artificial red roses to enliven the crape she had been wearing as mourning for her last parent, and to make shy awkward advances towards an elderly widower who had no intention of marrying her, but had no objection to walking home from church with her on Sundays in return for the free washing and mending of his clothes. Her eager adoration and his lumpish indifference had made poor Sally's matrimonial designs the talk of the parish.

'No, no! Sally won't do at all. I'm sure Cousin Oliver'd never fancy Sally,' said Mercy, who always took literally all that was said. Then, after a moment's thought, she added, 'I can't think of anybody in this place at all likely for Oliver.'

Her father laughed and said, 'No, no! You didn't mean it seriously, did you, Poll? Although, mind you, there's many a man who might do worse than take a good hard-working maid like Sall for a wife. But this Oliver of ours you'll find'll be a smartish sort of chap, and such ones don't long go begging for a wife. There's more danger of 'em being mobbed by young women, and if he wants a wife he won't want any help from us; he'll soon set the church bells ringing. So don't you girls go worrying yourselves about gettin' him married, but have ready a bit of cousinly affection.' Then, as he took his hat down from its peg by the doorway, he said slyly over his shoulder, 'And don't go marrying him yourselves, for I can't spare neither of you!'

Mrs. Finch's letter from Oliver, not having been called for at the Mixlow Post Office, arrived on the Monday morning. Charity took in the thin, crackling foreign envelope with the regimental badge on the back. The letter expressed the same warm affection and pleasure at the prospect of meeting as the one to Waterside. 'Tell Cherry,' it ended, 'that I have not forgotten her, nor have I forgotten my promise to take her to Banbury. I'll warrant she's too grown up now to care about brandy-snaps, but I shall find something to pleasure her. Give her my love.'

─── XI ───

THE RETURN OF THE SOLDIER

BUT March had set in, mild as a lamb for once, and the daffodils were nodding in the Finches' garden when the soldier returned. Then, towards the close of a day of sunshine and showers, when the Finches were sitting round the table having tea by daylight and telling each other how the days were drawing out, Charity's father, who sat facing the window, exclaimed, 'God bless my soul! Here's the Crown turn-out stopping in front and a gentleman getting out, and he's coming this way. Somebody about a job of work, I s'pose.' 'Or to ask the way somewhere,' suggested his wife, and both she and Charity rose from the table to look out of the window. A tall, broad, well-dressed man was coming across the green, followed by the hotel groom carrying a stylish portmanteau. Not one of them recognized Oliver, but Oliver it was, and an Oliver who had changed less than suggested by his outward appearance, for he fairly lifted his Aunt Alice, as he still called her, from her feet as he kissed and hugged her. 'Not know me!' he cried. 'Well, that's a good joke! Why, I'd have known you if I'd meet you in the streets of Bombay! And Uncle George, too, you've not changed at all, either of you. And this is Charity? She *has* altered a bit. Too grown up now to be carried on my shoulder when we take our long-promised trip to Banbury Town!'

Then the groom had to be dismissed with a tip, and after a cup of tea pressed upon him by Mrs. Finch, whose rule it was that anyone whomsoever who entered the house while a meal was upon the table must be treated as a guest. But, soon, the young man had gulped down the tea, asked permission to take the wedge of cake with him to eat upon the way, and had gone. Then Oliver had to rummage in his portmanteau for the shawl he had brought for Mrs. Finch and the embroidered muslin dress-length for Charity. 'Just a few trifles to be going on with,' he said magnificently, as he handed a case of silver-mounted pipes to Mr. Finch, 'There's a packing case of curios on the way and there's something else there for all of you.'

In a very short time a ham had been reached down from the rack and slices had been

191

cut and fried with eggs for Oliver's tea, and, after Mrs. Finch had surreptitiously changed the tablecloth and substituted as much of the best china as she could without making what she called an upset, they all sat down to the table again. While they plied him with eatables and he ate, Oliver told them about some of his adventures, and they, in return, told him of the Restharrow changes. So-and-so had died, years ago, and So-and-so had married, been widowed, and married again, and such-and-such a house or farm had changed hands. And, all the time, the eyes of the three Finches were upon Oliver. His height, breadth, and the little bald spot on the top of his head amazed them no more than his improved accent and bearing. He was something quite new to them in the way of time-expired Service men, who, after serving abroad, usually re-turned to Restharrow with impaired health and empty pockets and ever afterwards spoke of their period of foreign service as a kind of purgatory.

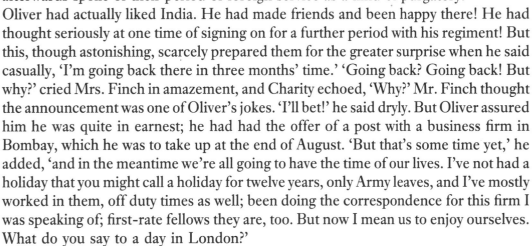

Oliver had actually liked India. He had made friends and been happy there! He had thought seriously at one time of signing on for a further period with his regiment! But this, though astonishing, scarcely prepared them for the greater surprise when he said casually, 'I'm going back there in three months' time.' 'Going back? Going back! But why?' cried Mrs. Finch in amazement, and Charity echoed, 'Why?' Mr. Finch thought the announcement was one of Oliver's jokes. 'I'll bet!' he said dryly. But Oliver assured him he was quite in earnest; he had had the offer of a post with a business firm in Bombay, which he was to take up at the end of August. 'But that's some time yet,' he added, 'and in the meantime we're all going to have the time of our lives. I've not had a holiday that you might call a holiday for twelve years, only Army leaves, and I've mostly worked in them, off duty times as well; been doing the correspondence for this firm I was speaking of; first-rate fellows they are, too. But now I mean us to enjoy ourselves. What do you say to a day in London?'

Before bedtime, Oliver had to go to Waterside to show himself to Reuben and the girls, and out in the larder Charity whispered to her mother, might she go, too? And her mother said, of course, if she wrapped up well against the night air. She would have gone with them herself if she had not had Oliver's bed to make up, for it had been agreed that Oliver should sleep at the Finches' cottage for the next few nights, then, perhaps, for a few nights at Waterside; after that, he thought he would put up at the Crown at Mixlow. He had made the acquaintance of the people there to-day and liked them. And when Mrs. Finch protested, he said he could not think of quartering himself on friends for so long. Besides, she must remember that he was now an old bachelor with odd bachelor's ways, and at an inn he could get up and go to bed and order his meals when he pleased, without disturbing family arrangements.

Mrs. Finch had never in her life before known a visitor who had relatives in a place stay at any but relatives' houses; but Oliver spoke so persuasively and at the same time so authoritatively that she was soon convinced that for him to put up at the Crown was the proper thing, and only stipulated that he should come daily to see them and eat his Sunday dinners at Restharrow and Waterside alternately. At that Oliver laughed and said he should come so often that they would get tired of seeing him. Besides, had he not promised Charity long ago to squire her around? What about a day in Oxford next week? He would find out at the Crown what was on at the theatre.

Charity smiled back into the merry blue eyes which were regarding her so intently. That would be lovely, she said, twisting a warm, knitted scarf round her head and neck before venturing out into the night air. She was glad that the scarf was one which became her, dim purple in colour, and lightly knitted and lacey, and when Oliver sprang forward to hold her coat while she put it on she was thrilled by the delicate attention.

At Waterside there was more happy, excited talk and more expressions of wonder. Elderberry wine was brought out in the tall glass decanter only used on special occasions, and biscuits and filberts and apples were placed on the table in the old-fashioned green leaf-shaped dessert dishes which had belonged to the girls' grandmother. To Reuben the occasion seemed to demand something even more special. He went to the cupboard known as 'Dad's' and brought out a dusty black bottle. 'Here's something you've not tasted on all your travels, a drop of fine old metheglin,' he told Oliver. ''Tis the last bottle of the half-dozen your Aunt Marianna made the first years of our marriage. I'd meant it for Bess's wedding, but somehow forgot all about it; maybe because it didn't seem to mix well with Arnold's champagne. I'm not going to offer you girls any; 'tis too strong and heady for maidens and you'd better stick to your wine.' He poured three glasses for the men of the party, then, holding his own glass up to the light and closing one eye, the better to focus the dark amber liquid, he said, 'Here's welcome home to the warrior, love to the absent, fond memories of our lost ones, and good luck to us all!' and they honoured the old country toast by draining their glasses.

Mercy, at first, had appeared to be a little overawed by Oliver. She said afterwards that he was so tall and big and somehow so important-looking that she could scarcely believe that he was a relative of theirs; but very soon she was sitting comfortably by his side, not saying much, beyond pressing upon him this and that on the table, but giving what he was saying the closest attention. Shyness was not one of Polly's failings; she was not content merely to listen, but asked so many questions about Oliver's travels that

her father had to remind her that it was long past her bedtime and tell her that, some day or other, she could bring out the map and put her cousin through a regular examination, but to-night was the turn of her elders; and she lighted her candle for bed with much jingling of the silver bangles which Oliver had given her and departed with many a backward look at the hero of the hour.

Going back by the footpath way between her father and Oliver, Charity felt a hand on her shoulder and a voice said, 'Will you not take my arm?' For a man to offer his arm to a lady to help her over an uneven road, or in darkness, or when hurry was called for, was still at that date but commonplace good manners, but Charity regarded the invitation as a great compliment from a man of the world, such as Oliver, to a country mouse like herself; and when Oliver patted the hand on his elbow and said, 'You and I, Charity, must always stick together,' her pulse bounded with delight.

For the next few days she seemed to herself to be floating on air, rather than walking on solid earth. Every day she hurried home from school, happy in the prospect of sitting beside Oliver at table and strolling with him afterwards through the village or out in the fields. Often he was waiting for her to go with him to Waterside, where later her parents would join them, and after tea there would be singing, or cards, or country games – Postman's Knock, or Blind Man's Buff, or Turn the Trencher. These parties were family parties; no outsiders were invited, for that was only done at Christmas, and Mrs. Pocock and Stella, who would have had to be included occasionally, were away on a visit to their London relations. They were a party in themselves; none of them wished to share Oliver with other company, and he himself seemed perfectly satisfied with that in which he found himself. For all his varied experience and knowledge of the world, he appeared to have remained at heart a simple, affectionate being whose present happiness it was to give pleasure to those who had befriended his orphaned childhood.

When Oliver walked through the village, with his upright carriage, good looks and good clothes and pleasant manners, looking, as one of his admirers said, 'every inch a gentleman', smiles greeted him on every side. No one whom he had known as a boy was forgotten; he remembered their names, their family histories, even their favourite ailments. He visited aged women in their cottages and knew by a kind of instinct where the gift of a shilling would be appreciated and where it would give more pleasure for himself to accept some hoarded trifle as a memento of his visit. One day when he came out of the *Magpie* and found four old men on the bench beneath the sign-post, taking the air, but with no visible sign of other refreshment, he went back and called for four

pints of the best and himself helped to carry the mugs out to them. The children followed him everywhere. He would beg little girls to give him one of their curls, clap little boys on the shoulder and tell them they would soon make fine soldiers, and compliment their elder sisters on their fine eyes or rosy complexions. All this, of course, made him extremely popular, but it was not done designedly for that purpose, it was merely the natural expression of his high spirits and good nature. And those who might have been thought to flatter him were not insincere. They naturally wanted to share his goodwill and generosity, but they also felt a less selfish pride in the young man whom they thought had got on in the world and yet had remained one of themselves. The general feeling was that Oliver Lathom was a credit to Restharrow and that somehow or other they had all had a hand in shaping his course.

At Waterside, Mercy spent what would have been her spare time thinking out and cooking unaccustomed dishes which she thought might please Oliver. Curry appeared for the first time on the Waterside table and was praised with overflowing eyes and contorted features by the girls, because Oliver praised it. Polly adored Oliver and on one occasion was seen sitting on his knee and singing to him one of his favourite old country songs. Like a young thrush sitting on a perch, said her father, though Charity, who happened to be present, thought she more nearly resembled a young hawk cooing.

Reuben liked Oliver, and when it came to discussing politics or improved farming methods found him a stimulating companion. But, surprisingly, there was a slight reserve in his liking, for one day, when told of some instance illustrating his nephew's popularity, he said thoughtfully, 'All things to all men. It's a cheap way to liking, and those who've got the knack o't are generally the sort that change with the wind. Though, mind you, there may be exceptions.'

Mr. Finch liked Oliver unreservedly. It was seldom he came in close contact with so travelled and well-informed a man, and by the fireside and out in the workshop, himself measuring and planing and Oliver perched on a corner of the bench with his legs swinging, they talked, as Mrs. Finch said, nineteen to the dozen. Mrs. Finch herself, though, as always, loving Oliver as she might have done her own son had she had one, was a little distrustful of his charm. Or perhaps it was her daughter's good sense she distrusted, for more than once she said to Charity, as she had done on other occasions, 'Beware the desire of the eye!'

Charity was almost in love with Oliver. Not quite; her time for loving and being loved was still far in the future, and, when it came, the desire of the eye had no part in it. She was rather in love with Oliver's good looks and gay spirits and with the distinction of being singled out by him as his chosen companion than with him as a man. It all culminated in their day in Oxford, a magic, never-to-be-forgotten day of April showers and sunshine, of budding green and hyacinth beds against grey stone buildings and wisps of amethyst mist floating around turrets and towers. They saw and did everything appropriate to such a visit, from walking shyly round such places as were open to the public to peering through holes in a screen at a sixpenny peepshow at such scenes as Queen Victoria on her way to open Parliament and the Prince of Wales leading one of the horses from his racing stable. They dined at the ordinary at one of the lesser hotels; roast sirloin with horseradish sauce and apple tart with cream; two shillings for the two of them and twopence left under Oliver's plate for the waiter. They drove home from the railway station at Mixlow in style. Oliver had ordered the hotel dog-cart to meet their train, and the quick, stimulating passage between budding hedgerows gave the last touch of delight to a perfect day. It was the last such day they

were to enjoy together, for within a week the Pococks returned from their holiday in London and all was changed.

Stella and her mother arrived, loaded with their own luggage and articles which had been given to them and tired after their walk from Mixlow. To save them the trouble of lighting their fire and pumping water, Mercy suggested that they should have tea with the Truman family. Charity was there with her mother, and when Reuben and Oliver came in from the farmyard there was a little bustle of fetching more chairs and rearranging places; but room and provisions were ample and other entertainment was unnecessary, as Mrs. Pocock was prepared to do most of the talking. Every room and practically every piece of furniture in her brother's house had to be described, and the superior position of himself and his friends had to be extolled. Stella and she had been to the theatre, seen the West End shops and the Crystal Palace and been on a Sunday to Kew Gardens. How, after a fortnight of civilized life, they would be able to exist in this dead-alive place she declared that she did not know.

She had so much to tell and took so long in telling it that probably no one but Charity noticed Oliver's unwonted silence. He sat, as she thought, gloomily, cutting his bread and butter fingers and spreading the fingers with jam with a finicking care very unlike his usually hearty enjoyment of food. Once or twice he cast a sidelong glance at Stella, who sat next to him, her lovely profile set off by the green window-curtains, and once asked her how she liked London. 'Very much, thanks', was her sweetly demure reply, which he seemed to find satisfying, for he did not take further advantage of the opening. Strangely enough, he seemed a little shy and awkward that day, which rather disappointed Charity, who had counted upon his making a good impression on Stella and her mother. She would have liked them to have seen that others besides them-selves had dashing relations. But, she concluded, it was quite natural that Oliver should show no particular interest in his cousin's housemates. Why should he, after all the more exciting people he had known?

It was a surprise to her when, the first moment they were alone together, he asked, 'Why didn't any of you tell me about Stella?' Charity said he must have heard them speaking of her at least a score of times. 'Do you mean to tell me you didn't know there were other people living in the house?' she asked. 'Other people! Other people!' he exclaimed almost rudely. 'Including in this case a perfect beauty! It makes a fellow look silly coming suddenly on one such as her without any preparation. A clumsy great idiot she must have thought me!' Charity, a little nettled, said that beauty was a matter of opinion; some people she knew did not care for Stella's looks, leaving him to suppose that she herself did not; and Oliver, also a little nettled, said that he could quite believe that some women did not care for Stella Pocock's looks, for they knew that she put them all in the shade. 'But she strikes a mere man as being too lovely for this earth, and too modest and gentle.'

Modest and gentle or not, Stella was certainly at her best in Oliver's company, and from that day on she was often in his company, for her former custom of dropping into the Truman's living kitchen at odd moments, which had declined since Bess's departure, was resumed. Oliver was usually there to entertain her, and with him she was never sarcastic or sulky, but at her gayest and most animated. It was remarked that her holiday in London had done wonders for Stella. 'I've never known her so bright and bonny,' her mother said. 'A change was all she needed, a change and good company,' and Mercy agreed. Charity, when this was repeated to her, thought bitterly that there had been no need for Stella to

198

go to London for change and good company, for Restharrow now provided both: the change for herself to digest as best she could while Stella enjoyed the good company. By that time Oliver was staying at the Crown at Mixlow, and every evening he would escort Stella home from her work, and the walk took longer and longer, until often the lamp would be lighted and supper would have begun before they reached Waterside.

This did not pass unnoticed. 'Our Oliver's not been here to tea for a week,' complained Mrs. Finch to her husband. 'I do hope he's not going to take up seriously with that Stella.'

Mr. Finch laughed. 'Oh, you women! You women!' he said. 'A man can't look at a pretty maid without you've got them wedded and bedded in fancy. Besides, what if he does take up with her, as you call it? I s'pose the man's got to marry somebody; most of us do at one time or another – you women take care we do that – and Ol's old enough to know his own mind and there's nothing against the girl that I know of.'

'But she's not good enough for our Ol,' persisted his wife. 'If he weds her he'll wed trouble.'

Again Mr. Finch laughed, this time a little sardonically. 'Well, come to that,' he said, 'matrimony at its best is no bed of roses. But don't you go frettin' yourself. Oliver's old enough and big enough to look after himself. Surely a man who can be trusted to keep a regiment of soldiers in order can manage a bit of a girl no bigger than three-hap'orth of soap,' and he went whistling out to his workshop.

Charity and her mother looked at each other. 'Men don't care,' sighed Mrs. Finch; 'and I s'pose what he says is right enough. Ol is a man in years and knows his own business best. He must do as he thinks fit.' Then, after a pause and with more spirit, 'Though I must say he's not treated you at all well.'

'Now, Mother,' said Charity loftily, 'please don't get the idea into your head that there was ever anything between Oliver and me, save what was cousinly. You know very well that I don't want to marry Oliver or anybody else. I want to be a schoolmistress.' Then, seeing her mother's hurt expression, she gave her a tight hug and ran upstairs to shed a few tears in privacy, for, though her heart was not broken, it was a little bruised. To see another preferred to oneself seems to the young hard to bear. We get used to it in later life.

The weeks went on and the time of Oliver's return to India drew near. Although Oliver came to see his Restharrow relatives less frequently than before, when with them he behaved in his old affectionate manner, but said not a word of the expected engagement. Nor was Stella more communicative. Once she let drop some chance remark about the innkeeper's wife at the Crown; she wore this or that, or had said something which Stella repeated; and, knowing that Oliver had become close friends with the family at the Crown, Mrs. Finch concluded that Stella had been invited there and had also become on friendly terms with the family. Several times Mrs. Pocock told Mercy that Stella was working late on a wedding or funeral order, which at the time was regarded as an invention to excuse her daughter's late hours; but it is quite likely that the excuse may have been Stella's, for it turned out afterwards that, for once, Mrs. Pocock had had no hand in shaping events. It was certainly not only a surprise, but also a shock to her when, late one evening, the pair walked hand in hand into the Waterside kitchen and announced their marriage.

It happened that Mrs. Pocock had herself been working late that evening and, when she reached home, had come downstairs to get water from the pump in the courtyard, and Mercy had told her that the kettle on the kitchen fire was on the point of boiling. If she liked to make her tea from it, it would save time, and she must be in need of a cup after her long, dusty walk. Mrs. Pocock had fetched her teapot and was stooping over the fire filling it, and Mercy, who had been pumping her water for her, was standing, pail in hand, in the doorway, when the couple came in and Oliver called gaily, 'Allow me to introduce you to Mrs. Oliver Lathom! Married to yours truly at Mixlow Registrar's Office this morning!'

'Married! You don't say so!' gasped Mercy; then, hurriedly collecting her wits, she added, 'I wish you joy!' But Stella's mother said nothing; she was not in a condition to do so, for she had fallen across the arms of Reuben's chair in a dead faint. She had barely recovered when Stella announced, 'I'm going to India with Oliver. My passage was booked weeks ago.' Her mother gave me one stricken look and moaned, 'You're never going to leave me!' Neither bride nor bridegroom troubled themselves to answer; they were too taken up with their own affairs to consider the position of an unloved mother. In less than an hour Stella had gathered together such of her belongings as she required for the time being and, except for one short visit a day or two later, had left the home of her childhood for ever. A room had been engaged for them for a few days at Mixlow; the rest of Oliver's leave was to be spent in London.

Charity met the bridal couple on the footpath, closely linked arm in arm, his head bent tenderly to catch her every expression. Stella, in a new grey suit and a fashionably small hat with a spotted veil to the chin, was a model of elegance. 'Congratulate us!' she cried as Charity drew near. 'This is our wedding day. Married this morning at Mixlow! No wonder you look astonished; everybody does when we tell them, and when they hear that I'm going to India

with Ol they flop down in faints!'

Charity did not flop down in a faint. Upon her the news had a different effect. It may have been her proneness to the desire of the eye, against which her mother had so often warned her, for they certainly were a handsome pair, which caused in her the sudden rush of sympathy, even of love. For all their assurance and their brave attire, there seemed to her something pathetic about the untried pair who, so rashly or bravely, had joined themselves together and were about to face the unknown. For the first time in years she threw her arms about Stella and kissed her. Oliver had gone on and was shouting, 'Hoi! Hoi!' to the groom who had brought the dog-cart to the stile – he came back for his kiss afterwards – and while for a few moments the girls were alone, Stella seized Charity's hand and whispered, 'You won't ever tell Oliver about those letters, will you? He thinks I'm a saint, and I do mean to be good, really!' And Charity said, 'Of course not! Never!'

It was Mercy who, that night, helped Stella's mother to undress and did what she could to console her. What she could do was but little, but that little could not have been done better; for the poor proud woman, with all her defences down, had less need of spoken than of practical sympathy. Mercy was not one to talk about another's weakness; but, years afterwards, in an unguarded moment, she did say that she had never in her life seen anyone so distressed as Mrs. Pocock on her daughter's wedding night. The next day, when she reappeared, Mrs. Pocock was as self-possessed as usual, and afterwards declared that the marriage was what she had wished and made a boast of Stella's prospects. But, as long as she remained at Waterside, she was more gentle and considerate than her wont towards Mercy. 'I don't include you, my dear; you're all right,' she would say when condemning the villagers in general. She did not remain long at Waterside after Stella had gone. One of her patrons, having one of the lodges on her husband's estate fall vacant, offered the post of lodgekeeper to 'that dear, kind, patient soul, Mrs. Pocock'. There happened to be a right of way through the park by way of the gate she controlled, and at great inconvenience to herself she blocked it by keeping the gate locked and only opening it to wheeled vehicles. The villagers, denied access to their short cut, were so enraged that a number of them assembled on a Sunday morning and tore a section of the park palings down, which caused almost as much commotion in the place as the anonymous letters had done at Restharrow. But that was later.

Before Oliver and Stella left, Oliver told Mrs. Finch that he had suggested to Stella that her mother should go with them to India and share their home; but Stella had at once rejected the proposal. 'Of course you know that Stella has never been happy at home,' he said. Mrs. Finch replied that that was the first word she had heard of it, and refrained by an effort from adding that if Stella had not been happy at home it was not for want of having her own way in everything.

'No, you wouldn't have heard of it,' continued Oliver gravely. 'I might have known that Stella would be too loyal to have told anyone of her sufferings. I fear my poor

darling has had a miserable childhood, shut up in two rooms with that bad-tempered old mother of hers and made to slave at the housework like a little Cinderella from the time she was tall enough to use a broom, and neglected and nagged at and dressed in old-cast-off clothes, given to her mother in charity, when the best and richest wouldn't be fit to show off her beauty as it deserves. But there's going to be a change now; she's going where she'll be appreciated. I wish you could be there to see her shine, for shine she will; nobody with a pair of eyes in their head could help but admire her. And it's not only her looks; she's got a nature to match her beauty, has my Stella!'

Before such doting, Mrs. Finch had not the heart to say all she had intended to say. 'He'll find her out only too soon,' she said afterwards. All she said at the time was: 'I think you ought to have told us you were going to get married, and you ought not to have let Stella deceive her mother'; but, as she told Charity afterwards, it was like talking to a man deaf and blind, and 'my heart bleeds for him when his eyes are open,' she ended.

Oliver may have been disillusioned; but, if so, there was no hint of disillusion in his letters. After he had returned with Stella to India, he still wrote occasionally to Mrs. Finch and to Reuben. Stella's pleasures, Stella's attainments, Stella's social triumphs, and, later, Stella's ailments was the main theme of his letters, though he still expressed his own warm affection and hopes for the well-being of his Restharrow friends. He never at any time appeared to be conscious that he himself had ever given cause for disappointment.

Many years afterwards, after a long letter-less period, when writing to tell Mrs. Finch of Stella's death, he wrote of her as 'my dear wife', 'my own lost angel, too good for this wicked world', and Charity, who by that time had gained more experience, wondered if Oliver had lived all those years in a fool's paradise, or if Stella in childhood had been a jewel misplaced and unappreciated.

XII

'ALL'S WELL!'

CHARITY'S generation at Restharrow was dispersing. The girls who had sat with her on the school benches in childhood had gone out to service, away from home; many of the boys had enlisted in the Army, or emigrated, or gone to work in towns; those who were left to work on the land were thinking of marrying. Other children, babes or unborn when their elders had been pupils, hung their clothes on their pegs and occupied their seats at the desks. From Waterside, Bess had gone, and Stella, and Mrs. Pocock had relinquished her free quarters there to keep the lodge gates of her Ladyship. Charity was teaching for her last term at Restharrow National School; after Christmas she was to enter the Training College for Teachers at Radley. Reuben, Mercy and Polly remained at Waterside. In that great barn of a place, Reuben said, the three of them rattled like shrunken kernels in a nutshell; but their part of the house was unchanged, being, as it had always been, an example of homely comfort. There, in a changing outside world, the old country customs and ways of life were observed, the old country principles were honoured, the tender ties of family affection and loyalties were preserved, and from there neighbourly sympathy and goodwill radiated. All this was soon to become but a memory.

It was towards the close of a close, overcast October day that Bob Purchase brought Champion II to Waterside. *Clip, clop! Clip, clop! Clip, clop! Jingle, jingle*, they had come along dusty roads and lanes from the farm of Champion's last engagement, Bob, small and monkey-like, straddling bow-leggedly beside the great, glossy stallion, linked to himself by a thin, loosely held leading-rein. There had been one of those hot, dry spells which so often follow a wet summer, the kind of autumn weather which exasperates a farmer who has had a wet haytime and harvest, and the narrow, flinty byways were padded with dust. But a change was at hand; towards evening the heavy grey canopy overhead parted to reveal an angry red sunset. Sharp little squalls shook the hedgerows and sent the dust whirling. Champion had taken every one of these

disturbances as a personal affront. 'Now! Now! Steady there! Steady, my beauty, steady!' Bob had urged, tightening his hold on the leading-rein, and, after a show of backing on the one side and soothing words and caresses on the other, the two had gone on as before. To anyone following them they must have appeared an ill-matched pair: Champion's great hooves and dust-whitened fetlocks planted firmly, his plaited and beribboned tail swinging across his hindquarters with the regularity of a pendulum; and, beside him, the little man, Bob, spidery of build, and, of gait, almost mincing.

Bob loved his charge and was its willing slave. All his days and sometimes part of his nights were devoted to its service, feeding and grooming and leading him from farm to farm, soothing his temper, smoothing his way, and supervising his engagements. In return, Champion gave Bob a grudging obedience. Perhaps affection also, who can tell? At least he would permit no one but Bob to attend him – an exclusiveness which sometimes troubled his owner, who, while appreciating Bob's expert management of the animal, saw himself at a loss if he should leave his service or fall ill. However, there seemed no likelihood of either event. Though small, Bob was wiry and, in his employer's phrase, hard as nails, and, setting aside his devotion to Champ, he knew a good job when he'd got one. You can't pick a pound a week off a furze bush, and Bob knows it, was the farmer's conclusion.

That day there had been other hindrances besides the dustwhorls. Champion was under the impression that any road upon which he travelled should be reserved for his own royal progress, and showed his resentment of other traffic by plunging and rearing. 'That 'oss be nout but a bundle o' narves,' a wagoner had remarked when he had had to halt his own team with their load while the backing stallion was coaxed past on the grass margin. That accomplished, Bob had looked back over his shoulder, 'A fat lot you know about 'osses what be 'osses!' he called. 'Narves, my elber! 'Tis his mettle what's talkin',' and they had gone on their way, the horse still twitching and trembling, the man whispering into its ear words of soothing.

'Ole Bob may say what he's a mind to; but if I've got any eyes in me yed that stallion of his'n's a mischief-maker,' called the carter to the man on the top of the load, and the other called back, 'You're right, mate. Champ'll be pickin' up ole Bob one o' these days an' shakin' him like a terrier shakes a rat at threshin' time. Lord! he could eat up ole Bob in one mouthful!'

Meanwhile Bob was carrying on a one-sided conversation with Champ. 'Now, now, my beauty! Never let it be said that you was frittened by a wagon-load o' straw! And these comin' now be but milkin' cows. Take no notice. Let 'em see how a tip-top gentleman can behave when he's a mind to. Eyes sore? Dust in 'em? If I had my way you should have a

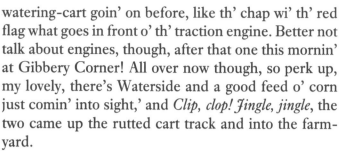

watering-cart goin' on before, like th' chap wi' th' red flag what goes in front o' th' traction engine. Better not talk about engines, though, after that one this mornin' at Gibbery Corner! All over now though, so perk up, my lovely, there's Waterside and a good feed o' corn just comin' into sight,' and *Clip, clop! Jingle, jingle*, the two came up the rutted cart track and into the farm-yard.

Reuben happened to be indoors at the moment of their arrival, but when Luke came running to tell him that Champion was there he hurried up to make sure that nothing was lacking for the animal's comfort. Champion was tired after his journey and, except for a whinny or two when he scented the mares, allowed himself to be led quietly into the smaller, less-used stable across the yard, which had been prepared for his reception, and soon had been rubbed down and was munching. Then, and not until then, Bob turned his attention to the steaming jug of tea Mercy had brought out for his own refreshment.

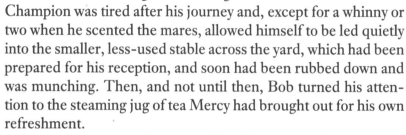

It was the custom, when away from home on such itineraries, for the man in charge to sleep at the farmhouse where the horse was stabled, the idea being that he should be at hand in case any harm threatened the valuable creature during the night; and when, on his travels with Champion, Bob reached Waterside, he slept there. At most other farms he remained about the place all the evening – on guard, as it were; but it happened that Bob was a native of Restharrow and had an old mother still living there, and when his travels brought him to Waterside it was his custom to take an hour or two off in order to visit her, leaving Champion as a sacred charge to Reuben, in whom he had perfect confidence. But, that evening, when all had been done that had to be done and all said that was necessary, he still lingered. 'I don't half like leaving him,' he said, as he closed the stable door.

'Why, man, what's going to harm him?' asked Reuben somewhat impatiently. 'It isn't his first night in that stable and I don't s'pose it's going to be his last. What's worrying you?'

'Nothin' that I knows on. 'Tis just a feelin', same as you might have for a nipper you was fond of and could hardly bring yourself to let out of your sight. But, as you says, he's safely bedded down for the night now, and if you'll give him a look in once or twice I'll be getting along,' and Bob went straddling over the footpath, a straw between his teeth, and in his hand a few comforts he had brought for his mother, tied up in a red, white-spotted handkerchief.

Reuben laughed when he told the girls about this at the supper-table. 'Talk about a mother putting her first bantling to bed!' he said when describing Bob's meticulous care. 'Not that I think any the worse of the chap for it. You can't spend your days and part of your nights with a creature without getting fond of it; besides, it's a valuable beast and old Bob's responsible.'

'You men and your old horses!' laughed Polly. 'I protest you think more of yours than you do of your daughters!' And Mercy ladled out more pickled cabbage on to her father's plate and begged him to cut himself another slice of cold bacon from the streaky end, to which he was partial. But though he knew that what he was saying was but partly comprehended by his listeners, Reuben continued meditatively: 'No! I don't think any the worse of the chap. A man who gives no more nor a dry bed and a feed of corn to his beast is but half a man. And Bob's a whole man. If you'd seen him as I've seen him, holding back and controlling Champ in his tantrums, and him but a midget himself, you'd have felt a sort of pride in him, as I've felt. No, thankee, Mercy, no more beer for me. When did you know me to go beyond my pint? Now you girls had better go to bed and get your beauty sleep, and I'll sit by the fire with my pipe till Bob comes in,' and he was about to withdraw to the chimney corner when the back door burst open and an agitated voice shouted, 'Mus' Truman! Mus' Truman! Come quick!' He went. There was a sound of hurrying feet on the courtyard cobbles, then silence.

'I wonder what's up!' said Polly, and she went over and drew back the window-curtain. 'Mercy,' she said wonderingly, 'the sky's all red. There must be a fire somewhere,' and both girls ran out to the gate to behold a scene which they never forgot. A hayrick in the rickyard beyond the farm buildings was alight. Already flames mounted high above the stable, or, puffed by the wind, bent down to lick the slated roof. The two men who had first seen the blaze from the road past the churchyard and given the alarm were dragging out pitchforks and other implements from the cart-house to fight the fire. Other men and boys rushed panting past the house, shouting, 'Fire! Fire! Fire!'

Polly ran at once to the rickyard and was soon organizing a chain of bucket-bearers from the horsepond. People said of her afterwards that, that night, she was as good as any two men, for she'd got the headpiece. Mercy turned back into the house and filled and put on the embers the big black kettle, to have hot water in readiness in case of accidents, or to make tea for the workers. So far her feeling was one of excitement, rather than of apprehension. It was no uncommon thing for a hayrick here and there about the countryside to fire after a wet summer, although, within her memory, it had not happened at Waterside. All would be well, thought Mercy. Dad was there with plenty of willing workers. If they found the burning rick could not be saved they would concentrate upon those surrounding it and all would be over in half an hour. Then she would have the helpers to feed; she must look to the bread and the bacon. But those out of doors already knew that fighting the fire was not going to be so simple a matter. The danger lay in the wind, which in the last hour had freshened and was bearing down and directing the flames to the farm buildings. The house, being situated at the farther end of the farmstead, was reasonably safe.

Mercy, running towards the rickyard, saw burning wisps of straw floating in the air. One fell to earth close beside her and she stopped to stamp out the smouldering mass, but another and another came floating over the roof of the stables until fire seemed to be falling all around her, and for the first time that night she felt afraid. The rickyard was alive with men, some up ladders, beating down the flames, others below with buckets or pitchforks, all working frantically, their dark, moving figures silhouetted against the blaze. Besides these serious helpers there were others, tearing around and shouting without visible object. At the rickyard gate stood a small group of women watchers, their frightened faces illuminated by the conflagration. 'Have you seen my sister?' Mercy asked one of these, but before she had succeeded in making herself heard Polly herself dashed past them. She had either lost or discarded her skirt and appeared in her short red flannel petticoat, with a man's red pocket-handkerchief tied gipsy-wise over her hair. If she saw Mercy, she had no time to stop to speak to her, but tore on towards the burning ricks with the coil of rope she was carrying. Mercy gazed after her helplessly. Though twice the size of Polly, she was not made of the same material. Frightened, confused, destitute of ideas, and of a too gentle nature to push her way through the throng, she was carried hither and thither. She heard someone about, 'Look to the stable roof!' and there was a stampede in that direction with ladders to reach the slates, through which puffs of smoke were issuing. 'Father! Where's Father?' she cried, seizing a man by the elbow. 'Gettin' out th' 'osses,' he shouted. 'But don't hold me – don't hinder me – we must fend th' roof,' and he shook himself free and was gone.

Mercy pushed her way out of the rickyard in time to see the end of a string of farm horses disappear down the lane towards the paddock, each horse led by a man or a youth by the mane, or by a hastily caught up bridle. There was some plunging and whinnying among them, but, with their backs to the fire and soothed by familiar voices, they went fairly quietly.

'All out?' shouted somebody as she neared the stable entrance, and another voice called in reply, 'All out but old Champ, and Mus' Truman's got he well in hand. We've sent for Bob, but he hasn't come yet.' Reuben had got Champ well in hand. By using all his wiles with horses, he had coaxed him out through the doorway and in another moment or two all would have been well had not a wisp of floating flame fallen so near to the horse's head that it lighted up his exposed teeth and glaring eyeballs. Whinnying loudly, he reared, carrying upward the small, frail-looking man who held to his bridle and jerking him violently up and down until he relaxed his hold and fell to the ground, to be, as it seemed, trodden to death by the great ironshod hooves. But Reuben fell clear and lay on his back a few feet away, apparently insensible. The first of his men

who tried to reach him received a glancing blow on his forehead which laid him low, but, regardless of their own lives, others sprung forward and dragged both men to comparative safety. Then Bob came up at a shambling run, seized Champion's bridle and, after a sharp tussle, led him away. All this had taken place in a few moments and all had taken place by the light of the flames.

Reuben was carried indoors and laid on the sofa beneath the living-kitchen window. When water was dashed on his forehead he opened his eyes, but he did not speak, and soon relapsed into unconsciousness. By that time the fire had been checked or burnt itself out in the rickyard, but the farm buildings were still in great danger and every pair of skilled hands were needed, so, after feeling Reuben's limbs and assuring Mercy that no bones were broken, that her father had but swooned and would come round in a few minutes, the men went away, saying that they would send a woman or two to keep her company. Mercy begged them to send a messenger for her aunt, Mrs. Finch, who, she

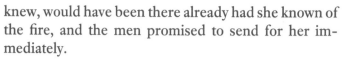

knew, would have been there already had she known of the fire, and the men promised to send for her immediately.

The Finches had not heard of the fire. They were all sleeping peacefully in their beds when knocked up by the messenger, when they quickly threw on their clothes and hurried towards the farm. Mercy fetched pillows for her father's head and blankets to cover him, filled the big stone hot-water bottle and put it to his feet, and sponged the soot and grime from his face, then sat down beside him and chafed his cold hands. Except for flashes of red light on the window when a roof collapsed and flames shot up, she could see nothing of the fire, though the crashes of falling rafters and tiles and the loud warning shouts of the men told her that it was still raging. In contrast with the turmoil without, the house seemed unnaturally silent. She could hear the loud, regular ticking of the grandfather's clock, the creaking of floorboards and the scuffling of mice behind the wainscot. She said afterwards, and repeated many times during the rest of her life, that what chiefly impressed her at that time was the unreality, the unbelievableness of it all – flames raging out of doors and the whole population of the parish gathered there at that time of night, yet, within doors, every familiar thing in place and herself watching alone beside the unconscious form of her father, who but little more than an hour before had been eating his supper at the table. She never for one moment doubted that he would revive. Indeed, one of her anxieties was how she should prevent him from rushing out to take charge of the fire-fighting before he had sufficiently recovered. But when he did at last open his eyes, she knew at once that she need have no further anxiety on that score, for he was obviously too weak even to raise himself. After she had got him to swallow a spoonful of brandy, he sank back in a doze which she thought it better not to disturb, and again she listened to the clock, ticking off moments which seemed to her hours.

She heard the fire-engine arrive and the firemen shouting to their horses as they backed it into the farmyard; then came the sound of hurrying feet on the courtyard cobbles and Mr. Virtue entered the kitchen. 'All alone, Mercy?' he said. 'Well, you won't be much longer. Your uncle and aunt and Charity are on their way; saw them getting over the church stile when I galloped past.' While he was speaking he was looking closely at Reuben. 'They told me your father had swooned,' he said, 'and I thought I'd just look in and see how he was,' and he felt Reuben's pulse, then opened his waistcoat and laid his hand on his heart. 'Have you ever known him to faint before, or to complain of his heart or anything?' he asked, and Mercy said no, her father had never ailed in any way. He leaned down again and listened to Reuben's breathing. 'Um, aye,' he said. 'Not come round yet, not properly round. But there's nothing for you to worry about; he'll be all right in time. He's not so young as he was and he's had a proper wrenching. I think perhaps we'd better send for the doctor; more satisfactory. I'll go and get Chump Nixey to go for him; he can borrow the landlord's bicycle. I know the young rip can ride, for I saw him fall off at the bottom of Toft Hill last Sunday,' and he replaced the blankets and was about to go when, slowly and languidly, Reuben opened his eyes. 'You all right, Mercy?' he asked weakly, then, 'Where's Polly?' and Mercy assured him that Polly was safe and out helping the men.

'Nobody hurt, I hope?'

'Only a few cuts and bruises.'

'And Bess? Is Bess safe?' he asked, which Mercy thought a curious question, as Bess was far away in her own home and knew nothing of that night's happenings; but, as she thought to humour him, she told him that Bess and Arnold and little Marianna were all safe and well.

'And the horses? Are they safe? And Champ?'

Mr. Virtue said that the horses were safe and had quieted down; he had had a look at them in the paddock as he passed; and Champion, too, was uninjured; Bob had led him off home or to another farm; and the fire-engine had come and the fire was well under. All Reuben had to do now was to lie still and rest. Reuben must have heard all this, though he said nothing. His breathing had become heavy and laboured. Mercy brought another pillow and they were about to raise his head, when he suddenly sat up and said, loudly and clearly, 'All's well!' and sank back upon his pillows.

As he had spoken those last words, Mr. and Mrs. Finch and Charity had come into the room. Mrs. Finch flung off her cloak and darted forward; Mercy and Charity clung together; Mr. Virtue leaned over and gently closed Reuben's eyelids. 'All is well with you, my good old friend,' he said; 'but you'll be missed here, my man, you'll be missed!'

It was Bess's wish that her father should be carried to his rest by the footpath way with his own men as bearers and followed only by his family. 'No hearse and no carriages,' she said. 'He would not have wished it. Let us bury him as he lived, in the old country way.' There were no flowers on his coffin, for he had disliked the custom, then coming into fashion, of loading the dead with flowers. 'When my time comes,' he had often said, 'I hope nobody'll spend their money or spoil their garden on my account. If any of you want to show your affection, you can plant a flower or two on my grave, where they'll have a chance of living;

though, to my mind, there's no better covering than a bit of green turf.'

It was a small, homely procession which on a moist, sunshiny October afternoon accompanied Reuben on the last of his many journeys along the footpath. Though the women wore black and the men showed some token of mourning, the scene was not one of unrelieved woe. In the sunshine the meadow turf, lately washed with rain, gleamed emerald; the richly-berried hedges shone scarlet and crimson, and, once, while the bearers were resting, the silvery sweet strain of a robin threaded the silence. 'The welcome home!' said Mrs. Finch, and her husband, who in a general way cared little for such country superstitions, listened a moment then echoed her words, 'The welcome home!'

'We've lost a good friend,' said one of the village spectators in the churchyard, and another replied, 'Aye, we have. It'll be some time before we see his likes again. Perhaps never.' And though doubtless they found other good friends, they never did, or could, see Reuben's like again, for he was one of the last of the old country breed, poor in this world's goods, obscure in position, not gifted with speech or any intellectual attainment, but for all that a man who stood out from his fellows in his complete mastery of all that pertains to the land, and in his tolerance, sympathy, and sturdy independence.

XIII

RUNNING WATER

AFTER her father's death, Mercy took a situation as housekeeper to a market gardener living near Mixlow. At that time Ben Franklin was a widower with four young children. His was a pretty and substantial cottage, situated in the part of his garden devoted to flower-growing; but since his wife's death a succession of incompetent or idle housekeepers had allowed everything within doors to go to rack and ruin. The children, too, had been neglected and had to be won back to obedience and orderly living, so Mercy had plenty of scope for her own peculiar qualities. But perhaps, as she said afterwards, the hard work and the overcoming of difficulties were good for her, for she had little leisure in which to brood on her own loss.

Soon the children had become a pattern of neatness and comfort, and the children, reclaimed and reclothed, were her joy and pride. A year later, she and Ben Franklin were married. When Mrs. Finch expressed some surprise that she should have married a man fifteen years her senior and the father of a ready-made family, Mercy said she had felt sorry for Ben, he had suffered so much and, not being very strong in health, he needed somebody to look after him. As to the children, she already loved them as if they were her own, and they seemed to love her, but she thought she could be more of a mother to them if she married their father. 'It's the children, not the father, she's marrying,' said Mrs. Finch to Charity afterwards. 'I hope she'll never have cause to regret it.' Mercy never regretted her marriage. Many years later, when someone spoke of her to one of her grown-up sons as 'your stepmother,' he looked confused, then laughed and said, 'We've never thought of our Mum as a step, but as what she's always been to us – the best mother in all the world, let whosoever may be the next best.'

Bess died at forty-three. Though full of life and energy, she had never been robust, and during her married life she had exerted herself in such public work as was then expected of the wives of village schoolmasters. She had had her own interests, too, and shortly before she died had taken part in a processional march organized by the Women's Suffrage Movement. Her daughter Marianna married an Australian soldier during the First World War, and afterwards joined him in Queensland. She had several children, some of whom must still be living and have children of their own, and it may be that this description of Waterside will be read by Bess's grandchildren and Reuben's great-grandchildren.

Time turned Polly, the Lammas lamb, into a tall, bony, somewhat grim, though thoroughly efficient hospital sister. Her life was cut short by a flying fragment of shell near a field hospital in France in 1915.

Luke never married. He became one of those odd bachelor men at that time to be found in every village. He cooked, washed and mended for himself, dug and planted his garden patch and kept his two-roomed cottage clean, if not very tidy according to feminine standards. The last time Charity saw Luke he was returning from a walk on a Sunday morning, accompanied by a crowd of little ones between the ages of three and seven. They had been in the meadows, and there the children had decked Uncle Luke, as they called him, with buttercup chains – a buttercup chain round his neck, another round his black bowler hat, buttercup wristlets, buttercup garters, and, in every buttonhole, from top to bottom of his Sunday coat, a buttercup bouquet. 'Looks a bit of a fool, don't he?' said one of two youths who were pushing their bicycles up the Restharrow street. But Luke was no fool; his only peculiarity was simple goodness.

After the debris of the fire had been cleared and the stock had been provided for elsewhere, the farmhouse for some time stood empty, the farmer having decided to let it as a small country house for gentlefolks as soon as a likely tenant appeared. But, although not far from a village, it was far from a town or a main road, and in what in those days before motor cars or the general use of the telephone was considered an isolated position; and although Mr. Mercer was prepared to let it at less than the present-day rent of a suburban bungalow, it remained unoccupied. At last he gave up all hope of the kind of tenant he desired and again offered the house rent-free to two of his workmen. Two families actually lived there for a time, but the two women could not agree and one family left, the husband saying that two shillings a week for a cottage in the village was a small price to pay for peace and quiet. After they had gone, the remaining housewife complained of the loneliness, caged up all day in that gert barracks of a place, with her husband

at work and her children at school and not so much as a neighbour to speak to. So they, too, departed, and although it was afterwards offered to several, no one else ever lived there. The house, once so well-kept and well-loved, stood empty, and damp and frost and high winds did their work on the structure, which ultimately was demolished and the stones were carted away to build pigsties and walls and for road metal.

On the last day of her Restharrow visit, Charity stood in the deserted field corner still known as Waterside. Where the orchard and farmyard had been the ground had been levelled and taken into the field. Of the buildings, only the big barn remained. That had been given a new corrugated iron roof, painted dark red, but was otherwise unchanged. Solid, four-square, silver-grey, the thick walls looked good for another century. A couple of hayricks stood beside the barn. The field was under grass that year and sheep were grazing the aftermath. The wind ruffled their fleeces, waved

through the clover and bent the hazel boughs in the lane. Although the sun was still hot overhead, the weather had broken and one more summer had gone.

The site of the house and the little walled garden had not been levelled sufficiently for cultivation. Long, overgrown mounds marked the foundations of the house, and by these the position of the different rooms could be traced. A flourishing bed of nettles filled the space once occupied by the living kitchen. Briars encroached on the little walled garden with its one remaining fruit tree. Charity remembered that tree in its prime. It was a Blenheim orange apple which had been a favourite with Reuben on account of the quality of its prolific yield. Now it had aged into a gnarled stump with one bough, which, sticking out at a right angle, had still persisted in putting out a few green leaves. Moreover, it had actually borne fruit, for, in the long grass beside it, she found one apple, eaten to a shell by wasps. Of herbs and flowers there was no trace at that season; but she had been told in the village that every year in February there was an abundance of snowdrops. Then on Sundays, after afternoon church, people crossed the meadow to pick the flowers to stand in jugs and pots on their window-sills, and many wondered how they had come to grow there, for it was not a wild snowdrop country. The little walled garden had been Bess's garden and she had planted the snowdrops. For a year or two they had not bloomed and she had feared they were dwindling; but they had recovered and now had spread, until, as the  woman had said, when out they lay as thick as snow on the grass. A fitting legacy, those graceful flowers, to be left by one so graceful as Bess.

For the rest of the year, but for a roving band of schoolboys who might light upon the old foundations and find them good for their camping games, or for men working in the nearby fields, who might go there to get an implement from the barn or to eat their dinner in its shelter or shade, the place was deserted. Yet that day it had about it none of the melancholy atmosphere which so often envelops once-occupied places from which human life has ebbed. The sunlit sweep of green field with its hayricks and grazing sheep was a wholesome sight. The wind waved the grasses, larks soared and sang, and all the time Charity was aware of another sound – a sound associated with her early memories of Waterside. It was the sound of running water.

Unchanged where all else had changed, the stream still wound through the fields between its margins of willow and willowherb; foaming around obstacles, lapping softly over shallows, dimpling in the sunshine, running dark in the shade. With its sound in her ears and the scent of meadowsweet and water-mint in her nostrils, Charity stood musing. Every year, she thought, new flowers had bloomed on its margins, new water had constantly poured down from its springs; yet the stream was the same stream.  So it had run and so it had sung before the house known for a century or so as Waterside had been built on its bank, so it had continued through all the changes in the lives of those who had dwelt in that house, and so it remained and would remain when the memory of that house and those lives had faded.

And so with us, she thought. We come, we go, and, as individuals, we are forgotten. But the stream of human life goes on, ever changing, but ever the same, and as the stream is fed by well-springs hoarded by Nature so the stream of humanity is fed by the store of accumulated wisdom and effort and hard-won experience of past generations. Lapping peacefully over the shallows, running dark in the shade, wrestling turbulently with the obstacles, ever changing, yet ever the same, it continues. And as she once more trod the old footpath way with the sound of running water in her ears, these thoughts gave her an extraordinary sense of comfort and reassurance.

SOURCES OF THE ILLUSTRATIONS

The thirteen woodcut engravings at the beginning of each chapter are by Thomas Bewick. The drawings and sketches reproduced throughout the book are taken from sketchbooks by Myles Birket Foster, in the collection of the Victoria and Albert Museum, London (Crown copyright). Pressed flowers were supplied by Jessie Parkes and Molly Wood, and photographed by Julie Fisher. Butterflies were supplied by Worldwide Butterflies, Compton, Dorset, and dragonflies by Mr L. Christie. The front cover label incorporates a photograph by Tony Evans.

The paintings are as follows:

Page	Artist and title	Source
5	John Atkinson Grimshaw, 'Thrush's Nest'	Fine Art Photographs
6	Charles Edward Wilson, 'Rustic Anglers'	Victoria and Albert Museum (Crown copyright)
9	Arthur Wilkinson, 'A Cottage Flower Garden'	Richard Hagen Fine Paintings, Broadway, Worcestershire
16	Ethel Atcherley, 'Scything'	Chris Beetles Ltd, London
25	Fred Hall, 'Cabbage Field'	Fine Art Photographs
30	George Vicat Cole, 'By the Haystack'	Fine Art Photographs
35	Charles James Adams, 'The Tinkers 1898'	Richard Hagen Fine Paintings
38	Charles Low, 'At the Gate'	Priory Gallery, Cheltenham
43	Charles Edward Wilson, 'The Meadow'	Richard Hagen Fine Paintings
46	Thomas Mackay, 'Evening'	Priory Gallery
53	Arthur Foord Hughes, 'Poll the Milkmaid'	Fine Art Photographs
61	Henry Earp, 'Logging'	Priory Gallery
66	Claude Hayes, 'The Shepherd'	Fine Art Photographs
69	Alfred Carlton Smith, 'By the Fire'	Chris Beetles Ltd
72	John Linnell, 'Sunset (1861)'	Fine Art Photographs
79	Myles Birket Foster, 'By the Bridge'	Fine Art Photographs
88	Thomas Mackay, 'The Bridge'	Priory Gallery
95	Ernest Albert Waterlow, 'The Reigate Hills'	Chris Beetles Ltd
100	David C. Jenkins, 'Spring 1891'	Fine Art Photographs
107	Henry William Banks Davis, 'Towards Evening in the Forest'	Bridgeman Art Library/Christopher Wood Gallery
110	John A. Lynas Gray, 'Golden Moments'	Priory Gallery
119	Isabel Naftel, 'The River at Sutton Courtney'	Priory Gallery

INDEX OF ARTISTS